Praise for Howard Waldrop:

"Waldrop subtly mutates the past, extrapolating the changes into some of the most insightful, and frequently amusing, stories being written today, in or out of the science fiction genre."
—*The Houston Post/Sun*

"The man's a national treasure!"
—*Locus*

"Clever, humorous, idiosyncratic, oddball, personal, wild, and crazy."
—*Library Journal*

"Wise and funny."
—*Publishers Weekly*

"An authentic master of gonzo sf and fantasy."
—*Booklist*

"Erudite and gonzo."
—*Science Fiction Weekly*

"The resident Weird Mind of his generation, he writes like a honkytonk angel."
—*Washington Post Book World*

T0126255

Also by Howard Waldrop

Novels
*The Texas-Israeli War: 1999* with Jake Saunders (1974)
*Them Bones* (1984)

Collections
*Howard Who?* (1986)
*All About Strange Monsters of the Recent Past: Neat Stories* (1987)
*Night of the Cooters: More Neat Stories* (1990)
*Going Home Again* (1997)
*Custer's Last Jump and Other Collaborations* (2003)
*Heart of Whitenesse* (2005)
*Things Will Never Be the Same: Selected Short Fiction* 1980-2005 (2007)
*Other Worlds, Better Lives: Selected Long Fiction* 1989-2003 (2008)
*Horse of a Different Color: Stories* (2013)

Chapbooks
*A Dozen Tough Jobs* (1989)
*A Better World's in Birth* (2003)
*The Horse of a Different Color (That You Rode In On)* / *The King of Where-I-Go* (2006)

Nonfiction
*Dream Factories and Radio Pictures* (2003)

Forthcoming
*I, John Mandeville*
*The Moon World*
*Moving Waters*

# Howard Who?

# Howard Who?
## stories

# Howard Waldrop

Peapod Classics
Easthampton, MA

Copyright © 1986 by Howard Waldrop. All rights reserved. First published as *Howard Who? Twelve Outstanding Stories of Speculative Fiction* by Doubleday in 1986.
Introduction copyright © 1986 by George R.R. Martin.

Peapod Classics is an imprint of Small Beer Press.

Small Beer Press
150 Pleasant St., #306
Easthampton, MA 01027
smallbeerpress.com
weightlessbooks.com
bookmoonbooks.com

Distributed to the trade by Consortium.

Library of Congress Cataloging-in-Publication Data

Waldrop, Howard.
  Howard who? : stories / Howard Waldrop. -- 1st ed.
    p. cm.
  ISBN-13: 978-1-931520-18-8 (pbk. : alk. paper)
  ISBN-10: 1-931520-18-6 (pbk. : alk. paper)
  1. Science fiction, American.  I. Title.
  PS3573.A4228H6 2006
  813'.54--dc22

First edition    3 4 5 6 7 8 9 10

Printed in the USA.
Text set in Centaur MT. Titles set in AlleyCat.
Cover art © 2006 by Kevin Huizenga: kevinhuizenga.com

# Contents

# Introduction by George R. R. Martin

Let's begin with some riddles. What do Dwight David Eisenhower and the dodo have in common? How are Japanese sumo wrestlers like Disney cartoon characters? What's the common link between Izaak Walton, Abbott & Costello, and George Armstrong Custer? If you ran into a gorilla in a powdered wig at a tractor pull, what would that remind you of? And while you're pondering all that, just who was that masked man anyway?

The last one is easy. The masked man is Howard Waldrop, a short squinty-eyed fellow with an atrocious accent and a wardrobe like Mork from Ork. He was born in Mississippi, grew up in Texas, and has bounced around the Lone Star State most of his adult life, from Arlington to Grand Prairie to Bryan to Austin, where he now resides. He knows everything there is to know about B movies, he can sing fifties rock and TV theme songs all night long (and often does), he likes to fish, and he just happens to be the most startling, original, and entertaining short story writer in science fiction today.

The word *unique* is much abused these days, but in Howard's case it applies. We live in a derivative age, and nowhere is that more apparent than in the books we read. Every new horror writer is compared to Stephen King. Our fantasists all seem to write in the tradition of J.R.R. Tolkien, Robert E. Howard, or Stephen R. Donaldson. The hot young talents in SF are routinely proclaimed as the next Robert A. Heinlein, the new Isaac Asimov, the angriest young man since Harlan Ellison, unless they happen to be female, in which case they are dutifully likened to Andre Norton,

I

Ursula K. LeGuin, and Marion Zimmer Bradley. If you listen to the blurb-writers, these days it seems that everybody writes like somebody else.

Howard Waldrop's short fiction is squarely in the tradition of Howard Waldrop. There's never been anyone like him, in or out of science fiction. His voice is his own; singular, distinctive, quirky, and—once you've encountered it—more than a little addictive. I'm tempted to say that the only thing that's like a Howard Waldrop story is another Howard Waldrop story, except that it wouldn't be true. Howard's stories differ as much from each other as from your run-of-the-mill SF and fantasy. The only thing they have in common is that they're all a little bit different.

Howard doesn't like to write the same thing twice. Well-meaning friends keep telling him that the best way to get rich and famous is to write the same thing over and over and over and over again, to keep frying up those robot duneburgers of gor and serving them to a hungry public, but Howard keeps wandering off and getting interested in Groucho Marx, Chinese proletarian novels, and the mound-builder Indians. Suddenly books start piling up in his office, a maniacal gleam lights his tiny little eyes, and he begins to talk incessantly about a strange new story he's going to write. Meanwhile, he consumes those piles of books during breaks in his daily regimen of building bookcases and watching old movies on television. Then, when all of his friends are just about ready to skin him alive, out it comes all in a rush: the latest Waldrop wonderment.

It's an odd way to work, but it's Howard's way, as uniquely his own as the stories it produces. He's been doing it for a long time. People have been paying him for it ever since 1970, but he started long before that, writing stories just for the love of writing. I couldn't tell you just when Howard began to scrawl words on paper, but I suspect that it was about nine seconds after he first learned to hold a Crayola in his stubby little fingers.

I do know that he was born in Mississippi on September 15, 1946 (a date he's immortalized in one of his recent short stories), that later on his family moved to Texas, and that he's been a thorough-going Texan ever since. He was already writing up a storm by the time he first came to my attention.

That was in 1963; we were both in high school, him in Arlington, Texas and me in Bayonne, New Jersey, and both of us were publishing our juvenilia in the comic book fan magazines of the day, tiny publications printed in purple with fast-fading ditto masters and circulated to literally *dozens* of eager readers, most of them high school kids, like Howard himself. Even then, Howard was unique. Everyone else who wrote for those tiny little fanzines (including, I blush to admit, myself) imitated the professional funny-books and wrote about superheroes. Howard wrote detective stories set in France at the time of the Musketeers. The readers loved him, but didn't quite know what to make of him, and they'd write in puzzlement to the fanzine letter columns to say, "Boy, Howard Waldrop's story was really great, but it was all about Cardinal Richelieu. What powers did *he* have, anyway?" He's been pleasing and puzzling readers ever since.

Everyone who read him back then knew right off that Howard was too good to stay an amateur for long, and sure enough we were all right. He made his first professional sale in 1970, just before he got drafted. The Army sent him to Georgia, gave him a typewriter, and taught him all the words to "I Want to Be an Airborne Ranger," but otherwise did him little good. The story had more lasting effects on his life and career. It was a little thing called "Lunchbox," and the editor who bought it was the legendary John W. Campbell, Jr. During the decades that he had edited *Astounding* (later *Analog*), Campbell had discovered and introduced an astonishing number of SF greats, and in fishing Howard Waldrop out of the slush pile, he demonstrated that his eye for talent hadn't deserted him. Campbell's untimely death came before he could actually print Howard's debut story, but in a very real sense it can still be said that Howard Waldrop was Campbell's last great gift to science fiction.

Two years as an army journalist slowed him down a little, but there was no stopping Howard permanently, and once he was discharged he returned to Texas to begin to write and sell all sorts of things. He even wrote a novel, a collaboration with his landlord. It was called *The Texas-Israeli War*, by Jake Saunders and Howard Waldrop, and it's still in print today.

Those were heady days in Texas, for reasons entirely unconnected with the Dallas Cowboys Cheerleaders. Hot young writers were popping up all over the Lone Star State, and selling stories to every contemporary market, large and small. The brilliant Tom Reamy was just beginning to publish, Lisa Tuttle was turning heads with her early stories, Bruce Sterling was in the process of becoming a Harlan Ellison Discovery, and all of them—along with Howard and a half-dozen others—were part of a loosely organized floating workshop they called the Turkey City Neopro Rodeo. Collaboration was endemic among the Turkey City writers, and Howard shared bylines with a number of them, producing some forgettable journeyman stories and others that are still being talked about, most notably "Custer's Last Jump," about the way Crazy Horse and the Plains Indian Air Force destroyed Custer's paratroops at the Battle of the Little Big Horn. It was berserk, brilliant, and an omen of the things soon to come from Howard's clanking manual typewriter.

It was around then that people finally started noticing Howard Waldrop. He was nominated for *two* Nebulas in 1977: for "Custer" and again for "Mary Margaret Road-Grader," Howard's solo tour de force about post-holocaust tractor pulls, which you'll find in this collection. He didn't take home any trophies that year, but it was only a matter of time. Other nominations for other awards followed, and in 1981 his classic story "The Ugly Chickens" (that's also included here) won both the Nebula and the prestigious World Fantasy Award, and came within a dodo feather of copping the Hugo as well, for a rare triple crown.

Nowadays, Howard seems to be just about everywhere. Once, to find the latest Waldrop stories, you had to buy Terry Carr's distinguished hardcover anthology series *Universe*, or seek out small circulation semi-professional magazines like *Shayol, Chacal,* and *Nickelodeon.* These days Howard is publishing in *Omni* and *Playboy* . . . but you'll still find him in *Universe* and *Shayol* as well. He's not the kind who forgets where he came from. His name turns up monotonously on the shortlists for every major award in the field and most of the minor ones, and no wonder. The stories keep getting stranger and stranger, but they're getting better and better too.

He even had another go at a novel recently, this time without any help from his landlord. The end result was called *Them Bones,* time travel as only Waldrop would write it, and it was published to loud huzzas as part of Terry Carr's revived Ace Specials line.

As good as it was, however, *Them Bones* still wasn't a patch on Howard's short stories. Short fiction remains Waldrop's forte, and believe me, nobody does it better. You've got a damned fine sampler of Waldrop in the pages that follow, the famous stories and the obscure ones, plucked from magazines with hundreds or hundreds of thousands of readers. The only thing they all have in common is their quality. If this is your first taste of Howard, I envy you. Bet you can't read just one.

Oh, yes, you'll be wanting the answers to the riddles. Howard Waldrop. Howard Waldrop. Howard Waldrop. And finally, Howard Waldrop. There's only one of him, but—lucky for us—he spreads himself around.

—*George R.R. Martin, 1986*

*To the editors who first bought them—Terry (Bob and Marta sorta for a few minutes), Pat & Arnie, Ellen, Damon, Tom, Alice; Pat (who bought the whole thing); Joe (who sold the whole thing); but mostly for Ruthie, who could have been a contender, instead of a bum, which is what I am.*

# The Ugly Chickens

My car was broken, and I had a class to teach at eleven. So I took the city bus, something I rarely do.

I spent last summer crawling through The Big Thicket with cameras and tape recorder, photographing and taping two of the last ivory-billed woodpeckers on the earth. You can see the films at your local Audubon Society showroom.

This year I wanted something just as flashy but a little less taxing. Perhaps a population study on the Bermuda cahow, or the New Zealand takahe. A month or so in the warm (not hot) sun would do me a world of good. To say nothing of the advance of science.

I was idly leafing through Greenway's *Extinct and Vanishing Birds of the World*. The city bus was winding its way through the ritzy neighborhoods of Austin, stopping to let off the chicanas, black women, and Vietnamese who tended the kitchens and gardens of the rich.

"I haven't seen any of those ugly chickens in a long time," said a voice close by.

A grey-haired lady was leaning across the aisle toward me.

I looked at her, then around. Maybe she was a shopping-bag lady. Maybe she was just talking. I looked straight at her. No doubt about it, she was talking to me. She was waiting for an answer.

"I used to live near some folks who raised them when I was a girl," she said. She pointed.

I looked down at the page my book was open to.

What I should have said was: "That is quite impossible, madam. This is a drawing of an extinct bird of the island of Mauritius. It is perhaps the most famous dead bird in the world. Maybe you are mistaking this drawing for that of some rare Asiatic turkey, peafowl, or pheasant. I am sorry, but you are mistaken."

I should have said all that.

What she said was, "Oops, this is my stop," and got up to go.

My name is Paul Linberl. I am twenty-six years old, a graduate student in ornithology at the University of Texas, a teaching assistant. My name is not unknown in the field. I have several vices and follies, but I don't think foolishness is one of them.

The stupid thing for me to do would have been to follow her.

She stepped off the bus.

I followed her.

I came into the departmental office, trailing scattered papers in the whirlwind behind me. "Martha! Martha!" I yelled.

She was doing something in the supply cabinet.

"Jesus, Paul! What do you want?"

"Where's Courtney?"

"At the conference in Houston. You know that. You missed your class. What's the matter?"

"Petty cash. Let me at it!"

"Payday was only a week ago. If you can't . . ."

"It's business! It's fame and adventure and the chance of a lifetime! It's a long sea voyage that leaves . . . a plane ticket. To either Jackson, Mississippi or Memphis. Make it Jackson, it's closer. I'll get receipts! I'll be famous. Courtney will be famous. *You'll* even be famous! This university will make even *more* money! I'll pay you back. Give me some paper. I gotta write

Courtney a note. When's the next plane out? Could you get Marie and Chuck to take over my classes Tuesday and Wednesday? I'll try to be back Thursday unless something happens. Courtney'll be back tomorrow, right? I'll call him from, well, wherever. Do you have some coffee? . . ."

And so on and so forth. Martha looked at me like I was crazy. But she filled out the requisition anyway.

"What do I tell Kemejian when I ask him to sign these?"

"Martha, babe, sweetheart. Tell him I'll get his picture in *Scientific American*."

"He doesn't read it."

"*Nature,* then!"

"I'll see what I can do," she said.


The lady I had followed off the bus was named Jolyn (Smith) Jimson. The story she told me was so weird that it had to be true. She knew things only an expert, or someone with firsthand experience, could know. I got names from her, and addresses, and directions, and tidbits of information. Plus a year: 1927.

And a place: northern Mississippi.

I gave her my copy of the Greenway book. I told her I'd call her as soon as I got back into town. I left her standing on the corner near the house of the lady she cleaned for twice a week. Jolyn Jimson was in her sixties.


Think of the dodo as a baby harp seal with feathers. I know that's not even close, but it saves time.

In 1507, the Portuguese, on their way to India, found the (then unnamed) Mascarene Islands in the Indian Ocean—three of them a few hundred miles apart, all east and north of Madagascar.

It wasn't until 1598, when that old Dutch sea captain Cornelius van Neck bumped into them, that the islands received their names—names which changed several times through the centuries as the Dutch, French, and English changed them every war or so. They are now know as Rodriguez, Réunion, and Mauritius.

The major feature of these islands were large flightless birds, stupid, ugly, bad-tasting birds. Van Neck and his men named them *dod-aarsen,* stupid ass, or dodars, silly birds, or solitaires.

There were three species—the dodo of Mauritius, the real grey-brown, hooked-beak clumsy thing that weighed twenty kilos or more; the white, somewhat slimmer dodo of Réunion; and the solitaires of Rodriguez and Réunion, which looked like very fat, very dumb light-colored geese.

The dodos all had thick legs, big squat bodies twice as large as a turkey's, naked faces, and big long downcurved beaks ending in a hook like a hollow linoleum knife. They were flightless. Long ago they had lost the ability to fly, and their wings had degenerated to flaps the size of a human hand with only three or four feathers in them. Their tails were curly and fluffy, like a child's afterthought at decoration. They had absolutely no natural enemies. They nested on open ground. They probably hatched their eggs wherever they happened to lay them.

No natural enemies until van Neck and his kind showed up. The Dutch, French, and Portuguese sailors who stopped at the Mascarenes to replenish stores found that besides looking stupid, dodos were stupid. They walked right up to them and hit them on the head with clubs. Better yet, dodos could be herded around like sheep. Ship's logs are full of things like: "Party of ten men ashore. Drove half-a-hundred of the big turkey-like birds into the boat. Brought to ship where they are given the run of the decks. Three will feed a crew of 150"

Even so, most of the dodo, except for the breast, tasted bad. One of the Dutch words for them was *walghvogel,* disgusting bird. But on a ship three months out on a return from Goa to Lisbon, well, food was where you found it. It was said, even so, that prolonged boiling did not improve the flavor.

That being said, the dodos might have lasted, except that the Dutch, and later the French, colonized the Mascarenes. These islands became plantations and dumping-places for religious refugees. Sugar cane and other exotic crops were raised there.

With the colonists came cats, dogs, hogs, and the cunning *Rattus norvegicus* and the Rhesus monkey from Ceylon. What dodos the hungry sailors left were chased down (they were dumb and stupid, but they could run when they felt like it) by dogs in the open. They were killed by cats as they sat on their nests. Their eggs were stolen and eaten by monkeys, rats, and hogs. And they competed with the pigs for all the low-growing goodies of the islands.

The last Mauritius dodo was seen in 1681, less than a hundred years after man first saw them. The last white dodo walked off the history books around 1720. The solitaires of Rodriguez and Réunion, last of the genus as well as the species, may have lasted until 1790. Nobody knows.

Scientists suddenly looked around and found no more of the Didine birds alive, anywhere.

This part of the country was degenerate before the first Snopes ever saw it. This road hadn't been paved until the late fifties, and it was a main road between two county seats. That didn't mean it went through civilized country. I'd traveled for miles and seen nothing but dirt banks red as Billy Carter's neck and an occasional church. I expected to see Burma Shave signs, but realized this road had probably never had them.

I almost missed the turn-off onto the dirt and gravel road the man back at the service station had marked. It led onto the highway from nowhere, a lane out of a field. I turned down it and a rock the size of a golf ball flew up over the hood and put a crack three inches long in the windshield of the rent-a-car I'd gotten in Grenada.

It was a hot muggy day for this early. The view was obscured in a cloud of dust every time the gravel thinned. About a mile down the road, the gravel gave out completely. The roadway turned into a rutted dirt pathway, just wider than the car, hemmed in on both sides by a sagging three-strand barbed-wire fence.

In some places the fenceposts were missing for a few meters. The wire lay on the ground and in some places disappeared under it for long stretches.

The only life I saw was a mockingbird raising hell with something under a thorn bush the barbed wire had been nailed to in place of a post. To one side now was a grassy field which had gone wild, the way everywhere will look after we blow ourselves off the face of the planet. The other was fast becoming woods—pine, oak, some black gum and wild plum, fruit not out this time of the year.

I began to ask myself what I was doing here. What if Ms. Jimson were some imaginative old crank who—but no. Wrong, maybe, but even the wrong was worth checking. But I knew she hadn't lied to me. She had seem incapable of lies—good ol' girl, backbone of the South, of the earth. Not a mendacious gland in her being.

I couldn't doubt her, or my judgment, either. Here I was, creeping and bouncing down a dirt path in Mississippi, after no sleep for a day, out on the thin ragged edge of a dream. I *had* to take it on faith.

The back of the car sometimes slid where the dirt had loosened and gave way to sand. The back tire stuck once, but I rocked out of it. Getting back out again would be another matter. Didn't anyone ever use this road?

The woods closed in on both sides like the forest primeval, and the fence had long since disappeared. My odometer said six miles and it had been twenty minutes since I'd turned off the highway. In the rearview mirror, I saw beads of sweat and dirt in the wrinkles of my neck. A fine patina of dust covered everything inside the car. Clots of it came through the windows.

The woods reached out and swallowed the road. Branches scraped against the windows and the top. It was like falling down a long dark leafy tunnel. It was dark and green in there. I fought back an atavistic urge to turn on the headlights. The roadbed must have been made of a few centuries of leaf mulch. I kept constant pressure on the accelerator and bulled my way through.

Half a log caught and banged and clanged against the car bottom. I saw light ahead. Fearing for the oil pan, I punched the pedal and sped out.

I almost ran through a house.

It was maybe ten yards from the trees. The road ended under one of the windows. I saw somebody waving from the corner of my eye.

I slammed on the brakes.

A whole family was on the porch, looking like a Walker Evans Depression photograph, or a fever dream from the mind of a "Hee Haw" producer. The house was old. Strips of peeling paint a yard long tapped against the eaves.

"Damned good thing you stopped," said a voice. I looked up. The biggest man I had ever seen in my life leaned down into the driver's-side window.

"If we'd have heard you sooner, I'd've sent one of the kids down to the end of the driveway to warn you," he said.

Driveway?

His mouth was stained brown at the corners. I figured he chewed tobacco until I saw the sweet-gum snuff brush sticking from the pencil pocket in the bib of his overalls. His hands were the size of catchers' mitts. They looked like they'd never held anything smaller than an axe handle.

"How y'all?" he said, by the way of introduction.

"Just fine," I said. I got out of the car.

"My name's Lindberl," I said, extending my hand. He took it. For an instant, I thought of bear traps, sharks' mouths, closing elevator doors. The thought went back to wherever it is they stay.

"This is the Gudger place?" I asked.

He looked at me blankly with his grey eyes. He wore a diesel truck cap, and had on a checked lumberjack shirt beneath his overalls. His rubber boots were the size of the ones Karloff wore in *Frankenstein.*

"Naw, I'm Jim Bob Krait. That's my wife Jenny, and there's Luke and Skeeno and Shirl." He pointed to the porch.

The people on the porch nodded.

"Lessee? Gudger? No Gudgers round here I know of. I'm sorta new here," I took that to mean he hadn't lived here for more than twenty years or so.

"Jennifer!" he yelled. "You know of anybody named Gudger?" To me he said, "My wife's lived around here all her life."

His wife came down onto the second step of the porch landing. "I think they used to be the ones what lived on the Spradlin place before the Spradlins. But the Spradlins left around the Korean War. I didn't know any of the Gudgers myself. That's while we was living over to Water Valley."

"You an insurance man?" asked Mr. Krait.

"Uh . . . no," I said. I imagined the people on the porch leaning toward me, all ears. "I'm a . . . I teach college."

"Oxford?" asked Krait.

"Uh, no. University of Texas."

"Well, that's a damn long way off. You say you're looking for the Gudgers?"

"Just their house. The area. As your wife said, I understand they left during the Depression, I believe."

"Well, they musta had money," said the gigantic Mr. Krait. "Nobody around here was rich enough to leave during the Depression."

"Luke!" he yelled. The oldest boy on the porch sauntered down. He looked anemic and wore a shirt in vogue with the Twist. He stood with his hands in his pockets.

"Luke, show Mr. Lindbergh—"

"Lindberl."

"Mr. Lindberl here the way up to the old Spradlin place. Take him as far as the old log bridge, he might get lost before then."

"Log bridge broke down, daddy."

"When?"

"October, daddy."

"Well, hell, somethin' else to fix! Anyway, to the creek."

He turned to me. "You want him to go along on up there, see you don't get snakebit?"

"No, I'm sure I'll be fine."

"Mind if I ask what you're going up there for?" he asked. He was looking away from me. I could see having to come right out and ask was bothering him. Such things usually came up in the course of conversation.

"I'm a—uh, bird scientist. I study birds. We had a sighting—someone told us the old Gudger place—the area around here—I'm looking for a rare bird. It's hard to explain."

I noticed I was sweating. It was hot.

"You mean like a goodgod? I saw a goodgod about twenty-five years ago, over next to Bruce," he said.

"Well, no." (A goodgod was one of the names for an ivory-billed woodpecker, one of the rarest in the world. Any other time I would have dropped my jaw. Because they were thought to have died out in Mississippi by the teens, and by the fact that Krait knew they were rare.)

I went to lock my car up, then thought of the protocol of the situation. "My car be in your way?" I asked.

"Naw. It'll be just fine," said Jim Bob Krait. "We'll look for you back by sundown, that be all right?"

For a minute, I didn't know whether that was a command or an expression of concern.

9

"Just in case I get snakebit," I said. "I'll try to be careful up there."

"Good luck on findin' them rare birds," he said. He walked up to the porch with his family.

"Les go," said Luke.

Behind the Krait house was a henhouse and pigsty where hogs lay after their morning slop like islands in a muddy bay, or some Zen pork sculpture. Next we passed broken farm machinery gone to rust, though there was nothing but uncultivated land as far as the eye could see. How the family made a living I don't know. I'm told you can find places just like this throughout the South.

We walked through woods and across fields, following a sort of path. I tried to memorize the turns I would have to take on the way back. Luke didn't say a word the whole twenty minutes he accompanied me, except to curse once when he stepped into a bull nettle with his tennis shoes.

We came to a creek which skirted the edge of a woodsy hill. There was a rotted log forming a small dam. Above it the water was nearly three feet deep, below it, half that much.

"See that path?" he asked.

"Yes."

"Follow it up around the hill, then across the next field. Then you cross the creek again on the rocks, and over the hill. Take the left-hand path. What's left of the house is about three quarters the way up the next hill. If you come to a big bare rock cliff, you've gone too far. You got that?"

I nodded.

He turned and left.

The house had once been a dog-run cabin, like Ms. Jimson had said. Now it was fallen in on one side, what they call sigoglin (or was it antisigoglin?). I once heard a hymn on the radio called "The Land Where No Cabins

Fall." This was the country songs like that were written in.

Weeds grew everywhere. There were signs of fences, a flattened pile of wood that had once been a barn. Further behind the house were the outhouse remains. Half a rusted pump stood in the backyard. A flatter spot showed where the vegetable garden had been; in it a single wild tomato, pecked by birds, lay rotting. I passed it. There was lumber from three outbuildings, mostly rotten and green with algae and moss. One had been a smokehouse and woodshed combination. Two had been chicken roosts. One was larger than the other. It was there I started to poke around and dig.

Where? Where? I wish I'd been on more archaeological digs, knew the places to look. Refuse piles, midden heaps, kitchen scrap piles, compost boxes. Why hadn't I been born on a farm so I'd know instinctively where to search?

I prodded around the grounds. I moved back and forth like a setter casting for the scent of quail. I wanted more, more. I still wasn't satisfied.

Dusk. Dark, in fact. I trudged into the Kraits' front yard. The toe sack I carried was full to bulging. I was hot, tired, streaked with fifty years of chicken shit. The Kraits were on their porch. Jim Bob lumbered down like a friendly mountain.

I asked him a few questions, gave them a Xerox of one of the dodo pictures, left them addresses and phone numbers where they could reach me.

Then into the rent-a-car. Off to Water Valley, acting on information Jennifer Krait gave me. I went to the postmaster's house at Water Valley. She was getting ready for bed. I asked questions. She got on the phone. I bothered people until one in the morning. Then back into the trusty rent-a-car.

On to Memphis as the moon came up on my right. Interstate 55 was a glass ribbon before me. WLS from Chicago was on the radio.

I hummed along with it, I sang at the top of my voice.

The sack full of dodo bones, beaks, feet and eggshell fragments kept me company on the front seat.

Did you know a museum once traded an entire blue whale skeleton for one of a dodo?

Driving. Driving.

*the dance of the dodos*

I used to have a vision sometimes—I had it long before this madness came up. I can close my eyes and see it by thinking hard. But it comes to me most often, most vividly when I am reading and listening to classical music, especially Pachelbel's *Canon in D.*

It is near dusk in The Hague and the light is that of Frans Hals, of Rembrandt. The Dutch royal family and their guests eat and talk quietly in the great dining hall. Guards with halberds and pikes stand in the corners of the room. The family is arranged around the table; the King, Queen, some princesses, a prince, a couple of other children, and invited noble or two. Servants come out with plates and cups but they do not intrude.

On a raised platform at one end of the room an orchestra plays dinner music—a harpsichord, viola, cello, three violins, and woodwinds. One of the royal dwarfs sits on the edge of the platform, his foot slowly rubbing the back of one of the dogs sleeping near him.

As the music of Pachelbel's *Canon in D* swells and rolls through the hall, one of the dodos walks in clumsily, stops, tilts its head, its eyes bright as a pool of tar. It sways a little, lifts its foot tentatively, one then another, rocks back and forth in time to the cello.

The violins swirl. The dodo begins to dance, its great ungainly body now graceful. It is joined by the other two dodos who come into the hall, all three in sort of a circle.

The harpsichord begins its counterpoint. The fourth dodo, the white one from Réunion, comes from its place under the table and joins the circle with the others.

It is most graceful of all, making complete turns where the others only sway and dip on the edge of the circle they have formed.

The music rises in volume; the first violinist sees the dodos and nods to the King. But he and the others at the table have already seen. They are silent, transfixed—even the servants stand still, bowls, pots and, kettles in their hands forgotten.

Around the dodos dance with bobs and weaves of their ugly heads. The white dodo dips, takes half a step, pirouettes on one foot, circles again.

Without a word the King of Holland takes the hand of the Queen, and they come around the table, children before the spectacle. They join in the dance, waltzing (anachronism) among the dodos while the family, the guests, the soldiers watch and nod in time with the music.

Then the vision fades, and the afterimage of a flickering fireplace and a dodo remains.

The dodo and its kindred came by ships to the ports of civilized men. The first we have record of is that of Captain van Neck who brought back two in 1599—one for the King of Holland, and one which found its way through Cologne to the menagerie of Emperor Rudolf II.

This royal aviary was at Schloss Neugebau, near Vienna. It was here the first paintings of the dumb old birds were done by Georg and his son Jacob Hoefnagel, between 1602 and 1610. They painted it among more than ninety species of birds which kept the Emperor amused.

Another Dutch artist named Roelandt Savery, as someone said, "made a career out of the dodo." He drew and painted them many times, and was no doubt personally fascinated by them. Obsessed, even. Early on, the paintings are consistent; the later ones have inaccuracies. This implies he worked from life first, then from memory as his model went to that place soon to be reserved for all its species. One of his drawings has two of the

Raphidae scrambling for some goodie on the ground. His works are not without charm.

Another Dutch artist (they seemed to sprout up like mushrooms after a spring rain) named Peter Withoos also stuck dodos in his paintings, sometimes in odd and exciting places—wandering around during their owner's music lessons, or with Adam and Eve in some Edenic idyll.

The most accurate representation, we are assured, comes from half a world away from the religious and political turmoil of the seafaring Europeans. There is an Indian miniature painting of the dodo which now rests in a museum in Russia. The dodo could have been brought by the Dutch or Portuguese in their travels to Goa and the coasts of the Indian subcontinent. Or they could have been brought centuries before by the Arabs who plied the Indian Ocean in their triangular-sailed craft, and who may have discovered the Mascarenes before the Europeans cranked themselves up for the First Crusade.

At one time early in my bird-fascination days (after I stopped killing them with BB guns but before I began to work for a scholarship), I once sat down and figured out where all the dodos had been.

Two with van Neck in 1599, one to Holland, one to Austria. Another was in Count Solm's park in 1600. An account speaks of "one in Italy, one in Germany, several to England, eight or nine to Holland." William Boentekoe van Hoorn knew of "one shipped to Europe in 1640, another in 1685" which he said was "also painted by Dutch artists." Two were mentioned as "being kept in Surrat House in India as pets," perhaps one of which is the one in the painting. Being charitable, and considering "several" to mean at least three, that means twenty dodos in all.

There had to be more, when boatloads had been gathered at the time.

What do we know of the Didine birds? A few ships' logs, some accounts left by travelers and colonists. The English were fascinated by them. Sir Hamon L'Estrange, a contemporary of Pepys, saw exhibited "a Dodar from the Island of Mauritius . . . it is not able to flie, being so bigge." One was stuffed when it died, and was put in the Museum Tradescantum in South Lambeth. It eventually found its way into the Ashmolean Museum. It grew ratty and was burned, all but a leg and the head, in 1740 By then there were no more dodos, but nobody had realized that yet.

Francis Willughby got to describe it before its incineration. Earlier, old Carolus Clusius in Holland studied the one in Count Solm's park. He collected everything known about the Raphidae, describing a dodo leg Pieter Pauw kept in his natural history cabinet, in *Exoticarium libri decem* in 1605, eight years after their discovery.

François Leguat, a Huguenot who lived on Réunion for some years, published an account of his travels in which he mentioned the dodos. It was published in 1690 (after the Mauritius dodo was extinct) and included the information that "some of the males weigh forty-five pounds. One egg, much bigger than that of a goose, is laid by the female, and takes seven weeks' hatching time."

The Abbe Pingre visited the Mascarenes in 1761. He saw the last of the Rodriguez solitaires, and collected what information he could about the dead Mauritius and Réunion members of the genus.

After that, only memories of the colonists, and some scientific debate as to *where* the Raphidae belonged in the great taxonomic scheme of things—some said pigeons, some said rails—were left. Even this nitpicking ended. The dodo was forgotten.

When Lewis Carroll wrote *Alice in Wonderland* in 1865, most people thought he invented the dodo.


The service station I called from in Memphis was busier than a one-legged man in an ass-kicking contest. Between bings and dings of the bell, I finally realized the call had gone through.

The guy who answered was named Selvedge. I got nowhere with him. He mistook me for a real estate agent, then a lawyer. Now he was beginning to think I was some sort of a con man. I wasn't doing too well, either. I hadn't slept in two days. I must have sounded like a speed freak. My only progress was that I found that Ms. Annie Mae Gudger (childhood playmate of Jolyn Jimson) was now, and had been, the respected Ms. Annie Mae Radwin. This guy Selvedge must have been a secretary or toady or something.

We were having a conversation comparable to that between a shrieking macaw and a pile of mammoth bones. Then there was another click on the line.

"Young man?" said the other voice, an old woman's voice, Southern, very refined but with a hint of the hills in it.

"Yes? Hello! Hello!"

"Young man, you say you talked to a Jolyn somebody? Do you mean Jolyn Smith?"

"Hello! Yes! Ms. Radwin, Ms. Annie Mae Radwin who used to be Gudger? She lives in Austin now. Texas. She used to live near Water Valley, Mississippi. Austin's where I'm from. I . . ."

"Young man," asked the voice again, "are you sure you haven't been put up to this by my hateful sister Alma?"

"Who? No, ma'am. I met a woman named Jolyn . . ."

"I'd like to talk to you, young man," said the voice. Then offhandedly, "Give him directions to get here, Selvedge."

Click.

I cleaned out my mouth as best I could in the service station restroom, tried to shave with an old clogged Gillette disposable in my knapsack and succeeded in gapping up my jawline. I changed into a clean pair of jeans, the only other shirt I had with me, and combed my hair. I stood in front of the mirror.

I still looked like the dog's lunch.


The house reminded me of Presley's mansion, which was somewhere in the neighborhood. From a shack on the side of a Mississippi hill to this, in forty years. There are all sorts of ways of making it. I wondered what Annie Mae Gudger's had been. Luck? Predation? Divine intervention? Hard work? Trover and replevin?

Selvedge led me toward the sun room. I felt like Philip Marlowe going to meet a rich client. The house was filled with that furniture built some-time between the turn of the century and the 1950s—the ageless kind. It never looks great, it never looks ratty, and every chair is comfortable.

I think I was expecting some formidable woman with sleeve blotters and a green eyeshade hunched over a roll-top desk with piles of paper whose acceptance or rejection meant life or death for thousands.

Who I met was a charming lady in a green pantsuit. She was in her sixties, her hair still a straw wheat color. It didn't look dyed. Her eyes were blue as my first-grade teacher's had been. She was wiry and looked as if the word fat was not in her vocabulary.

"Good morning, Mr. Lindberl." She shook my hand. "Would you like some coffee? You look as if you could use it."

"Yes, thank you."

"Please sit down." She indicated a white wicker chair at a glass table. A serving tray with coffeepot, cups, tea bags, croissants, napkins, and plates lay on the tabletop.

After I swallowed half a cup of coffee at a gulp, she said, "What you wanted to see me about must be important?"

"Sorry about my manners," I said. "I know I don't look it, but I'm a biology assistant at the University of Texas. An ornithologist. Working on my master's. I met Ms. Jolyn Jimson two days ago . . ."

"How is Jolyn? I haven't seen her in oh, Lord, it must be on to fifty years. The times gets away."

"She seemed to be fine. I only talked to her half an hour or so. That was . . ."

"And you've come to see me about? . . ."

"Uh. The . . . about some of the poultry your family used to raise, when they lived near Water Valley."

She looked at me a moment. Then she began to smile.

"Oh, you mean the ugly chickens?" she said.

I smiled. I almost laughed. I knew what Oedipus must have gone through.

It is now 4:30 in the afternoon. I am sitting at the downtown Motel 6 in Memphis. I have to make a phone call and get some sleep and catch a plane.

Annie Mae Gudger Radwin talked for four hours, answering my questions, setting me straight on family history, having Selvedge hold all her calls.

The main problem was that Annie Mae ran off in 1928, the year *before* her father got his big break. She went to Yazoo City, and by degrees and stages worked her way northward to Memphis and her destiny as the widow of a rich mercantile broker.

But I get ahead of myself.

Grandfather Gudger used to be the overseer for Colonel Crisby on the main plantation near McComb, Mississippi. There was a long story behind that. Bear with me.

Colonel Crisby himself was the scion of a seafaring family with interests in both the cedars of Lebanon (almost all cut down for masts for His Majesty's and others' navies) and Egyptian cotton. Also teas, spices, and any other salable commodity which came their way.

When Colonel Crisby's grandfather reached his majority in 1802, he waved good-bye to the Atlantic Ocean at Charleston, S.C. and stepped westward into the forest. When he stopped, he was in the middle of the Chickasaw Nation, where he opened a trading post and introduced slaves to the Indians.

And he prospered, and begat Colonel Crisby's father, who sent back to South Carolina for everything his father owned. Everything—slaves, wagons, horses, cattle, guinea fowl, peacocks, and dodos, which everybody thought of as atrociously ugly poultry of some kind, one of the seafaring uncles having bought them off a French merchant in 1721. (I surmised these were white dodos from Réunion, unless they had been from even earlier stock. The dodo of Mauritius was already extinct by then.)

All this stuff was herded out west to the trading post in the midst of the Chickasaw Nation. (The tribes around there were of the confederation of the Dancing Rabbits.)

And Colonel Crisby's father prospered, and so did the guinea fowl and the dodos. Then Andrew Jackson came along and marched the Dancing Rabbits off up the Trail of Tears to the heaven of Oklahoma. And Colonel Crisby's father begat Colonel Crisby, and put the trading post in the hands of others, and moved his plantation westward still to McComb.

Everything prospered but Colonel Crisby's father, who died. And the dodos, with occasional losses to the avengin' weasel and the egg-sucking dog, reproduced themselves also.

Then along came Granddaddy Gudger, a Simon Legree role model, who took care of the plantation while Colonel Crisby raised ten companies of men and marched off to fight the War of the Southern Independence.

Colonel Crisby came back to the McComb plantation earlier than most, he having stopped much of the same volley of Minié balls that caught his commander, General Beauregard Hanlon, on a promontory bluff during the Siege of Vicksburg.

He wasn't dead, but death hung around the place like a gentlemanly bill collector for a month. The colonel languished, went slap-dab crazy and freed all his slaves the week before he died (the war lasted another two years after that). Not having any slaves, he didn't need an overseer.

Then comes the Faulkner part of the tale, straight out of *As I Lay Dying*, with the Gudger family returning to the area of Water Valley (before there was a Water Valley), moving through the demoralized and tattered displaced persons of the South, driving their dodos before them. For Colonel Crisby had given them to his former overseer for his faithful service. Also followed the story of the bloody murder of Granddaddy Gudger at the hands of the Freedman's militia during the rising of the first Klan, and of the trials and tribulations of Daddy Gudger in the years between 1880 and 1910, when he was between the ages of four and thirty-four.

Alma and Annie Mae were the second and fifth of Daddy Gudger's brood, born three years apart. They seemed to have hated each other from the very first time Alma looked into little Annie Mae's crib. They were kids by Daddy Gudger's second wife (his desperation had killed the first) and their father was already on his sixth career. He had been a lumberman, a stump preacher, a plowman-for-hire (until his mules broke out in farcy buds and died of the glanders), a freight hauler (until his horses died of overwork and the hardware store repossessed the wagon), a politician's roadie (until the politician lost the election). When Alma and Annie Mae were born, he was failing as a sharecropper. Somehow Gudger had made it through the Depression of 1898 as a boy, and was too poor after that to notice more about economics than the price of Beech-Nut tobacco at the store.

Alma and Annie Mae fought, and it helped none at all that Alma, being the oldest daughter, was both her mother and father's darling. Annie Mae's life was the usual unwanted poor-white-trash-child's hell. She vowed early to run away, and recognized her ambition at thirteen.

All this I learned this morning. Jolyn (Smith) Jimson was Annie Mae's only friend in those days—from a family even poorer than the Gudgers. But somehow there was food, and an occasional odd job. And the dodos.

"My family hated those old birds," said the cultured Annie Mae Radwin, née Gudger, in the solarium. "He always swore he was going to get rid of them someday, but just never seemed to get around to it. I think there was more to it than that. But they were so much *trouble*. We always had to keep them penned up at night, and go check for their eggs. They wandered off to lay them, and forgot where they were. Sometimes no new ones were born at all in a year.

"And they got so *ugly*. Once a year. I mean, terrible-looking, like they were going to die. All their feathers fell off, and they looked like they had mange or something. Then the whole front of their beaks fell off, or worse, hung halfway on for a week or two. They looked like big old naked pigeons. After that they'd lose weight, down to twenty or thirty pounds, before their new feathers grew back.

"We were always having to kill foxes that got after them in the turkey house. That's what we called their roost, the turkey house. And we found their eggs all sucked out by cats and dogs. They were so stupid we had to drive them into their roost at night. I don't think they could have found it standing ten feet from it."

She looked at me.

"I think much as my father hated them, they meant something to him. As long as he hung on to them, he knew he was as good as Granddaddy Gudger. You may not know it, but there was a certain amount of family pride about Granddaddy Gudger. At least in my father's eyes. His rapid fall in the world has a sort of grandeur to it. He'd gone from a relatively high position in the old order, and maintained some grace and stature after the Emancipation, and though he lost everything, he managed to keep those ugly old chickens the colonel had given him as sort of a symbol.

"And as long as he had them, too, my daddy thought himself as good as his father. He kept his dignity, even when he didn't have anything else."

I asked what happened to them. She didn't know, but told me who did and where I could find her.

That's why I'm going to make a phone call.

"Hello. Dr. Courtney. Dr. Courtney? This is Paul. Memphis. Tennessee. It's too long to go into. No, of course not, not yet. But I've got evidence. What? Okay, how do trochanters, coracoids, tarsometatarsi, and beak sheaths sound? From their henhouse, where else? Where would you keep *your* dodos, then?

"Sorry. I haven't slept in a couple of days. I need some help. Yes, yes. Money. Lots of money.

"Cash. Three hundred dollars, maybe. Western Union, Memphis, Tennessee. Whichever one's closest to the airport. Airport. I need the department to set up reservations to Mauritius for me. . . .

"No. No. Not wild goose chase, wild *dodo* chase. Tame dodo chase. I *know* there aren't any dodos on Mauritius! I know that. I could explain. I know it'll mean a couple of grand . . . if . . . but . . .

"Look, Dr. Courtney. Do you want *your* picture in *Scientific American,* or don't you?"

I am sitting in the airport cafe in Port Louis, Mauritius. It is now three days later, five days since that fateful morning my car wouldn't start. God bless the Sears Diehard people. I have slept sitting up in a plane seat, on and off, different planes, different seats, for twenty-four hours, Kennedy to Paris, Paris to Cairo, Cairo to Madagascar. I felt like a brand-new man when I got here.

Now I feel like an infinitely sadder and wiser brand-new man. I have just returned from the hateful sister Alma's house in the exclusive section of Port Louis, where all the French and British officials used to live.

Courtney will get his picture in *Scientific American,* me too, all right. There'll be newspaper stories and talk shows for a few weeks for me, and I'm sure Annie Mae Gudger Radwin on one side of the world and Alma Chandler Gudger Molière on the other will come in for their share of the glory.

I am putting away cup after cup of coffee. The plane back to Tananarive leaves in an hour. I plan to sleep all the way back to Cairo, to Paris, to New York, pick up my bag of bones, sleep back to Austin.

Before me on the table is a packet of documents, clippings and photographs. I have come half the world for this. I gaze from the package, out the window across Port Louis to the bulk of Mt. Pieter Boothe, which overshadows the city and its famous racecourse.

Perhaps I should do something symbolic. Cancel my flight. Climb the mountain and look down on man and all his handiworks. Take a pitcher of martinis with me. Sit in the bright semitropical sunlight (it's early dry winter here). Drink the martinis slowly, toasting Snuffo, God of Extinction. Here's one for the Great Auk. This is for the Carolina Parakeet. Mud in your eye, Passenger Pigeon. This one's for the Heath Hen. Most importantly, here's one each for the Mauritius dodo, the white dodo of Réunion, the Réunion solitaire, the Rodriguez solitaire. Here's to the Raphidae, great Didine birds that you were.

Maybe I'll do something just as productive, like climbing Mt. Pieter Boothe and pissing into the wind.

How symbolic. The story of the dodo ends where it began, on this very island. Life imitates cheap art. Like the Xerox of the Xerox of a bad novel. I never expected to find dodos still alive here (this is the one place they would have been noticed). I still can't believe Alma Chandler Gudger Molière could have lived here twenty-five years and not know about the dodo, never set foot inside the Port Louis Museum, where they have skeletons and a stuffed replica the size of your little brother.

After Annie Mae ran off, the Gudger family found itself prospering in a time the rest of the country was going to hell. It was 1929. Gudger delved into politics again, and backed a man who knew a man who worked for Theodore "Sure Two-Handed Sword of God" Bilbo, who had connections everywhere. Who introduced him to Huey "Kingfish" Long just after that gentleman lost the Louisiana governor's election one of the times. Gudger stumped around Mississippi, getting up steam for Long's Share the Wealth plan, even before it had a name.

The upshot was that the Long machine in Louisiana knew a rabble-rouser when it saw one, and invited Gudger to move to the Sportsman's Paradise, with his family, all expenses paid, and start working for the Kingfish at the unbelievable salary of $62.50 a week. Which prospect was like turning a hog loose under a persimmon tree, and before you could say Backwoods Messiah, the Gudger clan was on its way to the land of pelicans, graft, and Mardi Gras.

Almost. But I'll get to that.

Daddy Gudger prospered all out of proportion with his abilities, but many men did that during the Depression. First a little, thence to more, he rose in bureaucratic (and political) circles of the state, dying rich and well-hated with his fingers in *all* the pies.

Alma Chandler Gudger became a debutante (she says Robert Penn Warren put her in his book) and met and married Jean Carl Molière, only heir to rice, indigo, and sugar cane growers. They had a happy wedded life, moving first to the West Indies, later to Mauritius, where the family sugar cane holdings were one of the largest on the island. Jean Carl died in 1959. Alma was his only survivor.

So local family makes good. Poor sharecropping Mississippi people turn out to have a father dying with a smile on his face, and two daughters who between them own a large portion of the planet.

I open the envelope before me. Ms. Alma Molière had listened politely to my story (the university had called ahead and arranged an introduction through the director of the Port Louis Museum, who knew Ms. Molière socially) and told me what she could remember. Then she sent a servant out to one of the storehouses (large as a duplex) and he and two others came back with boxes of clippings, scrapbooks and family photos.

"I haven't looked at any of this since we left St. Thomas," she said. "Let's go through it together."

Most of it was about the rise of Citizen Gudger.

"There's not many pictures of us before we came to Louisiana. We were so frightfully poor then, hardly anyone we knew had a camera. Oh, look. Here's one of Annie Mae. I thought I threw all those out after Mamma died."

This is the photograph. It must have been taken about 1927. Annie Mae is wearing some unrecognizable piece of clothing that approximates a dress. She leans on a hoe, smiling a snaggle-toothed smile. She looks to be ten or eleven. Her eyes are half hidden by the shadow of the brim of a gapped straw hat she wears. The earth she is standing in barefoot has been newly turned. Behind her is one corner of the house, and the barn beyond has its upper hay-windows open. Out-of-focus people are at work there.

A few feet behind her, a huge male dodo is pecking at something on the ground. The front two-thirds of it shows, back to the stupid wings and the edge of the upcurved tail feathers. One foot is in the photo, having just scratched at something, possibly an earthworm, in the new-plowed clods. Judging by its darkness, it is the grey, or Mauritius, dodo.

The photograph is not very good, one of those 3½ x 5 jobs box cameras used to take. Already I can see this one, and the blowup of the dodo, taking up a double-page spread in *S.A.* Alma told me around then they were down to six or seven of the ugly chickens, two whites, the rest grey-brown.

Besides this photo, two clippings are in the package, one from the Bruce *Banner-Times*, the other from the Oxford newspaper; both are columns by the same woman dealing with "Doings in Water Valley." Both mention the Gudger family moving from the area to seek its fortune in the swampy state to the west, and telling how they will be missed. Then there's a yellowed clipping from the front page of the Oxford newspaper with a small story about the Gudger Farewell Party in Water Valley the Sunday before (dated October 19, 1929).

There's a handbill in the package, advertising the Gudger Family Farewell Party, Sunday Oct. 15, 1929 Come One Come All. (The people in Louisiana who sent expense money to move Daddy Gudger must have overestimated the costs by an exponential factor. I said as much.)

"No," Alma Molière said. "There was a lot, but it wouldn't have made any difference. Daddy Gudger was like Thomas Wolfe and knew a shining golden opportunity when he saw one. Win, lose, or draw, he was never coming back *there* again. He would have thrown some kind of soirée whether there had been money for it or not. Besides, people were much more sociable then, you mustn't forget."

I asked her how many people came.

"Four or five hundred," she said. "There's some pictures here somewhere." We searched awhile, then we found them.

Another thirty minutes to my flight. I'm not worried sitting here. I'm the only passenger, and the pilot is sitting at the table next to mine talking to an RAF man. Life is much slower and nicer on these colonial islands. You mustn't forget.

I look at the other two photos in the package. One is of some men playing horseshoes and washer-toss, while kids, dogs, and women look on. It was evidently taken from the east end of the house looking west. Everyone must have had to walk the last mile to the old Gudger place. Other groups of people stand talking. Some men in shirtsleeves and suspenders stand with their heads thrown back, a snappy story, no doubt, just told. One girl looks directly at the camera from close up, shyly, her finger in her mouth. She's about five. It looks like any snapshot of a family reunion which could have been taken anywhere, anytime. Only the clothing marks it as backwoods 1920s.

Courtney will get his money's worth. I'll write the article, make phone calls, plan the talk show tour to coincide with publication. Then I'll get some rest. I'll be a normal person again; get a degree, spend my time wading through jungles after animals which will be dead in another twenty years, anyway.

Who cares? The whole thing will be just another media event, just this year's Big Deal. It'll be nice getting normal again. I can read books, see movies, wash my clothes at the laundromat, listen to Jonathan Richman on the stereo. I can study and become an authority on some minor matter or other.

I can go to museums and see all the wonderful dead things there.

"That's the memory picture," said Alma. "They always took them at big things like this, back in those days. Everybody who was there would line up and pose for the camera. Only we couldn't fit everybody in. So we had two made. This is the one with us in it."

The house is dwarfed by people. All sizes, shapes, dresses, and ages. Kids and dogs in front, women next, then men at the back. The only exceptions are the bearded patriarchs seated towards the front with the children—men whose eyes face the camera but whose heads are still ringing with something Nathan Bedford Forrest said to them one time on a smoke-filled field. This photograph is from another age. You can recognize

Daddy and Mrs. Gudger if you've seen their photograph before. Alma pointed herself out to me.

But the reason I took the photograph is in the foreground. Tables have been built out of sawhorses, with doors and boards nailed across them. They extend the entire width of the photograph. They are covered with food, more food than you can imagine.

"We started cooking three days before. So did the neighbors. Everybody brought something," said Alma.

It's like an entire Safeway had been cooked and set out to cool. Hams, quarters of beef, chickens by the tubful, quail in mounds, rabbit, butterbeans by the bushel, yams, Irish potatoes, an acre of corn, eggplant, peas, turnip greens, butter in five-pound molds, cornbread and biscuits, gallon cans of molasses, redeye gravy by the pot.

And five huge birds—twice as big as turkeys, legs capped like for Thanksgiving, drumsticks the size of Schwarzenegger's biceps, wholeroasted, lying on their backs on platters large as cocktail tables.

The people in the crowd sure look hungry.

"We ate for days," said Alma.

I already have the title for the *Scientific American* article. It's going to be called "The Dodo Is *Still* Dead."

# Der Untergang des Abendlandesmenschen

They rode through the flickering landscape to the tune of organ music.

Bronco Billy, short like an old sailor, and William S., tall and rangy as a windblown pine. Their faces, their horses, the landscape all darkened and became light; were at first indistinct, then sharp and clear as they rode across one ridge and down into the valley beyond.

Ahead of them, in much darker shades, was the city of Bremen, Germany.

Except for the organ and piano music, it was quiet in most of Europe.

In the vaults below the Opera, in the City of Lights, Erik the phantom played the *Toccata and Fugue* while the sewers ran blackly by.

In Berlin, Cesare the somnambulist slept. His mentor Caligari lectured at the University, and waited for his chance to send the monster through the streets.

Also in Berlin, Dr. Mabuse was dead and could no longer control the underworld.

But in Bremen . . .

In Bremen, something walked the night.

To the cities of china eggs and dolls, in the time of sawdust bread and the price of six million marks for a postage stamp, came Bronco Billy and William S. They had ridden hard for two days and nights, and the horses were heavily lathered.

They reined in, and tied their mounts to a streetlamp on the Wilhelmstrasse.

"What say we get a drink, William S.?" asked the shorter cowboy. "All this damn flickering gives me a headache."

William S. struck a pose three feet away from him, turned his head left and right, and stepped up to the doors of the *Gasthaus* before them.

With his high-pointed hat and checked shirt, William S. looked like a weatherbeaten scarecrow, or a child's version of Abraham Lincoln before the beard. His eyes were like shiny glass, through which some inner hellfires shone.

Bronco Billy hitched up his pants. He wore Levis, which on him looked too large, a dark vest, lighter shirt, big leather chaps with three tassels at hip, knee and calf. His hat seemed three sizes too big.

Inside the tavern, things were murky grey, black and stark white. And always, the flickering.

They sat down at a table and watched the clientele. Ex-soldiers, in the remnants of uniforms, seven years after the Great War had ended. The unemployed, spending their last few coins on beer. The air was thick with grey smoke from pipes and cheap cigarettes.

Not too many people had noticed the entrance of William S. and Bronco Billy.

Two had.

"Quirt!" said an American captain, his hand on his drinking buddy, a sergeant.

"What?" asked the sergeant, his hand on the barmaid.

"Look who's here!"

The sergeant peered toward the haze of flickering grey smoke where the cowboys sat.

"Damn!" he said.

"Want to go over and chat with 'em?" asked the captain.

"&%#*$% no!" cursed the sergeant. "This ain't our #%&*!*ing picture."

"I suppose you're right," said the captain, and returned to his wine.

"You must remember, my friend," said William S. after the waiter brought them beer, "that there can be no rest in the pursuit of evil."

"Yeah, but hell, William S., this is a long way from home."

William S. lit a match, put it to a briar pipe containing his favorite shag tobacco. He puffed on it a few moments, then regarded his companion across his tankard.

"My dear Bronco Billy," he said. "No place is too far to go in order to thwart the forces of darkness. This is something Dr. Helioglabulus could not handle by himself, else he should not have summoned us."

"Yeah, but William S., my butt's sore as a rizen after two days in the saddle. I think we should bunk down before we see this doctor fellow."

"Ah, that's where you're wrong, my friend," said the tall, hawknosed cowboy. "Evil never sleeps. Men must."

"Well, I'm a man," said Bronco Billy. "I say let's sleep."

Just then, Dr. Helioglabulus entered the tavern.

He was dressed as a Tyrolean mountain guide in *Lederhosen* and feathered cap, climbing boots and suspenders. He carried with him an alpenstock, which made a large *clunk* each time it touched the floor.

He walked through the flickering darkness and smoke and stood in front of the table with the two cowboys.

William S. had risen.

"Dr.—" he began.

"Eulenspiegel," said the other, an admonitory finger to his lips.

Bronco Billy rolled his eyes heavenward.

"Dr. Eulenspiegel, I'd like you to meet my associate and chronicler, Mr.

Bronco Billy."

The doctor clicked his heels together.

"Have a chair," said Bronco Billy, pushing one out from under the table with his boot. He tipped his hat up off his eyes.

The doctor, in his comic opera outfit, sat.

"Helioglabulus," whispered William S., "whatever are you up to?"

"I had to come incognito. There are . . . others who should not learn of my presence here."

Bronco Billy looked from one to the other and rolled his eyes again.

"Then the game is afoot?" asked William S., his eyes more alight than ever.

"Game such as man has never before seen," said the doctor.

"I see," said William S., his eyes narrowing as he drew on his pipe. "Moriarty?"

"Much more evil."

"More evil?" asked the cowboy, his fingertips pressed together. "I cannot imagine such."

"Neither could I, up until a week ago," said Helioglabulus. "Since then, the city has experienced wholesale terrors. Rats run the streets at night, invade houses. This tavern will be deserted by nightfall. The people lock their doors and say prayers, even in this age. They are reverting to the old superstitions."

"They have just cause?" asked William S.

"A week ago, a ship pulled into the pier. On board was—one man!" He paused for dramatic effect. Bronco Billy was unimpressed. The doctor continued. "The crew, the passengers were gone. Only the captain was aboard, lashed to the wheel. And he was—drained of blood!"

Bronco Billy became interested.

"You mean," asked William S., bending over his beer, "that we are dealing with—the undead?"

"I am afraid so," said Dr. Helioglabulus, twisting his mustaches.

"Then we shall need the proper armaments," said the taller cowboy.

"I have them," said the doctor, taking cartridge boxes from his backpack.

"Good!" said William S. "Bronco Billy, you have your revolver?"

"What!? Whatta ya mean, 'Do you have your revolver?' Just what do you mean? Have you ever seen me without my guns, William S.? Are you losing your mind?"

"Sorry, Billy," said William S., looking properly abashed.

"Take these," said Helioglabulus.

Bronco Billy broke open his two Peacemakers, dumped the .45 shells on the table. William S. unlimbered his two Navy .36s and pushed the recoil rod down in the cylinders. He punched each cartridge out onto the tabletop.

Billy started to load up his pistols, then took a closer look at the shells, held one up and examined it.

"Goddam, William S.," he yelled. "Wooden bullets! Wooden bullets?"

Helioglabulus was trying to wave him to silence. The tall cowboy tried to put his hand on the other.

Everyone in the beer hall had heard him. There was a deafening silence, all the patrons turned toward their table.

"Damn," said Bronco Billy. "You can't shoot a wooden bullet fifteen feet and expect to hit the broad side of a corncrib. What the hell we gonna shoot wooden bullets at?"

The tavern began to empty, people rushing from the place, looking back in terror. All except five men at a far table.

"I am afraid, my dear Bronco Billy," said William S., "that you have frightened the patrons, and warned the evil ones of our presence."

Bronco Billy looked around.

"You mean those guys over there?" he nodded toward the other table.

"Hell, William S., we both took on twelve men one time."

Dr. Helioglabulus sighed. "No, no, you don't understand. Those men over there are harmless; crackpot revolutionists. William and I are speaking of *nosferatu* . . ."

Bronco Billy continued to stare at him.

". . . the undead . . ."

No response.

". . . er, ah, vampires . . ."

"You mean," asked Billy, "like Theda Bara?"

"Not vamps, my dear friend," said the hawknosed wrangler. "Vampires. Those who rise from the dead and suck the blood of the living."

"Oh," said Bronco Billy. Then he looked at the cartridges. "These kill 'em?"

"Theoretically," said Helioglabulus.

"Meaning you don't know?"

The doctor nodded.

"In that case," said Bronco Billy, "we go halfies." He began to load his .45s with one regular bullet, then a wooden one, then another standard.

William S. had already filled his with wooden slugs.

"Excellent," said Helioglabulus. "Now, put these over your hatbands. I hope you never have to get close enough for them to be effective."

What he handed them were silver hatbands. Stamped on the shiny surface of the bands was a series of crosses. They slipped them on their heads, settling them on their hat brims.

"What next?" asked Bronco Billy.

"Why, we wait for nightfall, for the *nosferatu* to strike!" said the doctor.

"Did you hear them, Hermann?" asked Joseph.

"Sure. You think we ought to do the same?"

"Where would we find someone to make wooden bullets for pistols such as ours?" asked Joseph.

The five men sitting at the table looked toward the doctor and the two cowboys. All five were dressed in the remnants of uniforms belonging to the war. The one addressed as Hermann still wore the Knight's Cross on the faded splendor of his dress jacket.

"Martin," said Hermann. "Do you know where we can get wooden bullets?"

"I'm sure we could find someone to make them for the automatics," he answered. "Ernst, go to Wartman's; see about them."

Ernst stood, then slapped the table. "Every time I hear the word vampire, I reach for my Browning!" he said.

They all laughed. Martin, Hermann, Joseph, Ernst most of all. Even Adolf laughed a little.

Soon after dark, someone ran into the place, white of face. "The vampire!" he yelled, pointing vaguely toward the street, and fell out.

Bronco Billy and William S. jumped up. Helioglabulus stopped them. "I'm too old, and will only hold you up," he said. "I shall try to catch up later. Remember . . . the crosses. The bullets in the heart!"

As they rushed out past the other table, Ernst, who had left an hour earlier, returned with two boxes.

"Quick, Joseph!" he said as the two cowboys went through the door, "Follow them! We'll be right behind. Your pistol!"

Joseph turned, threw a Browning automatic pistol back to Hermann, then went out the doors as hoofbeats clattered in the street.

The other four began to load their pistols from the boxes of cartridges.

The two cowboys rode toward the commotion.

"Yee-haw!" yelled Bronco Billy. They galloped down the well-paved streets, their horses' hooves striking sparks from the cobbles.

They passed the police and others running toward the sounds of screams and dying. Members of the Free Corps, ex-soldiers and students, swarmed the streets in their uniforms. Torches burned against the flickering black night skies.

The city was trying to overcome the *nosferatu* by force.

Bronco Billy and William S. charged toward the fighting. In the center of a square stood a coach, all covered in black crepe. The driver, a plump, cadaverous man, held the reins to four black horses. The four were rearing high in their traces, their hooves menacing the crowd.

But it was not the horses which kept the mob back.

Crawling out of a second-story hotel window was a vision from nightmare. Bald, with pointed ears, teeth like a rat, beady eyes bright in the flickering night, the vampire climbed from a bedroom to the balcony. The front of his frock coat was covered with blood, his face and arms were smeared. A man's hand stuck halfway out the window, and the curtains were spattered black.

The *nosferatu* jumped to the ground, and the crowd parted as he leaped from the hotel steps to the waiting carriage. Then the driver cracked his whip over the horses—there was no sound—and the team charged, tumbling people like leaves before the night wind.

The carriage seemed to float to the two cowboys who rode after it. There was no sound of hoofbeats ahead, no noise from the harness, no creak of axles. It was as if they followed the wind itself through the nighttime streets of Bremen.

They sped down the flickering main roads. Once, when Bronco Billy glanced behind him, he thought he saw motorcycle headlights following. But he devoted most of his attention to the fleeing coach.

William S. rode beside him. They gained on the closed carriage.

Bronco Billy drew his left-hand pistol (he was ambidextrous) and fired at the broad back of the driver. He heard the splintery clatter of the wooden bullet as it ricocheted off the coach. Then the carriage turned ahead of them.

He was almost smashed against a garden wall by the headlong plunge of his mount, then he recovered, leaning far over in the saddle, as if his horse were a sailboat and he a sailor heeling against the wind.

Then he and William S. were closing with the hearse on a long broad stretch of the avenue. They pulled even with the driver.

And for the first time, the hackles rose on Bronco Billy's neck as he rode beside the black-crepe coach. There was no sound but him, his horse, their gallop. He saw the black-garbed driver crack the long whip, heard no *snap*, heard no horses, heard no wheels.

His heart in his throat, he watched William S. pull even on the other side. The driver turned that way, snapped his whip toward the taller cowboy. Bronco Billy saw his friend's hat fly away, cut in two.

Billy took careful aim and shot the lead horse in the head, twice. It dropped like a ton of cement, and the air was filled with a vicious, soundless image—four horses, the driver, the carriage, he, his mount and William S. all flying through the air in a tangle. Then the side of the coach caught him and the incessant flickering went out.

He must have awakened a few seconds later. His horse was atop him, but he didn't think anything was broken. He pushed himself out from under it.

The driver was staggering up from the flinders of the coach—strange, thought Bronco Billy, now I hear the sounds of the wheels turning, the screams of the dying horses. The driver pulled a knife. He started toward the cowboy.

Bronco Billy found his right-hand pistol still in its holster. He pulled it, fired directly into the heart of the fat man. The driver folded from the recoil, then stood again.

Billy pulled the trigger.

The driver dropped as the wooden bullet turned his heart to giblets.

Bronco Billy took all the regular ammo out of his pistol and began to cram the wooden ones in.

As he did, motorcycles came screaming to a stop beside him, and the five men from the tavern climbed from them or their sidecars.

He looked around for William S. but could not see him. Then he heard the shooting from the rooftop above the street—twelve shots, quick as summer thunder.

One of William S.'s revolvers dropped four stories and hit the ground beside him.

The Germans were already up the stairs ahead of Bronco Billy as he ran.

When the carriage had crashed into them, William S. had been thrown clear. He jumped up in time to see the vampire run into the doorway of the residential block across the way. He tore after while the driver pulled himself from the wreckage and Bronco Billy was crawling from under his horse.

Up the stairs he ran. He could now hear the pounding feet of the living dead man ahead, unlike the silence before the wreck. A flickering murky hallway was before him, and he saw the door at the far end close. William S. smashed into it, rolled. He heard the scrape of teeth behind him, and saw the rat-like face snap shut inches away. He came up, his pistols leveled at the vampire.

The bald-headed thing grabbed the open door, pulled it before him.

William S. stood, feet braced, a foot from the door and began to fire into it. His Colt .36 inches in front of his face, he fired again and again into the wooden door, watching chunks and splinters shear away. He heard the vampire squeal, like a rat trapped behind a trash can, but still he fired until both pistols clicked dry.

The door swung slowly awry, pieces of it hanging. The *nosferatu* grinned, and carefully pushed the door closed. It hissed and crouched.

William S. reached up for his hat.

And remembered that the driver had knocked it off his head before the collision.

The thing leaped.

One of his pistols was knocked over the parapet.

Then he was fighting for his life.

The five Germans, yelling to each other, slammed into the doorway at the end of the hall. From beyond, they heard the sound of scuffling, labored breathing, the rip and tear of cloth.

Bronco Billy charged up behind them.

"The door! It's jammed," said one.

"His hat!" yelled Bronco Billy. "He lost his hat!"

"Hat?" asked the one called Joseph, in English. "Why his hat?" The others shouldered against the gaped door. Through it, they saw flashes of movement and the flickering night sky.

"Crosses!" yelled Bronco Billy. "Like this!" he pointed to his hatband.

"Ah!" said Joseph. "Crosses."

He pulled something from the one called Adolf, who hung back a little, threw it through the hole in the door.

"*Cruzen!*" yelled Joseph.

"The cross!" screamed Bronco Billy. "William S. The cross!"

The sound of scuffling stopped.

Joseph tossed his pistol through the opening.

They continued to bang on the door.

The thing had its talons on his throat when the yelling began. The vampire was strangling him. Little circles were swimming in his sight. He was down beneath the monster. It smelled of old dirt, raw meat, of death. Its rat eyes were bright with hate.

Then he heard the yell, "A cross!" and something fluttered at the edge of his vision. He let go one hand from the vampire and grabbed it up.

It felt like cloth. He shoved it at the thing's face.

Hands let go.

William S. held the cloth before him as his breath came back in a rush. He staggered up, and the *nosferatu* put its hands over its face. He pushed toward it.

Then the Browning Automatic pistol landed beside his foot, and he heard noises at the door behind him.

Holding the cloth, he picked up the pistol.

The vampire hissed like a radiator.

William S. aimed and fired. The pistol was fully automatic.

The wooden bullets opened the vampire like a zipper going off.

The door crashed outward, the five Germans and Bronco Billy rushed through.

William S. held to the doorframe and caught his breath. A crowd was gathering below, at the site of the wrecked hearse and the dead horses. Torchlights wobbled their reflections on the houses across the road. It looked like something from Dante.

Helioglabulus came onto the roof, took one look at the vampire and ran his alpenstock, handle first, into its ruined chest.

"Just to make sure," he said.

Bronco Billy was clapping William S. on the back. "Shore thought you'd gone to the last roundup," he said.

The five Germans were busy with the vampire's corpse.

William S. looked at the piece of cloth still clenched tightly in his own hand. He opened it. It was an armband.

On its red cloth was a white circle with a twisted black cross.

Like the decorations Indians used on their blankets, only in reverse.

He looked at the Germans. Four of them wore the armbands; the fifth, wearing an old corporal's uniform, had a torn sleeve.

They were slipping a yellow armband over the arm of the vampire's coat. When they finished, they picked the thing up and carried it to the roof edge. It looked like a spitted pig.

The yellow armband had two interlocking triangles, like the device on the chest of the costumes William S. had worn when he played *Ben-Hur* on Broadway. The Star of David.

The crowd below screamed as the corpse fell toward them.

There were shouts, then.

The unemployed, the war-wounded, the young, the bitter, the disillusioned. Then the shouting stopped . . . and they began to chant.

The five Germans stood on the parapet, looking down at the milling people. They talked among themselves.

Bronco Billy held William S. until he caught his breath.

They heard the crowds disperse, fill in again, break, drift off, reform, reassemble, grow larger.

"Well, pard," said Bronco Billy. "Let's mosey over to a hotel and get some shut-eye."

"That would be nice," said William S.

Helioglabulus joined them.

"We should go by the back way," he said.

"I don't like the way this crowd is actin'," said Bronco Billy.

William S. walked to the parapet, looked out over the city.

Under the dark flickering sky, there were other lights. Here and there, synagogues began to flicker.

And then to burn.

# Ike at the Mike

Ambassador Pratt leaned over toward Senator Presley.

"My mother's ancestors don't like to admit it," he said, "but they all came to the island from the Carpathians two centuries ago. Their name then was something like Karloff." He smiled, then laughed through his silver mustache.

"Hell," said Presley, with the tinge of the drawl which came to his speech when he was excited, as he was tonight. "My folks been dirt farmers all the way back to Adam. They don't even remember coming from anywhere. That don't mean they ain't wonderful folks, though."

"Of course not," said Pratt. "My father was a shopkeeper. He worked to send all my older brothers into the Foreign Service. But when my time came, I thought I had another choice. I wanted to run off to Canada or Australia, perhaps try my hand at acting. (I was in several local dramatic clubs, you know?) My father took me aside before my service exams. The day before, I remember quite distinctly. He said, 'William' (he was the only member of the family who used my full name), 'William,' he said, 'actors do not get paid the last workday of each and every month.' Well, I thought about it awhile, and next day passed my exams with absolute top grades."

Pratt smiled once more an ingratiating smile. There was something a little scary about it, thought Presley, sort of like Raymond Massey's smile in *Arsenic and Old Lace*. But the smile had gotten Pratt through sixty years of government service. It had been a smile which made the leaders of small countries grin back as Kings George, number after number, took yet more of their lands. It was a good smile; it made everyone remember his grandfather. Even Presley.

"Folks is funny," said Presley. "God knows I used to get up at barn dances and sing myself silly. I was just a kid, playing around."

"My childhood is so far behind me," said Ambassador Pratt. "I hardly remember it. I was small, then I had the talk with my father and went to Service school, then found myself in Turkey. Which at that time owned a large portion of the globe. The Sick Man of Europe, it was called. You know I met Lawrence, of Arabia, don't you? Before the Great War. He was an archaeologist then. Came to us to get the Ottomans to give him permission to dig up Petra. They thought him to be a fool. Wanted the standard 90 percent share of everything, just the same."

"You've seen a lot of the world change," said Senator E. Aaron Presley. He took a sip of wine. "I've had trouble enough keeping up with it since I was elected congressman six years ago. I almost lost touch during my senatorial campaign, and I'll be damned if everything hadn't changed again by the time I got back here."

Pratt laughed. He was eighty years old, far past retirement age, still bouncing around like a man of sixty. He had alternately retired and had every British P.M. since Churchill call him out of seclusion to patch up relations with this or that nation.

Presley was thirty-three, the youngest senator in the country for a long time. The U.S. was in bad shape, and he was one of the symbols of the new hope. There was talk of revolution, several cities had been burned, there was a war on in South America (again). Social change, lifestyle readjustment, call it what they would. The people of Mississippi had elected Presley senator after five years as representative, as a sign of renewed hope. At the same time they had passed a tough new wiretap act, and had turned out for massive Christian revivalist meetings.

1968 looked to be the toughest year yet for America.

But there were still things that made it all worth living. Nights like tonight. A huge appreciation dinner, with the absolute top of Washington society turned out in all its gaudiness. Most of Congress, President Kennedy, Vice President Shriver. Plus the usual hangers-on.

Presley watched them. Old Dick Nixon, once a senator from California. He came back to Washington to be near the action, though he'd lost his last election in '58.

The President was there, of course, looking as young as he had when he was reelected in 1964, the first two-term president since Huey "Kingfish" Long, Jr., thought Presley. He was a hell of a good man in his Yankee way. His three young brothers were in the audience somewhere, representatives from two states.

Waiters hustled in and out of the huge banquet room. Presley watched the sequined gowns and the feathers on the women; the spectacular pumpkin-blaze of a neon orange suit of some hotshot Washington lawyer. The lady across the table had engaged Pratt in conversation about Wales. The ambassador was explaining that he had seen Wales once, back in 1923 on holiday, but that he didn't think it had changed much since then.

E. Aaron studied the table where the guests of honor sat—the President and First Lady, the veep and his wife, and Armstrong and Eisenhower, with their spouses.

Armstrong and Eisenhower. Two of the finest citizens of the land. Armstrong, the younger, in his sixty-eighth year, getting a little jowly. Born with the century, thought Presley. Symbol of his race and of his time. A man deserving of honor and respect.

But Eisenhower. Eisenhower was Presley's man. The senator had read all the biographies, reread all the old newspaper files, listened to him every chance he got.

If Presley had an ideal, it was Eisenhower. As both a leader and a person. A little too liberal, maybe, in his personal opinions, but that was the only possible drawback the man had. When it came time for action, Eisenhower, the "Ike" of the popular press, came through.

Senator Presley tried to catch his eye. He was only three tables away, and could see Ike through the hazy pall of smoke from after-dinner cigarettes and pipes. It was no use, though.

Eisenhower looked worried, distracted. He wasn't used to testimonials. He'd come out of semiretirement to attend, only because Armstrong had convinced him to do it. They were both getting presidential medals.

But it wasn't for the awards that all the other people were here, or the speeches that would follow, it . . .

Pratt turned to him.

"I've noticed his preoccupation, too," he said.

Presley was a little taken aback. But Pratt is a sharp old cookie, and he'd been around god knows how many people through wars, floods, conference tables. He'd probably drank enough tea in his life to float the Battleship *Kropotkin*.

"Quite a man," said Presley, afraid to let his true misty-eyed feelings show themselves. "Pretty much man of the century, far as I'm concerned."

"I've been with Churchill, and Lenin and Chiang," said Ambassador Pratt, "but they were just cagey, politicians, movers of men and material, as far as I'm concerned. I saw him once before, early on, must have been '38. Nineteen thirty-eight. I was very, very impressed then. Time has done nothing to change that."

"He's just not used to this kind of thing," said Presley.

"Perhaps it was that Patton fellow."

"Wild George? That who you mean?"

"Oh, didn't you hear?" asked Pratt, eyes all concern.

"I was in committee most of the week. If it wasn't about the new drug bill, I didn't hear about it."

"Oh. Of course. This Patton fellow died a few days ago, it seems. Circumstances rather sad, I think. Eisenhower and Mr. Armstrong just returned from his funeral this afternoon."

"Gee, that's too bad. You know they worked together, Patton and Ike, for thirty years or so—"

The toastmaster, one of those boisterous, bald-headed, abrasive California types, rose. People began to applaud and stub out their cigarettes. Waiters disappeared as if a magic wand had been waved.

Well, thought Presley, an hour of pure boredom coming up, as he and Pratt applauded also. Some jokes, the President, the awarding of the medals, the obligatory standing ovation (though all of the editor's feelings were going to be in his part of it, anyway). Then the entertainment.

Ah, thought Presley. The thing everybody has come for.

Because, after the ceremony, they were going to bring out the band, Armstrong's band. Not just the one he toured with, but what was left of the old guys, *The* Armstrong Band, and they were going to rip the joint.

But also, also . . .

For the first time in twenty years, since Presley had been a boy, a kid in his teens . . .

Eisenhower was going to break his vow. Eisenhower was going to dust off that clarinet.

For two hours, Ike was going to play with Armstrong, just like in the old days.

"Cheer up," said gravelly-voiced Pops, while the President was making his way to the rostrum. Armstrong smiled at Eisenhower. "You're gonna blow 'em right outta the grooves."

"All reet," said Ike.

The thunderous applause was dying down. Backstage, Ike handed the box with the Presidential medal to his wife of twenty years, Helen Forrest, the singer. "Here goes, honey," he said. "Come out when you feel like it."

They were in the outer hall back of the platform set up behind the head tables. Some group of young folksingers, very nervous but very good, were out there killing time while Armstrong's band set up.

"Hey hey," said Pops. He'd pinned the Presidential medal, ribbon and all, to the front of his jacket through the boutonniere hole. "Wouldn't old Jelly Roll like to have seen me now?"

"Hey hey," yelled some of the band right back.

"Quiet, quiet!" yelled Pops. "Let them kids out there sing. They're good. Listen to 'em. Reminds me of when I was young."

Ike had been licking his reed and doing tongue exercises. "You never were young, Pops," he said. "You were born older than me."

"That's a lie!" said Pops. "You could be my father."

"Maybe he is!" yelled Perkins, the guitar man.

Ike nearly swallowed his mouthpiece. The drummer did a paradiddle.

"Hush, hush, you clowns!" yelled Pops.

Ike smiled and looked up at the drummer, a young kid. But he'd been with Pop's new band for a couple of years, so he must be all right.

Eisenhower heaved a sigh when no one was looking. He had to get the tightness out of his chest. It had started at George S.'s funeral, a pain crying did not relieve. No one but he and Helen knew that he had had two mild heart attacks in the last six years. Hell, he thought. I'm almost eighty years old. I'm entitled to a few heart attacks. But not here, not tonight.

They dimmed the work lights. Pops had run into the back kitchen and blown a few screaming notes which they had heard through two concrete walls. He was ready.

"When you gonna quit playing, Pops?" asked Ike.

"Man, I ain't ever gonna quit. They're gonna have to dig me up three weeks after I die and break this horn to stop the noise comin' outta the ground." He looked at the lights. "Ease on off to the left there, Ike. Let us get them all ready for you. Come in on the chorus of the third song."

"Which one's that?" asked Ike, looking for his play sheet.

"You'll know it when you hear it," said Pops. He took out his handkerchief. "You taught it to me."

Ike went into the wings.

The crowd was tasteful, expectant.

The band hit the music hard, from the opening, and Armstrong led off with the "King Porter Stomp." His horn was flashing sparks, and the medal on his jacket front caught the spotlight like a big golden eye.

Then they launched into "Basin Street Blues," the horn sweet and slow and mellow, the band doing nothing but carrying a light line behind. Armstrong was totally in his music, staring not at the audience but down and at his horn.

He had come a long way since he used to hawk coal from the back of a wagon; since he was thrown in the Colored Waifs Home in New Orleans for firing off a pistol on New Year's Eve, 1913. One noise more or less shouldn't have mattered on that night, but it did, and the cops caught him. It was those music lessons at the Home that started him on the way, through New Orleans and Memphis and Chicago to the world beyond.

Armstrong might have been a criminal, he might have been a bum, he might have been killed unknown and unmourned in some war somewhere. But he wasn't: He was born to play that music. It wouldn't have mattered what world he would have been born into. As soon as his fingers closed around the cornet, music was changed forever.

The audience applauded wildly, but they weren't there just for Armstrong. They were waiting. And they got him.

The band hit up something that began nondescriptly—a slow blues beginning with the drummer heavy on his brushes.

The tune began to change, and as it changed, a pure sweet clarinet began to play above the other instruments, and Ike walked onstage playing his theme song, "Don't You Know What It Means to Miss New Orleans?"

His clarinet soared above the audience. Presley wasn't the only one who got chill bumps all the way down the backs of his ankles.

Ike and Armstrong traded off slow pure verses of the song; Ike's the sweet music of a craftsman, Armstrong's the heartfelt remembrance of things as they were. Ike never saw Storyville; Armstrong had to leave it when the Navy closed it down.

Together they built to a moving finale, and descended into a silence like the dimming of lights, with Ike's clarinet the last one to wink out.

The cream of Washington betrayed its origins with applause.

And before they knew what to do, the tune was the opening screech of "Mississippi Mud."

Ike and Armstrong traded licks, running on and off the melody. Pops wiped his face with his handkerchief; his face seemed all teeth and sweat. Ike's bald head shone, the freckles standing out above the wisps of white hair on his temples.

They played and played.

Ike's boyhood had been on the flat pan of Kansas, small-town church America at the turn of the century. A town full of laborers and business-men, barbershops, milliners and ice cream parlors.

He had done all the usual things—swum naked in the creek, run through town finding things to build up or tear down. He had hunted and fished and gone to services on Sunday; he had camped out overnight or for days at a time with his brothers, made fun of his girl cousins, stolen watermelons.

He first heard recorded music on an old Edison cylinder machine at the age of eight, long-hair music and opera his aunt collected.

There was a firehouse band which played each Wednesday night in the park across the street from the station. There were real band concerts on Sunday, mostly military music, marches and the instrumental parts of ballads, on the courthouse lawn.

Eisenhower heard it all. Music was part of his background, and he didn't think much of it. His brother had taken piano lessons for a while, but gave it up as, in his words, "sissy."

So Ike grew up in Kansas, where the music was as flat as the land.

Daniel Louis Armstrong was rared back, tooting out some wild lines of "Night and Day." In the old days it didn't matter how well you played; it was the angle of your back and the tilt of your horn. The band was really tight; they were playing for their lives.

The trombone player came out of his seat, jumped down onto the stage on his knees and matched Armstrong for a few bars.

The audience yelled.

Eisenhower tapped his foot and smiled, watching Armstrong and the trombone man.

The drummer was giving a lot of rim shots. The whole ballroom sounded like the overtaxed heart of a bird ready to fly away to meet Jesus.

Ike took off his coat and unknotted his tie down to the first button.

The crowd went wild.

Late August 1908.

The train was late. Young Dwight David Eisenhower hurried across the endless steel grid of the Kansas City rail yards. He was catching the train to New York City. There he would board another bound for West Point.

He carried his admission papers, a congratulatory letter from his congressman (gotten after some complicated negotiations—it looked for a while like he would be Midshipman Eisenhower), his train ticket and twenty-one dollars emergency money in his jacket.

He'd asked the porter for the track number. It was next to the station proper. A spur track confused him. He looked down the tracks, couldn't see a number (trains waited all around, ready to hurl themselves toward distant cities . . .) and went to the station entrance.

Four black men, ragged of dress, were smiling and playing near the door. What they played young David had never heard before—it was syncopated music, but not like a rag, not a march, something in between, something like nothing else. He had never heard polyrhythms like them before—they stopped him dead.

The four had a banjo, a cornet, a violin, and a clarinet. They played, smiled, danced a little for the two or three people watching them. A hat lay on the ground before them. In it were a few dimes, pennies, and a single new half-dime.

They finished the song. A couple of people said, "Very nice, very nice" and added a few cents to the hat. They walked away.

The four men started to talk among themselves.

"What was that song?" asked young David.

The man with the cornet looked at him through large horn-rimmed spectacles. "That song was called 'Struttin' with Some Barbecue,' young sir," he said.

Dwight David reached into his pocket and took out a shiny one-dollar gold piece.

"Play it again," he said.

They nearly killed themselves this time, running through it. Is was great art, it was on the street, and they were getting a whole dollar for it. David watched them, especially the clarinet player, who made his instrument soar above the others. They finished the number and all tipped their hats to him.

"Is that hard to learn to play?" he asked the man of the clarinet.

"For some it is," he answered.

"Could you teach me?" asked David.

The black man looked at the others, who looked away; they were no help at all. "Let me see your fingers," he said.

Eisenhower held out his hands, wrists up, then down.

"I could probably teach you to play in six weeks," he said. "I don't know if I could teach you to play like that. You've got to feel that music." He was trying not to say that Eisenhower was white.

"Wait right here," said Ike.

He went inside the depot and cashed in his ticket. He sent two telegrams, one home and one to the Army. He was back outside in fifteen minutes, with thirty-three dollars in his pocket, total.

"Let's go find me a clarinet," he said to the black man.

He knew he would not sleep well that night, and neither would anybody back on the farm. He probably wouldn't sleep good for weeks. But he sure knew what he wanted.

Armstrong smiled, wiped his face and blew the opening notes of "When It's Sleepy Time Down South."

Ike joined in.

Then they went into "Just a Closer Walk with Thee," quiet, restrained, the horn and clarinet becoming one instrument for a while, then Ike bent his notes around Armstrong's, then Pops lifted Eisenhower up, then the instruments walked arm in arm toward Heaven.

Ike listened to the drummer as he played. He sure missed Wild George.

The first time they had met, Ike was the new kid in town, just another guy with a clarinet that some gangster had hired to fill in with a band, sometime in 1911.

Ike didn't say much. He was working his way south from KC, toward Memphis, toward New Orleans (which he would never see until after New Orleans didn't mean the same anymore).

Ike could cook anyone with his clarinet—horn player, banjo man, even drummers. They might make more noise but when they ran out of things to do, Ike was just starting. He'd begun at the saloon filling in, but the bandleader soon had sense enough to put him out front. They took breaks, leaving just him and the drummer up there, and the crowds never noticed. Ike was hot before there was hot music.

Till one night a guy came in—a new drummer. He was a crazy man.

"My name is Wild George S. Patton," he said before the first set.

"What's the S. stand for?" asked Ike.

"Shitkicker!" said the drummer.

Ike didn't say anything.

That night they tried to cut each other, chop each other off the stage. Patton was doing two-hand cymbal shots, paradiddles, and flails. His bass foot never stopped. Ike wasn't a show-off, but this guy drove him to it. He blew notes that killed mice for three square blocks. Patton ended up by kicking a hole through the bass drum and ramming his sticks through his snare like he was opening a can of beans with them.

The bandleader fired Patton on the spot and threatened to call the cops. The crowd nearly lynched the manager for it.

As soon as the hubbub died, Patton said to Ike, "The S. stands for Smith," and shook his hand.

He and Ike took off that night to start up their own band.

And were together for almost thirty years.

Armstrong blew "Dry Bones."

Ike did "St. Louis Blues."

They had never done either better. This Washington audience loved them.

So had another, long ago.

The first time he and Armstrong had met had been in Washington, too. A hot bleak July day in 1932.

The Bonus Army had come to the capital, asking their congressmen and their nation for some relief in this third year of the Depression. President Al Smith was powerless; he had a Republican Congress under him.

The bill granting the veterans of the Great War their bonus, due in 1945, had been passed back in the twenties. All the vets wanted was it to be paid immediately. It had been sitting in the Treasury, gaining interest, and was already part of the budget. The vote was coming up soon.

Thousands, dubbed the B.E.F., had poured into Washington, camping on Anacostia Flats, in tin boxes, towns of shanties dubbed "Smithvilles," or under the rain and stars.

Homeless men who had slogged through the mud of Europe, been gassed and shelled, and who had lived with rats in the trenches for democracy, now they found themselves back in the mud again.

This time they were out of money, out of work, out of luck.

The faces of the men were tired. Soup kitchens had been set up. They tried to keep their humor. It was all they had left. May dragged by, then June, then July. The vote was taken in Congress on the twelfth.

Congress said no.

They accused the Bonus Marchers of being Reds. They said they were armed rabble. Rumors ran wild. Such financial largesse, said Congress, could not be afforded.

Twenty thousand of the thirty thousand men tried to find some way back home, out of the city, back to No Place, U.S.A.

Ten thousand stayed, hoping for something to happen. Anything.

Ike went down to play for them. So did Armstrong. They ran into each other in town, got together their bands and equipment. They set up a stage in the middle of the Smithville, now a forlorn-looking bunch of mud-strewn shacks.

About five thousand of the jobless men came to hear them play. They were in a holiday mood. They sat on the ground, in the mud. They didn't much care anymore.

Armstrong and Ike had begun to play that day. Half the band, including Wild George, had hangovers. They had drunk with the Bonus Marchers the night before, and well into the morning before the noon concert.

They played great jazz that day anyway. A cloud of smoke had risen up from some of the abandoned warehouses the veterans had been living in, just before the music began. There was some commotion from over toward the Potomac. The band just played louder and wilder.

The marchers clapped along. Wild George smiled a bleary-eyed smile toward the crowd. They were doing half his job.

Automatic rifle fire rang out, causing heads to turn.

The Army was coming. Sons and nephews of some of the Bonus Marchers there were coming toward them on orders from Douglas MacArthur, the Chief of Staff. He had orders to clear them out.

The men came to their feet, picking up rocks and bottles.

Marching lines of soldiers came into view, bayonets fixed. Small two-man tanks, armed with machine guns, rolled between the soldiers. The lines stopped. The soldiers put on gas masks.

The Bonus Marchers, who remembered phosgene and the trenches, drew back.

"Keep playing!" said Ike.

"Keep goin'. Let it roll!" said Armstrong.

Tear gas grenades flew toward the Bonus Marchers. Rocks and bottles sailed toward the soldiers in their masks. There was a real explosion a block away.

The troops came on.

The gas rolled toward the marchers. Some picked up the spewing canisters to throw them back, fell coughing to the ground, overcome.

The tanks and bayonets came forward in a line.

The marchers broke and ran.

Their shacks and tents were set afire by the chemical corpsmen behind the tanks.

"Let it roll! Let it roll!" said Armstrong, and they played "Didn't He Ramble" and the gas cloud hit them, and the music died in chokes and vomiting.

That night the Bonus Marchers were loaded on Army trucks, taken fifty miles due west and let out on the sides of the roads.

Ike and Louis went up before the Washington magistrate, paid ten dollars each fine for them and their band members, and took trains to New York City.

The last time he had seen Wild George alive was two years ago. Patton had been found by somebody who'd known him in the old days.

He'd been in four bad marriages, his only kid had died in the taking of the Japanese Home Islands in early '47, and he'd lost one of his arms in a car wreck in '55. He had been in a flophouse when the guy found him. They'd put him in a nursing home and paid the bills.

Ike had gone to visit. The last time they had seen each other in those intervening twenty-odd years had been the day of the fistfight in 1943, just before the Second World War broke out. Patton had joined the Miller band for a while, but was too much for them. He'd gone from band to band and marriage to marriage to oblivion.

He was old, old. Wild George was only five years older than Ike. He looked a hundred. One eye was almost gone. He had no teeth. He was drying out in the nursing home, turning brittle as last winter's leaves.

"Hello, George," said Ike, shaking his only hand.

"I knew you'd come first," said Patton.

"You should have let somebody know."

"What's to know? One old musician lives, another one dies."

"George, I'm sorry. The way things have turned out."

"I've been thinking it over, about that fight we had." Patton stopped to cough up some bloody spittle into a basin Ike held for him.

"God, oh, jees. If I could only have a drink." He stared into Ike's eyes. Then he said:

"About that fight. You were still wrong."

Then he coughed some more.


Ike was crying as they went into the final number. He stepped forward to the mike Helen had used when she came out to sing with them for the last three numbers.

"This song is for the memory of George Smith Patton," he said.

They played "The Old, Rugged Cross." Ike, nor anybody else, had ever played it just like that before.

Ike broke down halfway through. He waved to the crowd, took his mouthpiece off, and walked into the wings.

Pops kept playing. He tried to motion Ike back. Helen was hugging him. He waved and brushed the tears away.

Armstrong finished the song.

The audience tore the place apart. They were on their feet and stamping, screaming, applauding.

Presley, out there, sat in his chair.

He was crying too, but quickly stood up and cheered.

Then the whole thing was over.

❀

At home, later, in Georgetown, Senator Presley was lying in bed beside his wife Muffy. They had made love. They had both been excited. It had been terrific.

Now Muffy was asleep.

Presley got up and went to the bathroom. Then he went to the kitchen, poured himself a Scotch, and stood with his naked butt against the countertop.

It was a cold night. Through the half curtains on the window he saw stars over the city. If you could call this a city.

He went into the den. The servants would be asleep.

He turned the power on the stereo, took down four or five of his Eisenhower records, looked through them. He put on *Ike at the Mike*, a four-record set made for RCA in 1947, toward the end of the last war.

Ike was playing "No Love, No Nothing," a song his wife had made famous three years before. She wasn't on this record, though. This was all Ike and his band.

Presley got the bottle from the kitchen, sat back down, poured himself another drink. Tomorrow was more hearings. And the day after.

Someday, he thought, someday, E. Aaron Presley will be President of these here United States. Serves them right.

Ike was playing "All God's Chillun Got Shoes."

I didn't even get to shake his hand, thought Presley.

I'd give it all away to be like him, he thought.

He went to sleep sitting up.

# Dr. Hudson's Secret Gorilla

I do not remember anything, after the wreck, until I put my finger to my ear.

And felt the fur scratch against my hairy neck.

The fur from the back of my hand.

Later, after I had tried to rip the bandages from my head, and from somewhere behind me a needle had descended and pricked me, and I passed out; later, I awoke.

I lay still. I was on my back and watched the rise and fall of my smooth chest. My head was ringing from the drug used on me. Little blue circles swirled like a gnat swarm in my eyes. Slowly I raised my hand into my line of sight and saw its hairy back, like a glove made from a shag rug.

I pulled it to my head, found the edges of the bandages which started just above my brow. The brow was thick and long as a bicycle handlebar.

I lay back. Even that small movement caused my head to scream and slip sideways, and I went over.

Late for showtime. Critic's screening of new, solid blockbuster movie, seventeen stars, studio hype. Wet night, slick streets. Down the Canyon road, around the turn, headlights catch a dog or a cat or a small child, stomp the brake, good Michelin tires grab the road, Triumph says good-bye highway, sailing, sailing the lights of LA look nice tonight and are they getting close no time to scream now . . .

✻

I come up from the memory and shiver to find I have awakened myself groaning.

The groan is a hurricane inside an echo chamber, long, low, wet, with lungs and strength, hurt strength behind it.

The head pain is gone. Again, I look down at my body at the hugeness, the shagginess, the alienness. My body.

I need to take a dump. I cannot move well enough to get—where? To the corner of the cage. For I am barred in. It is ten body lengths long, five wide. Through one corner is a slanted running trough of water. Through the other, a fountain with a steel foot pedal. Outside the cage is dark. It is night, or the lights are off.

I am hurt. I do not understand what has happened. I do not think I am still dreaming. So this is what it is like to begin to lose the mind. I am afraid. I try to cry.

I see him staring at me while I open my eyes. The place is bright again and the light hurts.

He looks like Albert Einstein. He looks like a thousand mad scientists. He looks like . . . he has a large nose, unkempt white mustache, a fringe of hair from the temples around his head. His eyes are grey and quite gone. I have seen those tombstone eyes on the Strip, asking for change to support a habit. I saw them once in the Army, in Nam, on a guy who'd lived through an ambush when on one else had. He was over the edge. He was gone. His eyes looked like those in photographs of factory workers from the 1890's, all shiny like little steel balls.

Little steel balls with lights burning inside them.

"Tuleg! Tuleg!" He yells. "He is awake."

I twitched from the loudness of his voice. The blue gnats threaten my sight, then subside.

I try to move.

He watches me. He does not say anything. He studies the way I try to use my fingers. I cannot place them flat so I can push myself up. I realize I am trying to use them as my own hands. And that will not work. These are twice as large.

A door opens somewhere. My vision is still fuzzy. Beyond the bars of the cage is a blur. Light comes from somewhere, then goes.

And before me stands the Evil Assistant.

He is huge, he must be huge. He looks like an oak stump stretched out by chains. He is bald, a muscular Erich von Stroheim, and he moves like an acrobat. He is wearing khaki pants (I can only see the waistband. The cage is raised about a meter off the flooring of the—room?—the cage is in) and a real undershirt, the kind with thin shoulder straps and no sleeves. He is rubbing pizza sauce from his mouth as he walks in. He looks at me and scratches his chest with his right hand.

"So?" he says to the madman.

"So!?" says the other. "I have succeeded. You helped with the operation, you saw! A man's brain in the body of a gorilla. He lives! He will live, of that I'm sure."

"Mmm," grunted the man. He turned to leave. "Call me if you *really* need me."

I listened to them talk. I could not believe it. Was I making up this dialogue? Was I still asleep?

I looked at the Mad Scientist. He stared back as if I were golden, silver, a flying saucer, the Loch Ness monster.

The Evil Assistant went out the door. There was something about him I did not like. He seemed familiar.

Rondo Hatton. He reminded me of Rondo Hatton, the Creeper. He did not need acromegaly. He was an ugly man.

The Mad Scientist leaned on the cage and stared at me.

❁

Time passed and the scientist was gone. I managed to get up and hobble my way to the trough. I took a dump.

Gorilla shit is dry, almost all the liquid is gone from it. What I had eaten, or rather what the former owner of the body had last eaten, I do not know.

When I finished I lay back down. My head hurt. My body hurt. I sank into slumbers.

Sometimes later I felt another needle go into my skin. I was too weak to fight back. My sleep was filled with dim nightmares.

I saw beyond the cage a hospital stand with an empty IV bottle attached. Intravenous feeding, saves time, saves trouble.

I stood, went to the latrine, shuffled my weight across to the water fountain, stepped on the pedal and doused my face with water.

It did not feel the same as it did when I had done it . . . when I was a man. It felt as if the skin there were made of leather sewn on the outside of my normal face. I pushed on it, pulled at it with my clumsy hands. I pulled my fingers and tried my toes.

I stepped on the pedal, ran water into the fountain. I held my hairy, notebook-sized hand over the drain. There was light, from an indirect source, in the room.

I watched the drain fill, the water rise over my hand like a river flood covering a forest. Then I took my foot away from the handle.

I stared into the basin.

Gorilla eyes. Tiny. Brow swept back to a sagittal crest. Head like a cinderblock. Thick. Ugly.

I sat on the floor, my toes curled in. I could not believe it. I sat that way until I realized how I must look. Like a gorilla. A gorilla trying to solve the mysteries of the universe. I got up and began to pace the cage, slowly. Then I stood with my hands through the bars. Gorillas don't do that. Humans do that.

※

*gorilla gorilla.*

The most nearly human, the most frightening primate. No one believed the stories the natives told. Old men of the woods. They lived there, they beat their chests, they drive you off. They kill. They have teeth the size of knives. Pliny wrote about them. The Romans knew them, and later the Spanish and the Portugee. And they did not believe, either.

Two gorillas. The lowland, first, the one of the rain forest, and the mountain gorilla, he of the open hillsides. Dying, now, the bands breaking down, to the bulldozer, the city, the poachers.

Huge, the gorilla. Fierce-looking. Bestial, perhaps because he is so close to man, yet so far away. So strong, so heavy. Men twisted by nightmares.

The gorilla will fight, is shy. The beating of the chest is liable to be replaced by some other harmless activity. The males will protect the young and the females. They usually run and do not charge.

*See the gorilla. Terror of the jungle. Killer of the Congo. King of the Apes. gorilla gorilla.*

The Mad Scientist was named Hudson.

The Evil Assistant called him that next day.

I watched them come into the room while they talked.

Then I stood.

"You see?" said Hudson. "He stands on two legs."

I walked to the bars. I motioned with my hands. I wanted to know *why?*

Hudson watched me.

"You see?" he said to Tuleg. "He understands. He is still a man."

I was clumsy. I couldn't walk so well on two legs. I didn't know *how* to walk on all fours. You can't walk on four legs like a man would. I couldn't do anything right. I sat down.

"He is uncoordinated," said Hudson. "He can learn, though."

63

"So, who's gonna teach him?" asked Tuleg.

"We are," said Hudson.

For the first time, there was authority in his voice.

The days passed. At first they still gave me intravenous feedings and kept me groggy with drugs.

Then Hudson began to speak to me, like a child.

I tried to talk. What came out was *nnnngmnnnnnnnnng*.

I wanted to write. I moved my hands like writing.

Hudson handed me a pen and paper, happy as a child.

My fingers were like tree limbs. My thumb was like a sledgehammer. One letter took up most of the page. I tried.

"You will get better with it," said the Mad Scientist. "Don't worry."

I threw the pen down, tore the paper, clumsily, in half. I couldn't even do that well.

"Nod if you understand me," he said.

I nodded.

Hudson laughed and clapped his hands. "You do!" he said, dancing in little steps. "You do!"

I nodded again, my insides were turning with joy.

"Wait until I tell Tuleg!" he said, and ran from the room. I stood dumbfounded. We had been communicating, no matter how crudely. And he left. He left.

I did not want to be alone. I roared. I yelled, I shook the bars until my head began to spin and I had to sit. I sank to the floor and shivered.

I found that gorillas can cry.

I held the ballpoint pen in my hand and rocked myself to sleep.

The next morning, I realized what was wrong. Dr. Hudson was crazy, really mad. I had never thought of the meaning of the words "mad scientist" before. He must be mad to experiment so. But his madness did not end there. No. He is *mad*. He walked away when we were ready to communicate. He works to make me a gorilla, then he works to bring the man back out. And at the instant he does, he forgets me. He is *mad*.

Tuleg walked in by himself and shut the door.

I sat with the ballpoint in my hand, toes curled in, my knuckles flat on the floor. I stared back at him.

He stood with his arms akimbo. With his bald head, in the daylight, he reminded me of Boris Karloff in *Tower of London*. Mord, the Executioner.

He said nothing. Then he went to the cabinet in the far corner and drew out a long thin stick.

I jumped. I had seen one like it before.

"Ha ha ha," he said. His eyes said, "So you recognize the cattle prod, eh?"

He came toward me, moving his head to always keep eye contact with me through the bars. He reached the prod in and the sharp spark leapt like a knife. I felt as if I had been stabbed and clubbed at the same time. Smoke curled, and there was the smell of burnt hair in the air. I roared and leapt away from him.

But he moved far faster than I, and the prod touched again

and again

and again

and

I wrote with the pen, though he shocked me each second or so, and laughed as he did. I was quivering.

NO, I wrote, and he saw it, and knocked the pen from my hand. I reached for it, and he struck at me. The spark made my hand go numb. I watched the hair burn. I looked into his eyes.

"Fight me," he said. "Why don't you fight me?" He stuck the prod at my face. I tried to push it away.

Its touch blasted through my elbows to my teeth. I was crying, whimpering now. I lay down and curled up as best I could. He kept jabbing me, sending pain into me. I almost let go at each jolt. I bit my tongue in pain, felt blood run under my teeth.

The pain stopped.

"Damn you," he said, throwing the prod on the cabinet shelf. "Damn you to hell, why don't you fight me?"

He left. His words ran through my head. *Why don't you fight me?*

Because I am a man. Because . . .

The Evil Assistant was evil. Evil with all its connotations. Evil has motive. Evil strikes without warning. Sadism is an evil which needs no motivation. To give pain is human. Perhaps Tuleg gets sexual release in giving pain? I couldn't tell. I did not give him whatever he needed. I will not. Not ever.

I have learned the meaning of the word evil. I do not like it.

There were hands on me.

Tiny hands.

I opened my eyes and winced where one of the prod burns had seared the flesh of my brow. I moaned and rolled to my side.

"You poor thing," she said. "You frightened thing."

Why, why, why when there is a gorilla, and a mad scientist, and an evil assistant, why . . .

why must there be a beautiful woman?

I have seen all this before, I tell myself, as the doctor and the beautiful woman tend my wounds. I am so hurt, so stunned I can do nothing but lie and shiver. I am running a fever. My eyes feel made of grit and sand. I shake. Inside, I cry. They cover me with a blanket. I become dank, and cold by turns, and then burn for hours. I pass in and out of fever dreams. I see a jungle.

It is later, and I hear the Mad Doctor talk to the Beautiful Woman.

"I wouldn't have brought you here if I didn't want you to see it," he said. "I wouldn't have, if I had known what Tuleg was going to do. The brute! I hope he fries in hell. I'm going to send him away the moment he returns."

"I told you when he came to work for you that he was a terrible man," she said, her voice soft like an unswept floor.

"Well, he was a great help."

"I'm sure." Her voice sounded as if she had turned her back on him. "He helped you. Oh, Father," her voice quavered, then she continued. "Why?" she asked. "Why do something as stupid, as pointless as this? What use is it? What can you prove by it? What?"

"But, Blanche," he said. "If you could have known the heartache, the toil, the hours . . ."

"Can you imagine," she asked, turning toward him sharply, "what that poor man is going through? Can you?"

"He will make me immortal, Blanche."

"Oh Father, Father," she said. I heard her footsteps and the door open and close, hard.

"She doesn't understand. She just doesn't understand," said the old man, and moved some apparatus (the tinkling of glass and metal) around on the workbench.

I slept.

❋

Tuleg must have come back sometime during the night. I opened my eyes and he was walking around the room, preparing food and tasting it as he put it in a bowl.

He brought it over to the cage.

"Here," he said, putting it in through the bars. "Eat."

He went back to the workbench. He took down, and began to clean, a Thompson submachine gun. He looked at me from time to time as he worked with it. "Eat, I said."

I went to the bowl. It was filled with rolled oats, raisins, bits of celery and apple, sugar. I tried it and found it good. I was still running a fever, but I put the food in my mouth anyway.

My hand brushed my incisors. I felt them both. Long, curved, they were really there. They could crunch through meat as easily as a pair of pruning shears. They could punch open a tin can. They could kill a man. I shook my head.

I finished eating.

Hudson came in. He and Tuleg must have talked before, because the scientist was not surprised to see him.

"Today," he said to me, "we begin to teach you."


"You were Roger Ildell," said Dr. Hudson.

I nodded.

"You were killed in a wreck just beyond my home," he said. "At least, your body was. I was able to remove your brain before deterioration set in. I saved it. I saved your conscious mind."

I nodded again.

"I used to read your reviews," said Blanche, who was sitting at her father's side. "The police are still looking for your body. My father and Tuleg removed all traces. They were very thorough. They were very methodical," she said.

"We have to begin all over with you," said her father. "She tells me you were an intelligent man. There should be no problem. You'll be able to write again, though you'll never be able to talk. I regret that," he said. Then quietly, "I regret that."

I opened my hands wide, held them out towards the scientist. And his daughter. *Why? Why?*

Hudson was puzzled.

Tuleg snorted and left the room. He still wore the stained undershirt he'd had on the first time I'd seen him.

I made motions of writing. The gorilla body I wore was struggling with itself. I wanted to tell them, I wanted to ask them. What was wrong? Was my mind crippled in the wreck? Why couldn't I speak!? Why couldn't I write?

Blanche handed me a large pencil and a piece of paper the size of a tabloid. I wrote as best as I could, taking up most of the sheet, slipping, straining to make myself understood.

WHY ME? WHY DO THIS TO ME?

Blanche read it and looked deep into my piggy anthropoid eyes.

"Oh, Father!" she said, and turned to the Mad Scientist.

He stared at me with his Einstein looks, his fringe of hair.

"I did it to save your life! Don't you understand? You would have died out there!" He began to shout. Lines of saliva hung inside his mouth as it opened and closed. "I have to teach you! I have to! You have lived so I could carry on my research! Yarr!" he screamed, and fell to the floor in a convulsion.

I watched. Blanche screamed for Tuleg. Together, they got the madman up off the floor and out the doorway of the laboratory. After a while, Blanche came back.

"You poor man, you," she said. She came to the bars of the cage. She put her hand through and touched my hairy fingers.

I jerked as if with the shock from the cattle prod.

"No!" she said. "Don't. I'll help you all I can."

She leaned closer, still holding my hand.

"My father is not well," she said, staring at my eyes. "He is a sick man in many ways."

She kissed my fingers just above the nails, and licked the hair between the thumb and index finger.

Mad. She, too, is mad.

I sit in the corner of the cage, my back against the bars, my feet and legs sticking out before me. I look at my bent legs, at my hairy knees, the flat pad where the bottoms of my feet begin.

I think.

First, there are the movies. I saw them all, in that other life. The gorillas is the image of terror, the anthropoid killer of men and children, the despoiler of women.

(The penis of the male adult gorilla is only a couple of inches long. Ask me.)

*Gorilla at Large. White Pongo. Nabongo. Killer Gorilla.* In Poe's "Murders in the Rue Morgue," I was Old Man Pong, the orangutan. In the film, I was gorilla. Bela Lugosi. Poor, tired old Bela, shambling through role after role in which he had nothing to do but menace and laugh. *The Ape. Return of the Ape Man. The Ape Girl. Captive Wild Woman.* They put a horn on my head for *Flash Gordon. Konga. Unknown Island. Mighty Joe Young.*

*King Kong.*

I think of Blanche and I dream of Fay Wray. She does not look anything like her. I see Skull Island. I fight *Tyrannosaurus* for her. Through the dim eyes of the beast I pull the wings off the pterodactyl. I throw men from the log over the ravine to the waiting spiders. I roar my challenge from the Empire State Building.

I fall to the streets below.

Why does the gorilla always lust after the beautiful girl?

Why?

Why?

Tuleg has hurt me again.

Blanche found me quivering and shaking.

She came into the cage with me, opening it with a key from the workbench. I lay moaning.

"Oh, Roger, Roger," she said, cradling my head in her lap. "I'll kill him. I'll kill him if ever he hurts you again! My father will get rid of him."

She washes away the scored and scorched places, soothes me, rubs my chest where the prod has not bitten.

I DIDN'T FIGHT, I write.

"I know," she says, rocking me. "I know. It'll be all right."

But it is not all right. Tuleg comes into the room.

He stops dead still when he sees her in the cage with me.

"Get out of there!" he yells, and runs into the cage, pulling her away from me. He slams the door. The key falls to the floor and he kicks it away. I try to get up. I hurt too much.

I struggle up.

"Your father is dead," says Tuleg. "He went crazy and died."

"Oh no," she said, and ran up the stairs.

Tuleg followed her.

In a few moments, there is a scream, a woman's scream, and then another and another.

"No. No!" yells Blanche as she falls through the door, her clothes torn from her. I hear Tuleg laughing outside, and he comes into the room, still holding part of her dress.

I shamble to my feet and roar. I slam against the cage. Tuleg laughs, then grabs Blanche by the hair and pulls her backward behind the workbench.

I mash my fist to paste against the door as I catch it between my shoulder and the bars. And still I push against it.

And still.

And still.

I have to watch the murder. And then the rape.

Then, only then, do I see the keys. I can't reach them. I try. Tuleg is not through with Blanche, though Blanche is finished with everything.

He is groaning.

The ballpoint pen. I find it with my hand. I stick it through the bars. Tuleg surely hears the jingle as I spear the brass ring. But he is busy, and finishing up.

I have the keys now, and I put them inside the cage lock.

I turn the key. The lock grates. "No," says Tuleg, as he looks up from behind the bench, his face twisted in release. He jerks from the body.

He is going for the submachine gun.

I am there first, cutting him off. He is half naked. He bolts for the door. He slams it shut. His feet run up the stairs.

The doors part for me like a curtain, flinders flying each way.

It is a beautiful house, and Tuleg has made it to a phone. He is screaming an address into it. He turns, and his eyes go strange as he tries to stick a knife in me.

I do not feel it. I grab him by the ankle and pull him down. I am four hundred pounds of muscle and sinew, and he is a paper doll. The phone smashes against the bannister. Tuleg tries to scream.

I use him like a pogo stick, my foot and weight on his neck, while I hold to his kicking feet. One jump, two. *Snap crunch snap.* I like the sound as his neck goes soft like a pair of socks. Then I smash his head, and use the knife like a hoe in his stomach.

I carry the body of Blanche Hudson, and the air is filled with sirens, all coming toward us.

I carry her into the garden, where there is a gazebo. It looks out over the rest of the Canyon, and above me, that must be where my car plunged over.

I also carry the Thompson submachine gun in my hand.

I place the body of Blanche on the floor of the grape arbor, and lay her dress over her as neatly as possible. She is sweet in death, if you ignore the blood.

The house is beginning to burn. Tuleg's smoke will rise up to Hell forever, like the doctor said.

Fire trucks, police cars, and spectators arrive around front.

Ah.

Two policemen run toward me, yelling.

It is night, and they could not have seen me. One turns the corner of the garden house and sees Blanche's body (the beautiful daughter of the Mad Scientist) and stops. His eyes go wide as I bite through his throat, my hand on his face in a grip like a vise.

One banana, two banana, three banana, four.

The second cop sees me and draws his pistol.

I break his arm and knock in his head with the butt of the Thompson.

There is a stinging on my cheek, and the sound of a bee going by. Bullets. Oh so many of them. Pop pop pop.

I turn and say my name, but it must sound like a roar to them.

I turn the selector switch on automatic and open fire.

The Thompson says *its* name.

(A: A gorilla with a submachine gun.)

There is the sound of glass exploding and brick dust powdering wherever I point. *Tinkle tinkle crash.*

Little points of light wink, and the air fills with whines and screams. I fire again, and run into the bushes where the yard ends.

They are after me. I show them. They are afraid for what I am. I'll show them how near they are to me. I show them my teeth, up close.

Someone gets in the way and I kill him as I run.

I have the machine gun. They will not take me alive. You have sent me after the Three Stooges. You have visited my nightmare form on Abbott and Costello. You have run me across a footbridge where I snarled at Laurel and Hardy.

I am funny. Gorillas are funny.

I will show you funny.

This ape can think. It can pick locks and plant dynamite charges and use an MI6. Oh, there will be deaths! Run, Kong, shamble away before they catch you.

Careful, there. Almost crouched as I ran. Have to watch it.

Not to go on all fours. That is the Law.

# "... The World, As We Know't."

The neptunists and vulcanists were going at it hammer and tongs.

The fight had begun just after Curwell's demonstration on counteracting the effects of garlic on the compass. His methods, which would open the seas to safe passage of condiments and spices, had been wildly applauded by his peers in the Lunatick Society.

He had graciously accepted their accolades, and was making a few extemporary remarks. He seemed the essence of charm and grace as he answered questions from the audience, until he made the unfortunate mistake of mentioning the age of the earth.

Canes had begun rapping on the floor, there were whistles, words of dispute, and then the yelling had begun.

The president of the Society gaveled for quiet. Fists were brandished in faces. "Gentlemen! Order, please. Order."

This only infuriated them the more.

"I maintain," someone shouted from the back of the hall, "that the earth is no less than . . ."

They yelled him down.

To make matters worse, the argument began to eddy and splinter around the main one. The gradualist uniformitarians, who thought the land masses had been uncovered from a once all-pervading ocean, were yelling at the catastrophic vulcanists who were gathered in one corner of the hall.

"... The earth has been made over," yelled one of the latter in the face of one of the former, "by terrible volcanic upheavals something approaching twenty-seven consecutive times!"

"Faddle."

"Hear, hear!"

Across the aisle, a catastrophic neptunist climbed atop his chair and shouted at both groups. "You people can't use your own eyes to see that the rocks of the Northwest Territory were carried there by the action of a series of deluges, more than seven, but no more than ten in number, as has . . ."

Instantly, members of *all* the other factions turned on him.

The president kept gaveling for order.

Sir Robert Athole, mounting the platform, shook hands with Curwell, who was smiling and watching the uproar he had caused.

"They really are in some mood tonight," said Lawrence Curwell, who was a young man with a broad handsome face.

"It's really too bad you gave them no points to dispute in your presentation, which was quite remarkable," said Sir Robert.

They were bumped from behind by a black man who was taking models and equipment to the raised stage, where the gavel kept pounding and having absolutely no effect on the turmoil.

"Sorry, sir, so sorry," said the black.

Curwell took no notice.

"Thank you for the compliment," said Curwell. "I've already turned the results over to your Maritime Commission. I hope no more tragedies of the kind which took the *Bon Apetit* and the *Lucie Marie* to their watery graves will occur again because of my researches."

There were dull thuds from the back of the room. The two men turned to watch cane-brandishing men be pulled apart by their friends to the uttering of great vile oaths and epithets.

"Shall you be visiting the States long?" asked Sir Robert to Curwell.

"If it's at all possible, I should like you to come visit and see the progress of my researches. They might interest you."

"I'd love to. I hear you're doing splendid things. I look forward to your presentation tonight."

Sir Robert Athole began to bow, but paused to turn and watch as one of the more elderly philosophs bounded across the aisle and began to vigorously choke a younger man. They were absorbed in the crowd.

Then "oohs" and "ahhs" raced from the front of the room toward the back. It became very quiet and somber, and some bowed their heads.

For up on the dais, the president of the Society had signaled for the sergeant-at-arms to bring in a small square box and place it in the center of the president's desk.

"Franklin's spectacles," whispered someone. The whisper susurrated through the room. Persons righted their overturned chairs, straightened their wigs, took their seats.

"Order," said the president. The two raps of his small gavel now sounded like the slamming of the great gates of a fort in the still hall.

"The next item on the agenda," he said, "will be a presentation by Sir Robert Athole on the absolute nature of phlogiston."

The room itself was old, huge, and dark. It was lit by chandeliers and by candle sconces along the walls. The odor of wig powder, soot and sweat filled the hall. Through several doors leading in, household servants could be seen coming and going, preparing the traditional meal which would end the monthly meeting of the Lunatick Society.

Velvet and brocade rustled as the men moved about in their uphol-stered chairs. A snort, sniff and occasional sneeze broke the quiet as one or another of them took snuff. A cane rolled from a lap and clattered loudly to the floor.

The black man indicated to Sir Robert that the models were ready. He came a little closer. "Go easy on the cylinder," he said. "I think it might have cracked a little on the way over in the wagon."

"Very good, Hamp," said Sir Robert, and nodded to the president. There was polite applause for him as he stepped to the rostrum, on which sat a whale-oil lamp smoking quietly.

He looked out at the mass of faces and wigs flickering slowly in the dim light, and saw them as bubbles in the darkening pudding that was the world. No matter. He smiled and began.

He started with the history of combustion and with mention of the works of Becher and Stahl.

"Phlogiston is thought to permeate all things in finely inseparable parts. It is characterized by setting up a violent motion within substances in the presence of heat. This motion results in flame, and as long as the air is not kept from it, the motion will continue until only earthy ash remains."

He then described *terra pinguis* and the fatty earths, and the search for the phlogistic principle itself. His audience continued to listen intently, even a little restlessly. So far he had told them nothing new.

"Recently Cavendish thought he had found the most highly phlogiston-charged substance in his inflammable gas, which is lighter than common air, and is used to lift aerostatic vehicles to heretofore unheard-of heights. Inflammable gas burns violently in the air, sometimes to the point of detonation. But, as others, including Dr. Priestley, have shown, a mixture of inflammable gas and eminently respirable air explodes, but leaves as residue a wet liquid, indistinguishable from common water.

"And water, as you know, is the enemy of phlogiston, "It seems to me therefore, that a mixture of phlogiston and any other substance *could not* give a residue of its exact opposite. Cavendish, however . . ."

"Question!"

Sir Robert looked up.

"Yes?"

"According to the leading French theorists, eminently respirable air is . . ."

"The French," said someone else, "are a bunch of rabble who cannot even carry out a revolution in the accepted manner, as did we."

There was a matter of agreement.

"You were going to say, said Sir Robert to his questioner, "that the French New Chemistry, which denies the phlogistic principle, attributes other causes to combustion and calcination. Most of these concern the properties of the eminently respirable air, or oxygine, as it is named. Instead of phlogiston being given off by substances in combustion, the New Chemistry says substances combine with this oxygine in the presence of heat. And you are asking what I think of this theory?"

"Yes."

"Not much," said Sir Robert. "I *have* read in the French Chemistry. If you must deal with the devil, first you must know him." There was hearty applause from the back. "I have decided to ignore most of these theories, insofar as it is possible. For I believe it is now within the power of science to isolate phlogiston itself."

"No! No! Impossible! Wrong!" they shouted.

Oaths crossed the air again as others took his side.

Sir Robert raised his hand for quiet.

"I have come here tonight to outline my plans and to show you models of the operations by which I intend to carry out . . ."

"Phlogiston . . . ," said a voice, ". . . is present to some extent in all matter, and indivisible. Might as well try and weigh or separate sunlight itself!"

"Hear! Hear!"

Sir Robert looked them down. A tremor passed through his hand then, something he had noticed as happening more often since he began experimenting with his mercuric pneumatic troughs. He raised it as the tremor passed. "Some say phlogiston drifts down from the shooting stars through the aether. Others say it *comes* from the very sun. Perhaps if I succeed in isolating the phlogistic principle, we shall find, indeed, the true nature of even that great sun overhead."

That was too much for even the devout phlogistians in the audience. They came to their feet, arguing against him.

"Nevertheless," said Sir Robert, rolling up his manuscript. "Nevertheless, I have had special equipment ordered, and will carry through . . ." The president stood up and pounded with his gavel. ". . . I will prevail in my work, and expect within a fortnight to have all ready. Such of you as may want shall be invited to witness . . ." The roar rose above his words for a space and he paused. ". . . to witness this great thing, and those of you who don't can go to the very devil himself!"

He stomped from the dais. Hamp drove home in the wagon down the snow-covered ruts which passed for a road. The ground was lit by the cold still glow of the full moon, on whose closest Monday night the Lunatick Society sat, and for whose shining light it was named.

At noon two days later, Lawrence Curwell arrived. Sir Robert and Lady Margurite Athole met him on the wide carriage porch in the light of a bright cold sun.

Curwell bowed to Lady Margurite. "Your servant, madam."

"Sorry Hamp isn't here, too," said Sir Robert. "He's out in the laboratory, unpacking the new globe which arrived this forenoon from Philadelphia."

"I'm sure my note arrived rather late the night of the meeting," said Curwell. "I was surrounded by disputants during your speech. It's only luck we kept Hazzard from plunging his pen-knife into Revecher. What a contentious lot!"

Lawrence Curwell, like Sir Robert, was from Britain. Unlike the elder scientist, he could return, being in America to check on his brother's tobacco holdings. This was possible only because the new Constitution had been adopted, and relations between the two countries were normalizing again after the shaky years of the Confederation.

Sir Robert, who had once been a notorious supporter of the Colonies in their rebellion, had been hounded to the States, much like his contemporary Priestly who now lived in Pennsylvania.

Curwell, who was young and still loyal to Britain, and Sir Robert, in his fifties, experienced, but now apolitical, met only on the common ground of a devotion to knowledge and the empire of science. They shared another opinion that the American philosophs were hotheaded, opinionated, prejudiced, and had no science to match the new country's ideals. With a few exceptions: the late, lamented Franklin, Priestly, who really didn't count, Bartram of Carolina.

"I trust they'll sing another tune if you succeed," said Curwell.

"They'll have to," said Lady Margurite.

"Do we have time to see how Hamp's getting on before lunch?" asked Sir Robert.

Lady Margurite gave a knowing smile. "Surely," she said.

"Will you come with us?" asked Curwell, who was very taken with her beauty.

"Not presently. I have to see to the servants," she said, and turned to go into the house, which was an imposing, square, white three-story structure with a green roof.

"This way," said Sir Robert.

They followed a flagstone path around the house. A vista opened up to the flat rolling hills toward the west. Here was a barn, there poultry houses, stables and servant quarters larger than the cottage Curwell lived in. Past those was a wide field and beyond that a low squat edifice of fieldstones with many smokestacks and chimneys protruding from it. As Curwell neared it, he saw a huge pile of sand under the fire bell tower which stood near the doorway. One of the many large windows showed blackened signs of scorching.

"An accident late last year," said Sir Robert.

There were still a few patches of snow here and there in the shadows of the building and trees across the field. The wind was from the north but spring was in the air.

"This is quite a marvelous globe flask," said Sir Robert as they entered the building through a low rickety door. Several white servants and the black man were busy with crates and boxes. "It has a diameter of three feet, its sides are two and one-half inches in thickness, stoppable ports and conduits for sparking. I had it made especially for the grand experiment."

"Hamp," said Sir Robert. The black man looked up from his work, rubbed his hands on a chamois, came over. "Hamp. Lawrence Curwell. Lawrence, Hampton Hamilton."

"Pleased, indeed," said Hampton, and offered his hand.

It was the first time Lawrence Curwell had been offered the hand of a black man. He shook it nonetheless. He had assumed at the meeting that the man had been Sir Robert's slave.

"Hamp runs the laboratory for me, and is in charge of all the equipment and requisitioning. How's the globe, Hamp?"

"Excellent, indeed," said Hamp. Turning to the great transparent globe before them supported on sawhorses, he said, "The ports fit so tightly that I doubt we shall need wax and quicklime to seal the joints tight."

"Good, good," said Sir Robert. "Let me see the bill of lading, will you? Excuse me, Lawrence . . ."

While they put their heads together, Lawrence Curwell looked around the laboratory. He was struck by the spaciousness and cleanliness of the place and its supplies. Where most chemists got on with two or three small furnaces, Sir Robert had no less than seven—three of them large reverberatory cones, two forced-draft furnaces, two smaller ones spread down the length of the room, each with its own stack or chimney.

At one end stood large jugs—gallons of ether, vitriol, spirit of wine, acid, distilled waters. In other places were ceramic buckets marked sulfur, antimony, lead, earth of rhubarb, Mohr's salt.

Shelf after shelf stretched across the walls with tins, vials and flasks—the most completely stocked workroom Curwell had ever seen—syrup of violets, oil of Dippel, ley of oxblood, Icy Butter, Starkeys Soap, salt of Gall, Glauber's salt, liquor of flints, Minderer's spirit. Numberless others.

At the far end of the laboratory were pumps and basins for washing. Near each end were large workbenches covered with experiments in progress.

In the center of the room were pneumatic troughs for the recovery of gases. Two were filled with water, the third with four inches of mercury. Several glass bottles, some filled with a reddish air, stood upside down in each.

Curwell walked to the workbench where retorts and a Woulfe bottle caught his eye. In a few seconds he recognized it as the cohobation of some solid. At another spot he found lixiviation in process—how long it had been going on he did not know. He had seen some last for half a year, with virtually no result.

He followed to another spot where some matter was being edulcorated from acid by a water bath.

There seemed no order to the experiments, nowhere they should be leading. There was no thread holding them together, except perhaps that of refinement. Maybe Sir Robert was getting the best possible metals and calxes together before using them in his actual work.

"Lawrence," said Sir Robert. "Here, come over here." He was now standing near one of his pneumatic troughs, while behind him Hamp and the others busied themselves once more with the boxes.

"Here." He pointed at one of the inverted bottles. "I've been doing things with a gas collected over sulfur and nitre. Would you like to see?"

He began by showing Curwell some of the properties of the gas, talking occasionally of how it would be a part of the great experiment. They began moving from table to trough to bench as one or another thing they should try came to them. At one point they took off their frock coats, and sometime later their wigs. Curwell suggested other properties, other processes. They took bottles from workbench to crucible to mortar and pestle. The workmen came and left, came again. They ignored the two men huddling over the trough.

At some time Hamp lit candles in the room, finished the unpacking. Then he left. The candles burned down.

At 11 p.m. the two scientists stumbled back to the house, talking, gesturing, happy as mice and famished as wolves. Everyone was asleep.

It was the second week of Curwell's stay. Something was bothering Sir Robert, and both Margurite and Hampton could tell. Sir Robert seemed distracted in the middle of conversation or experiments. He drew plans on sheets of foolscap with a thick graphite pencil, then discarded them in lumps around the house or the laboratory.

Most of them dealt with clockwork devices, cogs, fuses. None seemed to satisfy him.

Curwell had begun to see that all the experiments and processes in the laboratory were coming together in a great design. It was ambitious, complicated, and to Curwell's mind it would probably not work. Most of it centered on fixing the phlogiston, much as fixed air is obtained from common air. He thought there were too many variables, and it depended on timing of at least four major processes. But Sir Robert's enthusiasm stirred him, and he and Hamp set about putting together minor portions of the apparatus and materials. Sir Robert talked less and less, worked more and more, and became still more dissatisfied.

One morning as he and Curwell walked toward the laboratory, they were interrupted by a halloo. Turning, they saw Athole's gamekeeper riding slowly toward them down the road. On the wagon-rut before him walked a trussed man dressed in deerskin trousers and a jacket who seemed much the worse for wear.

"Caught a live one, Your Lordship," said the gamekeeper, who was Irish. "He made the best shot I've ever seen. Right into one of your heath hens," he continued, and produced the feathered evidence from his saddlepack. "Am I to take him to the constable, or shall I pummel him unmercifully?"

"As if you haven't already!" grumbled the man in leather.

"Quiet, you!" said the gamekeeper, and yanked on the rope.

Sir Robert was staring as if transfixed. "What rifle did he use?"

"Here," said the gamekeeper, and handed down a Kentucky rifle.

"I didn't do anything," said the man.

"Quite right," said the gamekeeper, and dealt him a smart blow behind the ear with his own rifle butt.

"No need for that, McCartney," said Sir Robert.

"Ow Ow Ow!" said the man, who had fallen to the ground.

"How far was the hen?" asked Sir Robert.

"Between eighty and a hundred paces, my lord," said McCartney.

"It was a hundred or I'm damned," said the man on the road.

"And could you make a shot at a quarter mile?"

"How big a target, and with what gun?" asked the man.

Sir Robert thought a moment. "A target two feet across, and with whatever weapon you need."

"It'd take a Philadelphia rifle of .60 caliber," said the man, "and I could do it."

"Done!" said Sir Robert. "Be here at dawn on the twenty-first of the month. You shall have the Philadelphia rifle, and yours to keep, and a gold crown for making the shot."

"What's the catch?" asked the man.

"None whatever. You've solved a problem of great weight for me."

"I'm not going to have to kill a man, am I?"

"No, no! What's your name, man?"

"Bumppo," he said.

"Well, Bumppo, make this shot, you have all I named before and free hunting on my land besides, in perpetuity. What say?"

"But, sir——" said McCartney.

"Untie the man, McCartney," said Sir Robert, "so he can shake hands on the deal." Then he danced a little jig on the edge of the road.

The ropes came off. Humbly, Bumppo shook Sir Robert's hand.

They set up the apparatus for the Great Experiment in a field near the woods two miles from the house. It was a quarter mile from an old Indian mound which Sir Robert thought would serve as an excellent vantage point for the spectators.

The experiment had many stops, all leading to the great glass globe which was at the center of the setup. It was surrounded by charcoal buckets, basins and jars. Over all they had erected canvas to protect it from the elements.

The invitations had been posted for the morning of the twenty-first, weather permitting.

On the afternoon of the nineteenth, they were linking the last of the equipment in place. There cam to them a far-off noise, like low thunder or fireworks on the Fourth of July.

Sir Robert came out from under a basin he was installing. "What's that?"

Hampton turned to the south, from where the noise rose.

86

He smiled. "Pigeons," he said.

The rumble heightened like a great wind from a storm.

"Here they come," said Hamp.

To the south was a ragged blot on the horizon which wound in on itself, then spread.

"Pigeons?" asked Curwell, his face covered with soot from a charcoal bucket. "That noise?"

He stood beside the black man, who pointed.

"Passenger pigeons," he said. "Coming north again to nest. This time every year."

The line covered a quarter of the southern horizon. The sound was like a droning flutter, and the shape moved toward them with the inexorability of the rising tide. It seemed a solid mass which only resolved itself as they drew near the zenith.

They were brown and blue specks which flashed pink. They were packed more densely than Curwell had ever seen birds, ten or twenty sleek shapes to the cubic yard. They flew in a column thirty feet thick and two miles wide and—Curwell tried to count. "What's their rate of flight?"

"A mile to the minute," said Hamp, who watched a hawk diving at one of the edges of the flock. Where the predator flew the pigeons eddied and swirled, but still the column came on.

Curwell looked at his watch. The sun was blotted out as the pigeons passed over, and the fluttering roar was omnipresent.

"Under the awning!" said Hamp, and pulled Curwell back. White flashes like snow, and occasional feathers began to drift down. Passenger pigeon excrement dotted the ground in spots, then more, and fell like a gentle white rain.

Through the flutter of wings, shots could be heard from the neighboring estates. Curwell saw great clumps of pigeons drop a mile away on a surrounding farm.

Then one fell a few feet outside the canvas, struggled and lay still. It must have been hit some distance away and flown this far.

Curwell ran out, picked it up and brought it inside the tent.

It was the most beautiful bird he had ever seen, even in death. Its back was blue, its neck and stomach bronze, its chest pink and dull red, with an iridescent sheen to all the feathers. Its beak was dark, and its legs, feet and eyes were a brilliant orange-red. He placed it on the bench and examined it minutely.

Still the fluttering roared overhead, and the ground was as white as in a snow flurry. The sky outside was an interrupted play of darkness and light where the cloud of birds went in transit across the sun.

Curwell went back to work in the artificial gloom, occasionally looking out to make sure the flock was still traveling. Gunshots came more frequently from the nearby roads and fields.

Sometime later, the sound subsided. Curwell came out of the tent in time to see the last of the flock rocket overhead. The late evening sun began to shine again.

He looked at his watch. Two hours and forty minutes had elapsed. The column had been one hundred and sixty miles long. At ten birds to the yard, ten yards thick, 1,700 yards to the mile, two miles wide . . .

Sir Robert looked at Curwell. "About sixteen million birds, I'd say."

"I've seen more," said Hamp. "When I was a boy I saw a flock that took from noon to dusk to pass. It got dark at midday, and we never saw the sun go down. We had only morning that day." He pounded a copper pipe in place with a maul. He stopped to look at the encrusted ground for a moment.

Then they all went back to work.

All was in readiness.

The spectators, scientific men for the most part, had begun arriving in the early hours of the morn. Dawn was approaching. Then men on the

Indian mound waited while Curwell, Hampton, and Sir Robert Athole walked up the intervening field from the apparatus, which looked to be a jumble of metal and glass to the unaided eye at this distance.

Bumppo stood well back from the others. McCartney kept an eye on him. The leather-clad man was testing the feel of his new Philadelphia rifle, swinging it up and down from his shoulder.

Sir Robert came to the top of the mound and stood beside Lady Margurite.

"Gentlemen," he said. "Lady. Others.

"You are here to witness what I hope is a grand event in scientific progress. On yonder field," he pointed, "are working apparatus for the generation of gases and airs—of dephlogisticated, or eminently respirable, air; of flammable gas, of sulfur air, of phosphorus. They are all working and generating as we stand here, and shall be in fruition soon.

"They enter into conduits taken to the glass globe which you see at the center. They will enter the glass when Mr. Bumppo . . ." Here Bumppo held up his hand shyly, and a ragged cheer went up from the spectators, ". . . fires at his target disk. These phlosgiston-rich gases and liquids will rush together. They should produce the essence of fire, of combustion, of calcination viz. phlogiston itself. A clockwork will then be put in motion, and fifteen seconds later, the mixture will be sparked by means of a circuit from a Leyden jar. This should fix the phlogiston itself, much as common air becomes fixed air in the presence of the electric principle, and allow us the examination for the first time, of one of the principles, of one of the elements itself.

"That is my Great Experiment."

Some applauded.

"Question?"

"Yes?"

"You're mixing inflammable air, dephlogisticated air and phosphorus in the presence of common air, and sparking it?"

"That is my plan."

"Then what you'll get," said the voice, after a moment's reckoning, "is a gentle explosion, a small quantity of fixed air, and a small field fire to fight."

Some laughed.

"I doubt that," said Sir Robert Athole. "I have taken the precaution of removing us to this distance in case of some apparatus failure, and the leakage of noxious fumes."

The sun topped the small ridge to the east, and the field and mound were bathed in a frosty light.

"Win or lose," said Sir Robert, "I feel on the edge of great things."

"And I," said Curwell.

"I, too," said Lady Margurite, and took her husband's hand.

"Mr. Bumppo," said Sir Robert. "You see your target?"

"That I do," said Bumppo.

"Then earn your crown, man!"

The leather-clad man stepped to the front of the mound. Smoothly he raised the weapon as if it were part of him, pulled back the dog-ear hammer, aimed and fired.

The smoke from the muzzle wafted away.

Even without his spy-glass, Sir Robert saw the great globe turn milky white. But it was not the milk-white of residue gases. It roiled and swirled slowly. An "ooh" went up from the small crowd. Winks of light seemed to play across the equipment from the globe. All the apparatus was bathed in a white light.

Sir Robert felt the muscles of his stomach twitch.

For the requisite few more seconds, nothing happened.

Then it did.

Shaken and dazed, Sir Robert pulled himself from the ground in the blinding light. He was near the bottom of the mound. Some of the others were getting up as well as they could. One man lay with a branch through his chest. A few lay unmarked but unmoving. Hampton, near him, held his arm crookedly the wrong way.

There was a roaring in their ears, and it did not subside. Sir Robert stumbled back to the top of the mound, shielding his eyes.

To the west was a great rolling white cloud, too bright to be looked at directly. Bright blooms and bursts of light flew out from it like those from a pan of burning phosphorus. Sir Robert could tell that it was moving slowly away from him to the westward.

He turned. The cloud stretched to north and south, horizon to horizon, moving laterally to its progress westward. Ribbons of red flame shot through the bright white wall.

The smell of burnt wood permeated all the air. As the cloud moved away, it continued to grow in height.

The wind rose from the east, first gently, then in gusts, then faster and faster. The earth to the west was charred to the surface. Matchstick trees poked up. As Sir Robert watched, a puff of wind blew them to ash before his eyes.

The numbed scientists were milling around behind the mound. The wind rose to gale force.

"It's moving west with the rotation of the earth," said Hampton Hamilton. He knew, as did any schoolboy, that the air moves with the surface under it falling behind, from whence rise winds.

Sir Robert turned to see Curwell helping Lady Margurite up. They both seemed safe, though Lady Margurite's skirts flapped immodestly in the racking wind. Sir Robert noticed his wig was gone just as he saw Hamp's wig blow off and be lost in the western distance toward the bright cloud. They climbed down the Indian mound against the force of the wind.

"How long will it burn?" asked Curwell.

"I have no idea," said Sir Robert. "It was not supposed to burn at all."

It was supposed to fix in the globe. I just don't understand."

"It may burn until it reaches the Western Ocean," said Hampton, and he had voiced all their fears.

"Surely, surely not," said Athole, yelling to be heard above the wind.

"But you must have succeeded," said someone else. "You *must* have released all the phlogiston in the mixed matter. There's no telling what will happen with it. It could burn that far!"

"Then the water will put it out. The water!" said Sir Robert. He felt a spasm go through him and he lost consciousness.

He awakened with smoke and the smell of soot in his nostrils. The light outside was murky. A wind whistled around the rafters outside the house, but it was no longer the gale it had been. A brown darkness of smoke lapped against the windows.

He sat up on the couch where they had lain him.

Lady Margurite was crying on the sofa opposite.

"Everything to the west is gone, Robert," she said quietly when she saw him rouse.

"*Everything?*"

"As far as a horse and man can ride, before it becomes too hot to continue. And that was hours ago, when the scout from the township came back from his reconnoiter."

"The barometer," said Lawrence Curwell, tapping the great Dresden instrument atop the mantelpiece. "The barometer has dropped a full six inches since this morning, and is still falling."

"Oh, great Jehovah!" said Sir Robert. "What have I done?"

"Nothing any of us wouldn't have done," said Hampton Hamilton tiredly from another chair. "It only seems you succeeded much better than you had planned."

"Why didn't you stop me?"

"I don't know," said Hampton. "I doubt you would have stopped me."

"What time is it?"

"A little after five."

"We'll know in fourteen hours, then," said Curwell. He continued to stare at the barometer, as if to drag secrets from it.

They tried to eat after darkness fell, but no one was hungry. Tins of molasses had begun to pop their lids in the pantry. Sir Robert imagined it was harder to breathe, but knew better.

They sat in the parlor until no one could stand the waiting and the heat any longer.

"Damn it!" Sir Robert jumped to his feet. "If it's going to happen, I want to look it in the face. We'll go to the ocean."

They looked at him a moment, then climbed from their chairs. It was better than waiting here, where each ticking of the clock sounded loud as a carpenter's hammer to them.

The wagon bounced on the rutted road. The horse labored.

Sir Robert drove in front with Hampton; Curwell and Lady Margurite were in back with a picnic basket and blankets.

It was nearing midnight. The air was filled with the odors of burning—of a thousand things, burnt wood, grass, feathers, calcined metals, gunpowder smells. The wind brought warmth. Through rifts in the smoky sky they saw the stars—larger and colder than they had ever looked before, and they hardly twinkled.

The temperature was still rising, and the barometer had bottomed out an hour ago. It was now decidedly harder to breathe.

They topped the hill overlooking the port town of New Sharpton. Candles burned in the houses, torches moved in the streets as knots of people formed together and dispersed. An occasional rider left on the road down to the coast.

"Over here will be fine," said Sir Robert, guiding the horse to a spot beneath a group of trees atop the hill.

They spread the blankets on the seaward side of the hill and lay back, watching the still Atlantic.

Sir Robert drifted in and out of sleep as from fatigue. The air was hot and close, as if he were shut up in a chimney in the middle of summer.

Curwell had gone down the hill toward the bay. It had taken him a long time to go the few hundred yards. He had stopped frequently and rested.

The horse, which had been unhitched from the wagon, was in distress, as if it had been galloped miles, instead of being walked the few from the estate to the sea.

"The water temperature is rising, and the streams coming to it are out of their banks from melted snow," said Curwell, when he had labored up the hill and lay down. "There are shoals of dead fish away from the stream outlet. There are so many we could smell them from here were it not for this infernal smoke."

"It just can't be true," said Sir Robert. "It just cannot. Water *will not* burn!"

"Maybe," said Hampton, where he lay on the ground above them, holding his splinted and broken arm. "Maybe the New Chemistry has some truths. Perhaps water is *not* an element. Perhaps it, too, contains phlogiston, or inflammable gas, which . . ." For the first time in his life, Hampton was having trouble following a line of thought. He shook his head to clear it. ". . . Inflammable gas. Perhaps a constituent like the oxygine principle. Perhaps it was separated by the heat from the land. Perhaps the fire is fueled from it. Maybe it will have to pass over the Earth innumerable times before it is all combusted with phlogiston . . ."

Sir Robert lay back on the blanket. He held Lady Margurite's hand.

"All gone," he said at last.

"The buffalo. The Indians," said Margurite.

"The Chinese. The bold Russians. The Turks," said Hampton.

"The French. *Britain!*" said Curwell.

"Now us," said Hampton Hamilton, and pointed.

The east was beginning to lighten, though it was still an hour before dawn. The wind blew toward the sea, but it was still a gentle wind, a thin wind. It had very little force.

From north to south the bright white boiling line appeared, like the sun breaking through under a late afternoon storm. But much brighter.

"Shall we be burned?" asked Lady Margurite. Her arm sprouted gooseflesh. "The thought of burning is the worst."

"I think not," said Curwell. "Like the martyrs, I think the air will be too saturated with phlogiston for us to breathe before the fire reaches us." He paused as a great tongue of flame licked out of the roil toward them.

The hill and the village were bathed in the glaring artificial dawn. Screams came from the town from those who were still able to scream.

The thin wind rose more.

They watched the burning line quietly, each locked in their thoughts. The edge of the great combusting cloud was still more than two hundred miles away.

"Phlogiston!" said Sir Robert Athole and turned and passed away.

"I want to stand up," said Hamp. They heard him stir and fall behind them.

"The French *were* right, partly ..." said Curwell.

"Robert ... ?" asked Lady Margurite.

Curwell looked at the enormous burning wall.

"It's the end of ..."

The sentence was the only thing left unfinished.

# Green Brother

I am talking now about the time Red Cloud was fighting the Yellowlegs about the dirt road they put through our lands.

That started the last winter the Yellowlegs were beating the Grey White Men far to the east. We did not understand why they wanted to kill each other, but we did not mind so long as they left us alone.

I am Seldom Blanket. In those days I was a big medicine chief of my people. I would not have been down there in all the fighting with the soldiers if it had not been that my two sons-in-law wanted to go with the others. I don't give much of a damn for most of the rest of my people, but I did like my two daughters and the men who married them.

So early that spring we moved our lodges up to the places where the rest of the Lakota were camped, and we did the medicine dances and the younger men went off to fight the soldiers in their fort on the great dirt road.

I was in camp most of the time, though I would occasionally go up and watch the shooting and killing. Sometimes the war parties brought back one of our men, and we sang the death songs and wept. Sometimes we heard they caught a few of the soldiers and had fun with them and then killed them. It wasn't really a war at that time. We were just showing them how annoyed we were.

They had had a big meeting some years before, with representatives of the Great White Father, and we had all touched the pen, and got nice gifts and had a big supper. Then they brought us a lot of blankets and hardtack and beads. Then they built a road through our best hunting lands.

The road had filled up with wagons and the people who came through let us know they did not like us. There were afraid, too, so soon the soldiers came out while we were in the winter hunting grounds to the south and built a big wooden fort. It was there when our first scouts came back north. Also the soldiers were shooting the buffalo for their livers.

Red Cloud, the big talker for our people, went to the big fort and asked the main soldier there if they were going to move before it got cold again. The man said no.

They sent a man from the East who told Red Cloud that he had agreed to the building of the fort and the road.

Red Cloud said he didn't remember the subject ever coming up.

So they sent more white people to see Red Cloud.

"We ate real good for a week," he said to the Council, "but I don't think any one of them ever spoke from his heart the whole time." He said the white men complained that they were fighting with each other now over the Black White Men and needed the big dirt road.

Red Cloud told them the big wooden building was an eyesore in the Great Mystery's vision, and the dirt road was making the buffalo skittish and could they please move them both.

They said no, and waved the piece of paper around.

So Red Cloud and a few hundred warriors went out one night and burned the fort down.

Then the white men rebuilt it two winters ago. Now everybody was in on the fight. My sons-in-law were gone most of the time, except when they brought food back, and I was much in the company of older men, and women and children. It is pleasant occasionally to do this. It gives a man perspective.

The favorite of my grandchildren was then called Fall Colt, but that would change soon, as he was nearing his thirteenth birthday. He was a fast learner and picked up on the wisdom that I gave him very quickly. I could tell he wanted to be out there with the men fighting around the fort, but he was as yet too young.

I was smoking outside my lodge one day when he came to see me. I puffed on my pipe after offering some smoke to the winds. Then I sat facing the open end of the circled teepees. The sun had been up a few hours.

"Grandfather!" he said, all out of breath. He was thin and his hair was as black as night. He wore deerskin leggings even in the summer. It was all the fashion among young boys that year, as I remember.

"Yes? Something excites you?"

"Onion Boy is no longer Onion Boy. He went off three days ago and came back, and now he is Falcon Foot."

"Ah, that is good. I shall try to remember his new name. Is he changed much?"

"No, except that he now has a medicine bundle with a falcon foot in it. He said the hawk must have been shot, because as it flew over him, it lurched in the air and its foot dropped to the ground before him."

"Ah, a good sign. Did he dream of flying? Usually people who take bird's names have visions of flying while on their quest."

"I forgot to ask him."

"Not important," I said.

"Grandfather?"

"Yes?"

"What was your vision quest like?"

*I saw before me in my mind's eye the river valley, the wavering of my sight and my tiredness, felt the ache in my lids and the cuts between my toes where I had wedged the sharp rocks. I experienced again my shakes and sweats, and the heat of the day. Then I saw again*

98

*the man who was me walking through snow without a blanket, walking and walking, not cold, not tired, not sick or fevered. It would be forever on my brain.*

"Oh, that was a long time ago," I said. "I saw a man who did not need a blanket in the winter."

"Did you see a spirit animal?" he asked.

*The great beast reared up before me, huge and terrible, its eyes afire, its shaggy coat rippling with power, its claws large as knives, its teeth the size of bullets, its head wide as a hide shield, its breath rancid, its smell stifling, its charge unstoppable. I had evacuated my bowels.*

"A bear," I said. "Go and play now."

One of my sons-in-law was brought in with a bullet in his leg. I did the medicine and took out the bullet and chewed tobacco and invoked the Great Mystery to wrestle with death for him. He was up and about in no time.

I decided to ride up to the big dirt road where the fighting was going on and see it for myself.

"Can I go with you, Grandfather?" asked Fall Colt.

I looked at his mother. She shrugged her shoulders.

"Yipppppeeee!" he said, running to get his pony.

"You must remember we will not be able to see much," I said after him.

"I don't care!" he said. "I don't care!"

There were the three small hills before you got to the big wooden fort. Our people stayed on the third hill, just outside rifle range from the walls.

Between the first and second hills, woods used to grow, but the soldiers had cut those down to build the forts, and they had to come between the second and third hills for their firewood. That was still in sight of the fort, and occasionally they would send men out to get logs in a wagon. They would also send men out to shoot at us while the others gathered wood.

That was when we would try to kill them and they would try to kill us.

We did not like fighting this way, but other methods had failed. Early on, some of the warriors had attacked during the night and had been shot. Others had tried getting close during the day but the soldiers had used them for target practice. They seemed to have plenty of food and ammunition, but no firewood. So we waited till they came out.

It was boring work. Most of the time our men lay around and watched from the warm grass on the hills, polishing their coup sticks or sharpening their knives. Others would go hunting or fishing. They always cooked the game on the hills where the soldiers could see. The soldiers always shot at them when they did. That is how my son-in-law got the bullet in his leg.

Fall Colt and I walked up the hill where his father, Terrible Wolf, was dozing in the sun.

"Ho, father," he said, waking, as he saw us come up the draw. He sat up.

"Don't get up on our account," I said.

Fall Colt ran to his father and hugged him. "You embarrass me," said Terrible Wolf. The boy let go of him.

"How are things in camp?"

"Dull," I said. "Your brother is fine. He will come back this week." We sat down. Terrible Wolf and I started to talk.

It was a few minutes before I noticed that Fall Colt had not said anything. He was back down the draw toward the horses. But he kept looking toward the top of the hill behind me. He appeared nervous.

"Hey-A! Hey-A!" yelled someone from the top of the hill. Instantly Terrible Wolf and all the other men were up, rifles in hand and onto their horses. They swept up over the hill in a cloud of dust.

From the direction of the fort we could hear rifle fire. I went to my horse and pulled my shotgun from its holster and Fall Colt got his boy's bow and arrows from his mount. Then we went to the ridgetop.

Below us the ground swelled downward to the fort. Soldiers were on the walls, others milled around in the open gateway. Halfway between us and them, a wagon and several dozen mounted soldiers were on the near side of the first hill.

The warriors swept down toward them from all sides, yelling and raising a great bother. The soldiers came determinedly on, until they reached the timber on the near side of the second hill. Then the wagon stopped and the horsemen dismounted and began to shoot while others with axes started cutting up dead trees.

The braves rode toward them and stopped and dismounted and began firing. The soldiers all fired at once, the warriors whenever they wanted. The sound of axes could be heard intermittently.

Then came the formal charge from the fort, with another two dozen soldiers on horses riding out toward the braves. The warriors mounted and turned back up the third hill. Then they stopped and fired back at the blue-clad soldiers.

Then our second bunch of braves charged from the draw near the third rise, and the soldiers in the fort went wild. Smoke rose up everywhere on the walls as they shot. The wave of troops rushing the hill turned. Everywhere was motion and gunshots. A lot of dust was raised.

Some of the first braves had run back up the hill beside us and were yelling and taunting the soldiers. An occasional bullet whistled by. One man dropped his breechclout and danced ribaldly with his buttocks toward the fort. Then he held his ankles and hopped backwards down the hill toward the firing.

Many bullets began to hit around us.

The second wave of soldiers would never come up the third rise. Some started to, but the man with the sword and the two bars on his hat stopped them. They are usually more cautious than the ones with one bar on their hats.

Dust obscured everything. The warriors on the hill fired down into the woodchopping party, holding their rifles high. The soldiers there and in the fort were firing as fast as they could. The troops between them and us flitted in and out of the smoke and dust.

Then everything was quiet. The dust began to settle.

The wagon and the soldiers were going back into the fort, only a few logs bouncing in the back. The mounted soldiers kept a wary eye backward on the hills. Some of our people put their thumbs in their ears and stuck out their tongues, an old white man's insult.

The doors to the fort closed. We went back over the hill.

No one had been hurt.

I looked around, then up. Fall Colt was standing against the skyline, looking down at the fort. He was shaking and pale.

"Come down," I said. "They might hit you by mistake."

He shook himself, looked around.

"What is it?"

He looked down at the bow in his hand. "I don't know, Grandfather, . . . I . . . I . . ."

"Was the excitement too much for you?"

"No . . . I . . . I didn't pay much attention."

His eyes were troubled. I said no more to him, and we rode back to our camp.

It did not surprise me when I saw him calling his friends together two days later. He handed one his bow, another his arrows and knife. Then he passed out his leggings, his moccasins, his breechclout. Naked, he turned his back on the lodges and fires of our people and walked toward the distant mountains.

His mother came to me. "Father, did you see . . ."

I took my pipe from my mouth so her shadow wouldn't fall across it and harm the tobacco. "It is time," I said. "This has been coming on for days. He will be fine."

We watched him until he was lost in the evening sun.

Then we got busy for a few days, and I thought of Fall Colt rarely.

What we got busy doing was killing soldiers. It happened this way:

I accompanied my other son-in-law when he went back to the big dirt road. We got there when the sun stood straight up. The heat was already oppressive, the air still. Sound traveled a long way. We heard the gates of the fort open from up on our hill. The brave on watch let out his cry then. I looked up into the sky. A lone flycatcher chased a winged insect. I drew my shotgun from its scabbard and mounted up.

We did the same things we did the other day. The wagon came out, and we harassed it. Then the other soldiers charged out. Then our reserves came up out of their places. Then our warriors mounted up and came back up the hill.

I saw what was happening before the others did. I let out a cry and began my death chant.

Because the second wave of soldiers had not stopped at the near side of the second hill. They kept coming. They were led by a soldier with one bar on his hat. He pointed his sword at us and spurred his horse. I could see each of his horse's hoofbeats raise dust. His eyes locked on mine.

Supposing the ritual to be the same, some of our people had dismounted and were prancing on top of the hill.

"Yah-Yah-Yah!" they said, turning somersaults. "Yah-Yah-Can't catch us!" Then they noticed the mounted soldiers had not stopped but were bearing down on them. They fell all over each other for a second, then jumped on their horses.

Bullets whipped around me as the oncoming soldiers flew up the hill. As I jumped on my horse, I could see the man in charge of the wagon party shaking his fist at the man leading the charge up the hill. It was a very foolish thing for the man with one bar to do.

For a few seconds it seemed like a marvelous thing, but only because we did not expect it. But even as they neared the top of the hill and we spurred down into the open flat beyond, I saw that our reserves which had already made their ritual charge had turned and were heading up around the draw. Spotted Bull was in charge and he was a good man.

So we kicked our ponies and made them run. We could tell when the white men reached the top of the hill, because they started shooting everything in sight. Bullets hit all around us. Somebody on my left went down. The man to my right turned and fired, and we circled to the right so the white men would come sooner between us and the reserves. We turned on the soldiers as soon as their fire became scattered.

This was because Spotted Bull had gotten between them and the top of the hill. I turned to see the soldiers milling around as his bunch came down on them.

There were twenty or so mounted soldiers. There were a hundred of us. I sent Terrible Wolf back up to the top of the hill. "Tell us when the whole fort is coming," I said.

Then we turned back into battle.

I had no coup stick with me, so I leaned down next to my mount and swung up and out when I neared a soldier. He fired at me with his pistol. Powder burned my face and arms. I came up and hit him under the chin with the butt of my shotgun. He went limp and slid off his horse.

Then I saw the man with one bar and shot him in the face with both barrels. He died quickly.

A few of the soldiers had killed their horses and were shooting at us from behind them. We dismounted and began walking toward them, firing as we went. Smoke hung over everything.

"The whole fort is coming," yelled Terrible Wolf.

"Keep killing!" I said. "Keep killing!"

"They're on the second hill," yelled Terrible Wolf, but he hadn't mounted up yet.

We killed the last soldier just as the world filled with the sound of hooves. Terrible Wolf jumped on his mount and took off across the ridge. I got on mine and did the same. We divided up, half going east, half west.

Seventy soldiers came over the hill in brown and blue waves. Bullets went by like bees. Then we all turned and went over the same hill back down toward the fort. We caught the wagon party unprepared. We killed most of them and looted and set the wagon afire.

Somebody got off his horse and pissed on the face of a dead man. Then we rode as fast as we could away from there with everything we had taken from the wagon. They chased us until it was too dark to see.

We moved the camp some miles away from where it had been. Things calmed down in a few days, and our warriors were back on the hill and the soldiers were back in the fort.

It was evening. I sat smoking in front of my lodge. Then I saw a naked boy coming towards camp from a long way off. It was my grandson.

He paused often. He was limping. He kept turning to stare back toward the near mountains, in the direction the fort lay.

"Hello, Grandson," I said. "Did you follow our travois trail?"

He stared at me a moment.

"Grandfather," he said.

"Yes?"

"Can I sleep now? I will tell you about it later."

"Here," I said, moving over and giving him half of my buffalo robe.

He lay down slowly and then he was asleep. I patted his head while he dreamed.

He woke up late the next night.

"Could you help me with my new name?" asked my grandson.

"Most people do not need help with theirs," I said.

"That is because they have seen a totem animal spirit and know its name," he said.

"You saw no animal?"

"I saw an animal, Grandfather, but I do not know its name."

"That *is* a problem. Perhaps I can help."

He began to tell me what he remembered of his vision quest. It was disjointed, like most are up until a vision comes. He had roamed the hills, chanted, he did not sleep. He put rocks between his toes and scoured his eyes with brambles to keep him awake. He heard voices, but it was always the wind when he listened closer. He lay over a rock with his head down to help get a vision. One did not come until the third day.

"I turned in the direction of the big dirt road," he said. "And I saw it. I saw everything. There was water out there, much water. It was shining in the sun. The ground steamed and all was green and growing. Many small animals I did not know moved through the growths. In the water, things with long necks waded thick as buffalo on the plains. Animals like bats with long noses wheeled through the skies and dipped into the water for fish. All was large and out of proportion. All was cries and calls and roars like cougars. I did not understand."

"Visions are sometimes not meant to be understood, only acted upon," I said. "What was your animal like?"

"Then I *was* an animal, moving through the reeds. The wading animals that had seemed large were small to me now, my size. I brushed aside ferns. I chased one of the long-necked things which was trying to run from me.

Its eyes were filled with terror. I caught it in a jump. I bit into its head and it crushed like pecans. I felt blood and bone. I bit off the head and swallowed it, while the rest of the thing stumbled and staggered around, bleeding in great gouts. I waited and then I pushed it over and began eating while it flopped and heaved on the ground, mashing a place flat with its tail and legs. I threw my head back to eat and swallowed whole chunks without chewing.

"I was near the water and I saw my reflection. I was huge and green. I stood on two legs and had tiny claws where my arms were. My eyes were at the sides of a great head. I had a long mouth full of sharp teeth, and a long thick tail which I used to balance.

"I stood up from my prey and roared a challenge to all the world around me. The earth was silent for a moment, then all resumed as it was before."

My grandson looked at me. "I feel great kinship with that beast, Grandfather. I do not know what it is. It is a beast of terror and strength, and it had skin like a snake."

"There is no doubt it is a powerful animal."

"Grandfather, there is something else."

"What is that?"

"It is still here. Near the white man's fort."

My grandson looked around him, saw some of the booty from the attack on the wagon a few days before. "I will need that," he said, picking up a tool.

"There is no great magic in a shovel," I said.

"There is no great water near the white man's fort, either," he said. "But I saw it there."

He said he would choose a new name after he was done with his work.

The shovel was taller than he was. He strapped it on his pony and rode off toward the big dirt road.

"Where is Fall Colt going?" asked his mother.

"His name is not Fall Colt anymore."

"What is it, then?"

"He is going to find that out," I said.

"Aren't you going with him, Father?" she asked.

"I was just leaving," I said.

When I arrived, Terrible Wolf was standing on top of the hill scratching his head. He held his rifle across the crook of his left arm.

"He has been on his vision quest, hasn't he?" asked my son-in-law.

"Yes. He is troubled. It was inconclusive."

"I can . . . wait . . . what's he doing?"

We looked down the hill toward the fort. I saw that my grandson had been keeping to cover behind a clump of small trees, but now, shovel in hand, he took off running toward the fortress.

We saw puffs of smoke from the walls, then heard the crack of Army rifles. My grandson zigged and zagged like the woodpecker in flight. Puffs of dirt went up around him.

Some others had joined us on the hill, curious since they heard shots but no one had raised a cry. They watched the lone figure darting over the ground.

"Has he lost his wits?" asked someone.

"Great Mystery problems," I said.

"Oh."

Then he stopped. He looked around back and forth. Dust went up all around him, and the fire from the fort became heavy. I saw one of his braids whip in the air behind him.

He dropped down. I thought he was dead. He was obscured by a small bush barely big enough to hide a dog. Then we saw the flash of his shovel moving, the handle end sticking back up in the air like a great tongue.

"Yayyy!" we all yelled.

A few more shots came from the fort, then it was quiet.

Faintly we could hear the sound of the shovel, digging.

By nightfall he had disappeared behind a mound of dirt.

"I'm going down there soon to see if he is all right," said Terrible Wolf.

"Better take him some food and his bow," I said. "The white men might send someone out to try to hurt him."

My grandson was about two bowshots out from the fort but that seemed to worry the soldiers. The white men do not understand things dealing with the Great Mystery. I am sure they thought his digging had something to do with their fort. They were deathly afraid a thirteen-year-old was going to tunnel up under their building and kill them all in their sleep. So there was no telling what the soldiers would do.

After pitch dark, Terrible Wolf made his way out toward the sound of the shovel.

"I kept my eyes turned away," said Terrible Wolf later. "When I saw what he was doing."

"Oh," I said, smoking my pipe on the side of the hill away from the fort.

"There were parts of Storm Beasts around there. He was digging among them."

"That *is* bad," I said. We believe Storm Beasts dash themselves from the sky during rains. They are monsters who live in the heavens with the Thunderbird. They kill themselves with roars which is the thunder, and fall with a flash which is the lightning.

We believe this because you can always find their remains after storms, as they are exposed when the rain carry the earth away. Their bones litter our hunting grounds for miles after the spring rainstorms. We usually go around them, as they are unlucky animals.

"Did he mention Storm Beasts in his vision?" asked Terrible Wolf.

"There was no thunder and lightning in his story," I said.

"Do you think the Great Mystery has driven my son mad?" he asked.

"Let me get a reading on that," I said.

I was beginning to have a few doubts myself.

I performed three ceremonies, each more taxing than the one before it. I was sweating and tired, and my medicine bundle was oily and smelled bad when I finished.

"The Great Mystery is not punishing your son," I said to Terrible Wolf. "But there is magic at work out there, and it's so great I'd rather not be around when it happens."

"But you will."

"Of course I will."


The mound had grown. He was piling it up on the side toward the big dirt road. Occasionally a shovelful of dirt would clear the place he dug. Otherwise, the days were serene.

We could see men moving in the fort. Sometimes one would fire at the place where my grandson dug. Then they even quit doing that.

We settled into a routine. Terrible Wolf would take food and water out to his son at night, and we would watch and wait during the day, in case the soldiers came out for firewood or to harm my grandson. It was not the kind of thing we liked to do.

Terrible Wolf came back one night. He sat down tiredly, put his head between his knees and stared at the ground. I noticed in the moonlight that his moccasins had already started wearing out this early in the summer.

"I did not know one person could move so much dirt," he said.

❉

"Grandfather," someone said, shaking me awake.

"Yes," I said, sitting up on my robe where I had fallen asleep. I rubbed my eyes and sat up. It was some hours before dawn. There was a dull boom far away.

"I need some great medicine worked."

He was streaked with dirt, haggard. His eyes were clouded over with fatigue, barely reflecting the fires on the hill. He was as naked as he had been when he left on his vision quest.

In the distance, I heard another rumble of thunder, and the sky flashed light.

"If a storm is coming, and you are working among Storm Beasts, you are going to need more power than I can ask for. But I will see what I can do."

The first thing I did was to strip off naked and do a protection dance for myself. I am no fool. Then I did a small one for him, because he is so small. I didn't think that would stop the lightning from killing us, anyway. Then I picked up my medicine bundle.

"Have you thought of a name yet, Grandson?" I asked as we walked down the hill. The eastern horizon talked to itself in flashes of light. Great clouds walked toward us across the sky, their tops reaching far out in our direction.

"I am going to be called Green Brother," he said.

"Green Brother is a good name."

The small trees were being whipped about in the rising wind. Dust blew from the big dirt road. I was getting afraid, though my grandson did not know it.

Lightning slammed to the ground behind the white man's fort. Men moved on the walls. Possibly lightning would hit it and burn it to the ground and end all our troubles. I could not be concerned with the soldiers just now.

The pit was before us. Green Brother had dug a rampway down into the place he had scooped out of the ground. It started a long way back, the hole was so deep.

I did not know one person could move so much dirt, either.

"Guide me," I said, closing my eyes. I moved my lips in the death chant. If I saw the spirit animal all at once, it would be easier on me. I would either live or die in that instant.

I felt us go downward into the earthworks. The whistling wind stopped, only dust was blown onto my face from above. I felt my heart pound within my chest. I could not breathe right.

Green Brother turned to me. "It is before you, Grandfather."

"Is it terrible, Grandson?"

"Not after you get used to it."

My nerve failed then.

"Turn me away from it," I said. "The magic will be better if I am not used to it."

"There," he said, turning me.

I opened my eyes. The sides of the hole slanted down around me. The rampway went up from where I stood. A flash of lightning threw a horrible shadow on the ground before me. I felt the dead presence of the thing behind me.

"Make magic with it, Grandfather," said Green Brother.

"Is it upright? Are its legs and arms free? Will it step on us?"

"It is only bones, but they are iron. It is upright though curled toward us as if falling. Its body is stuck in the rock beneath us. I could not cut it away with the shovel.

"It is well you didn't. It might have fallen on you, and I would not know you new name." I wiped my brow. "This is going to be tough. What do you wish it to do?"

Green Brother looked up behind me. He smiled. "I want it to walk up this ramp and then across the big dirt road and into the fort."

"That would *probably* impress the white men," I said.

Thunder smashed outside the pit with a white flash. It unsettled me mightily. A few drops of rain hit my head. Soon the storm would open up. Perhaps more of the Storm Beasts would fall on us and kill us.

"Stand back," I said. "I need lots of room."

"Is there anything I can do?" asked my grandson Green Brother. "I feel kinship with this beast. I *was* this beast in my vision."

"If it moves," I said, "you can do *anything* you want."

I spread the things from my medicine bundle before me. It would take them all. I wished I had more sacred things. I had never tried anything so powerful before.

I called on the Great Mystery and reminded him that I was small before the storm, as are all men and women. I asked that he remember the things our people had done in gratitude for his blessings, and thanked him for the many times he had wrestled death for me.

When I had worked up his enthusiasm for me, I began to speak of specific things the soldiers had done to us, then asked him to intercede through the Storm Beast behind me.

As I paused for breath I heard the first gunshot. Then the warning cry from our people that meant the soldiers were coming from the fort.

"Sing your death song, Green Brother," I said. "I will try to finish this."

I had left my shotgun up on the hill because I did not like to carry it in a storm. Years ago I had seen a man melted to his rifle where he sat. It had not been pretty.

The storm crashed about us. There was a sound of firing, and hooves drummed near.

"Hurry, Grandfather!" said Green Brother, "Hurry!"

I was calling on the spirit of the Storm Beast to help us. I was really inspired, since it was no longer just my people, it was Green Brother and I who were in trouble. A gun fired from the dirt up near the mound from the pit, and voices called. The wind howled and roared. The sky danced with light and noise.

A bullet whipped into the ground near me. I closed my eyes tight. I heard men at the top of the ramp, nervous laughter.

"Thing!" I yelled, opening my eyes and dancing around. "Thing! Come alive! Come alive!"

A great bolt of lightning hit just outside the pit.

I saw many things at once:

I saw six soldiers on foot halfway down the ramp. Some were crouched down, rifles ahead of them. Two were upright, guns pointing toward me.

I saw Green Brother near me, head up, the shovel drawn back in his arms, ready to swing at the soldiers on the ramp.

I saw the shadow of the thing behind me on the ground.

*It moved.* It may have been only shadows from a different lightning flash.

I saw two of the soldiers jerk. I saw their hearts stop working in their chests. I saw six sets of eyes go wide as the doorknobs on the white man's houses. The eyes of the two men who died fell away to each side. The others disappeared backwards up the ramp.

Thunder crashed on top of us.

I turned and looked up at the thing behind me.

I wet myself all over my legs and fell forward into the soft ground.

Rain was falling in torrents, pushing at my face and eyes. I sat up. Water was running down into the pit. Green Brother lay sprawled across from me, his head bleeding where he had fallen against the shovel. I went to him after retrieving my medicine bag. Strangely there was no more thunder and lightning, just the rain.

I took the rifles from the two dead men and put them over one shoulder. I picked up Green Brother and walked up the muddy ramp. I did not look back. I did not care if the other soldiers were still there or not.

It was very calm under the cold rain.

Soon after the white men left and we burned down the fort again. After the snows melted the next spring, we signed another treaty, and a Doctor of Bones came out from the Great River Potomac to see the field of Storm Beasts.

He and Green Brother spent much time at the pit and all around there. Then men and a wagon came and took all the Storm Beasts away. The Doctor of Bones said Green Brother's vision animal was called in the white man's language *Tyrannosaurus rex*. He said this one was splendid.

Green Brother asked to go back East with the doctor and to learn more about all the spirit animals he had seen.

So he is at the university, and I miss him greatly. We are peaceful here now, and get our coffee and cattle and flour every month, and things are very boring.

Before he left, Green Brother said his spirit animal had been like the long-tailed yellow and brown lizard, only much bigger and much more fierce.

I am a simple man, and I am ignorant of many white men's things. But I do know one truth, and as long as there is a blue sky above me, and the Great Mystery smiles, I know this. That thing I saw that night in the pit was no lizard.

Please turn me toward the sun so I can smoke.

# Mary Margaret Road-Grader

It was the time of the Sun Dance and the Big Tractor Pull. Freddy-in-the-Hollow and I had traveled three days to be at the river. We were almost late, what with the sandstorm and the raid on the white settlement over to Old Dallas.

We pulled in with our wrecker and string of fine cars, many of them newly-stolen. You should have seen Freddy and me that morning, the first morning of the Sun Dance.

We were dressed in new-stolen fatigues and we had bright leather holsters and pistols. Freddy had a new carbine, too. We were wearing our silver and feathers and hard goods. I noticed many women watching us as we drove in. There seemed to be many more here than the last Sun Ceremony. It looked to be a good time.

The usual crowd gathered before we could circle up our remuda. I saw Bob One-Eye and Nathan Big Gimp, the mechanics, come across from their circles. Already the cook fires were burning and women were skinning out the cattle that had been slaughtered early in the morning.

"*Hoo!*" I heard Nathan call as he limped to our wrecker. He was old; his left leg had been shattered in the Highway wars, he went back that far. He put his hands on his hip and looked over our line.

"I know that car, Billy-Bob Chevrolet," he said to me, pointing to an old Mercury. "Those son-a bitch Dallas people stole it from me last year. I know its plates. It is good you stole it back. Maybe I will talk to you about doing car work to get it back sometime."

"We'll have to drink about it," I said.

"Let's stake them out," said Freddy-in-the-Hollow. "I'm tired of pulling them."

We parked them in two parallel rows and put up the signs, the strings of pennants, and the whirlers. Then we got in the wrecker and smoked.

Many people walked by. We were near the Karankawa fuel trucks, so people would be coming by all the time. Some I know by sight, many I had known since I was a boy. They all walked by as though they did not notice the cars, but I saw them looking out of the corners of their eyes. Music was starting down the way, and most people were heading there. There would be plenty of music in the next five days. I was in no hurry. We would all be danced out before the week was up.

Some of the men kept their strings tied to their tow trucks as if they didn't care whether people saw them or not. They acted as if they were ready to move out at any time. But that was not the old way. In the old times, you had your cars parked in rows so they could be seen. It made them harder to steal, too, especially if you had a fence.

But none of the Tractor Pullers had arrived yet, and that was what everybody was waiting for.

The talk was that Simon Red Bulldozer would be here this year. He was known from the Brazos to the Sabine, though he had never been to one of our Ceremonies. He usually stayed in the Guadalupe River area.

But he had beaten everybody there, and had taken all the fun out of their Big Pulls. So he had gone to the Karankawa Ceremony last year, and now was supposed to be coming to ours. They still talk about the time Simon Red Bulldozer took on Elmo John Deere two summers ago. I would have traded many plates to have been there.

"We need more tobacco," said Freddy-in-the-Hollow.

"We should have stolen some from the whites," I said. "It will cost us plenty here."

"Don't you know anyone?" he asked.

"I know everyone, Fred," I said quietly (a matter of pride). "But nobody has any friends during the Ceremonies. You pay for what you get."

It was Freddy-in-the-Hollow's first Sun Dance as a Raider. All the times before, he had come with his family. He still wore his coup-charm, a big VW symbol pried off the first car he'd boosted, on a chain around his neck. He was only seventeen summers. Someday he would be a better thief than me. And I'm the best there is.

Simon Red Bulldozer was expected soon, and all the men were talking a little and laying a few bets.

"You know," said Nathan Big Gimp, leaning against a wrecker at his shop down by the community fires, "I saw Simon turn over three tractors two summers ago, one after the other. The way he does it will amaze you, Billy-Bob."

I allowed as how he might be the man to bet on.

"Well, you really should, though the margin is slight. There's always the chance Elmo John Deere will show."

I said maybe that was what I was waiting for.

But it wasn't true. Freddy-in-the-Hollow and I had talked in English to a man from the Red River people the week before. He made some hints but hadn't really told us anything. They had a big Puller, he said, and you shouldn't lose your money on anyone else.

We asked if this person would show at our Ceremony, and he allowed as how maybe, continuing to chew on some willow bark. So we allowed as how maybe we'd still put our hard goods on Simon Red Bulldozer.

He said that maybe he'd be down to see, and then had driven off in his jeep with the new spark plugs we'd sold him.

The Red River people don't talk too much, but when they do, they say a lot. So we were waiting on the bets.

Women had been giving me the eye all day, and now there were a few of them looking openly at me; Freddy too, by reflected glory. I was thinking of doing something about it when we got a surprise.

At noon, Elmo John Deere showed, coming in with his two wreckers and his Case 1190, his families and twelve strings of cars. He was the richest man in the Nations, and his camp took a large part of the eastern end of the circle.

Then a little while later, the Man showed. Simon Red Bulldozer came only with his two wives, a few sons, and his transport truck. And in the back of it was the Red Bulldozer, which, they say, had killed a man before Simon had stolen it.

It's an old legend, and I won't tell it now.

And it's not important anymore, anyway.

So we thought we were in for the best Pull ever, between two men we knew by deeds. Simon wanted to go smoke with Elmo, but Elmo sent a man over to tell Simon Red Bulldozer to keep his distance. There was bad blood between them, though Simon was such a good old boy that he was willing to forget it.

Not Elmo John Deere, though. His mind was bad. He was a mean man.

Freddy said it first, while we lay on the hood of the wrecker the eve of the dancing.

"You know," he said, "I'm young."

"Obvious," I said.

"But," he continued, "things are changing."

I had thought the same thing, though I hadn't said it. I pulled my bush hat up off my eyes, looked at the boy. He was part white and his mustache needed trimming, but otherwise he was all right.

"You may be right," I answered, uneasily.

"Have you noticed how many horses there are this year, for God's sake?"

I had. Horses were usually used for herding our cattle and sheep. They were pegged out over on the north side with the rest of the livestock. The younger boys who hadn't discovered women were picking up hard goods by standing watch over the animals. I mean, there were always *some* horses, but not this many. This year, people brought in whole remudas, twenty-thirty to a string. Some were even trading them like cars. It made my skin crawl.

"And the women," said Fred-in-the-Hollow. "Loose is loose, but they go too far, really they do. They're not even wearing halters under their clothes, most of them. Jiggle-jiggle."

"Well, they're nice to look at. Times are getting hard," I said. The raid night before last was our first in two months, the only time we'd found anything worth the taking. Nothing but rusted piles of metal all up and down the whole Trinity. Not much on the Brazos, or the Sulphur. Even the white men had begun to steal from each other.

Pickings were slim, and you really had to fight like hell to get away with anything.

We sold a car early in the evening, for more plates than it was worth, which was good. But what Freddy had been talking and thinking about had me depressed. I needed a woman. I needed some good dope. Mostly, I wanted to kill something.

The dances started early, with people toking up on rabbit tobacco, shag bark and hemp. The whole place smelled of burnt meat and grease, and there was singing going on in most of the lodges.

Oh, it was a happy group.

I was stripped down and doing some prayers. Tomorrow was the Sun Dance and the next day the contests. Freddy tried to find a woman and didn't have any luck. He came through twice while I was painting myself and smoking up. Freddy didn't hold with the prayer parts. I figure they can't hurt, and besides, there wasn't much else to do.

Two hours after dark, one of Elmo John Deere's men knifed one of Simon Red Bulldozer's sons.

The delegation came for me about thirty minutes later.

I thought at first I might get my wish about killing something. But not tonight. They wanted me to arbitrate the judgement. Someone else would have to be executioner if he were needed.

"Watch the store, Freddy," I said, picking up my carbine.

I smoked while they talked. When Red Bulldozer's cousin got through, John Deere's grandfather spoke. The Bulldozer boy wasn't hurt too much, he wouldn't lose the arm. They brought the John Deere man before me. He glared at me across the smoke, and said not a word.

They summed up.

Then they all looked at me.

I took two more puffs, cleaned my pipe. Then I broke down my carbine, worked on the selector pin for a while. I lit my other pipe and pointed to the John Deere man.

"He lives," I said. "He was drunk."

They let him leave the lodge.

"Elmo John Deere," I said.

"Uhm?" asked fat Elmo.

"I think you should pay three mounts and ten plates to do this thing right. And give one man for three weeks to do the work of Simon Red Bulldozer's son."

Silence for a second, then Elmo spoke. "It is good what you say."

"Simon Red Bulldozer."

"Hmmm?"

"You should shake hands with Elmo John Deere and this should be the end of the matter."

"Good," he said.

They shook hands. Then each gave me a plate as soon as the others had left. One California and one New York. A 1993 and a '97. Not bad for twenty minutes' work.

It wasn't until I got back to the wrecker that I started shaking. That had been the first time I was arbiter. It could have made more bad trouble and turned hearts sour if I'd judged wrong.

"Hey, Fred!" I said. "Let's get real drunk and go see Wanda Hummingtires. They say she'll do it three ways all night."

She did, too.

The next dawn found us like a Karankawa coming across a new case of 30-weight oil. It was morning, quick. I ought to know. I watched that goddammed sun come up and I watched it go down, and every minute of the day in between, and I never moved from the spot. I forgot everything that went on around me, and I barely heard the women singing or the prayers of the other men.

At dusk, Freddy-in-the-Hollow led me back to the wrecker and I slept like a stone mother log for twelve hours with swirling violet dots in my head.

I had had no visions. Some people get them, some don't.

I woke with the mother of all headaches, but after I smoked awhile it went away. I wasn't a Puller, but I was in two of the races, one on foot and one in the Mercury.

I lost one and won the other.

I also won the side of beef in the morning shoot. Knocked the head off the bull with seven shots. Clean as a whistle.

At noon, everybody's life changed forever.

The first thing we saw was the cloud of dust coming over the third ridge. Then the outriders picked up the truck when it came over the second. It was coming too fast.

The truck stopped with a roar and a squeal of brakes. It had a long lumpy canvas cover on the back.

Then a woman climbed down from the cab. She was the most gorgeous woman I'd ever seen. And I'd seen Nellie Firestone two summers ago, so that was saying something.

Nellie hadn't come close to this girl. She had long straight black hair and a beautiful face from somewhere way back. She was built like nothing I'd seen before. She wore tight coveralls and had a .357 Magnum strapped to her hip.

"Who runs the Pulls?" she asked, in English, of the first man who reached her.

He didn't know what to do. Women never talk like that.

"Winston Mack Truck," said Freddy at my side, pointing.

"What do you mean?" asked one of the young men. "Why do you want to know?"

"Because I'm going to enter the Pull," she said.

Tribal language mumbles went around the circle. Very negative ones.

"Don't give me any of that shit," she said. "How many of you know of Alan Backhoe Shovel?"

He was another legend over in Ouachita River country.

"Well," she said, and held up a serial number plate from a backhoe tractor scoop, "I beat him last week."

"Hua, hua, hua!" the chanting started.

"What is your name, woman?" asked one of Mack Truck's men.

"Mary Margaret Road-Grader," she said, and glared back at him.

"Freddy," I said quietly, "put the money on her."

So we had a Council. You gotta have a council for everything, especially when honor and dignity and other manly virtues are involved.

Winston Mack Truck was pretty old, but he was still spry and had some muscles left on him. His head was a puckered lump because he had once crashed in a burner while raiding over on the Brazos. He only had one car, and it wasn't much of one.

But he did have respect, and he did have power, and he had more sons than anyone in the Nations, ten or eleven of them. They were all there in Council, with all the heads of other families.

Winston Mack Truck smoked awhile, then called us to session.

Mary Margaret Road-Grader wasn't allowed inside the lodge. It seemed sort of stupid to me. If they wouldn't let her in here, they sure weren't going to let her enter the Pull. But I kept my tongue. You can never tell.

I was right. Old man Mack Truck can see clear through to tomorrow.

"Brothers," he said. "We have a problem here."

*Hua Hua Hua*

"We have been asked to let a woman enter the Pulls."

*Silence.*

"I do not know if it's a good thing," he continued. "But our brothers to the East have seen fit to let her do so. This woman claims to have defeated Alan Backhoe Shovel in fair contest. She enters this as proof."

He placed the serial plate in the center of the lodge.

"I will listen now," he said, and sat back, folding his arms.

They went around the circle then, some speaking, some waving away the opportunity.

It was Simon Red Bulldozer himself who changed the tone of the Council.

"I have never seen a woman in a Pull," he said. "Or in any contest other than those for women."

He paused. "But I have never wrestled against Alan Backhoe Shovel, either. I know of no one who has bested him. Now this woman claims to have done so. It would be interesting to see if she were a good Puller."

"You want a woman in the contest?!" asked Elmo, out of turn.

Richard Ford Pinto, the next speaker, stared at Elmo until John Deere realized his mistake. But Ford Pinto saved face for him by asking the same question of Simon.

"I would like to see if she is a good Puller," said Simon, adamantly. He would commit himself no further.

Then it was Elmo's turn.

"My brothers!" he began, so I figured he would be at it for a long time. "We seem to spend all our time in Council, rather than having fun like we should. It is not good, it makes my heart bitter.

"The idea that a woman can get a hearing at Council revolts me. Were this a young man not yet proven, or an Elder who had been given his Service feather, I would not object. But, brothers, this is a woman!" His voice came falsetto now, and he began to chant:

> "I have seen the dawn of bad days, brothers.
> But never worse than this.
> A woman enters our camp, brothers!
> A woman! A woman!"

He sat down and said no more in the conference.

It was my turn.

"Hear me, Pullers and Stealers!" I said. "You know me. I am a man of my word and a man of my deeds. As are you all. But the time has come for deeds alone. Words must be put away. We must decide whether a woman can be as good as a man. We cannot be afraid of a woman! Or can some of us be?"

They all howled and grumbled just like I wanted them to. You can't suggest men in Council are afraid of anything.

Of course, we voted to let her in the contest, like I knew we would.

Changes in history come easy, you know?

They pulled the small tractors first, the Ford 250s and the Honda Fieldmasters and such. I wasn't much interested in watching young boys fly through the air and hurt themselves. So me and Freddy wandered over where the big tractor men were warming up. The Karankawas were selling fuel from the old Houston refineries hand over hose. A couple of the Pullers had refused, like Elmo at first, to do anything with a woman in the contest.

But even Elmo was there watching when Mary Margaret Road-Grader unveiled her machine. There were lots of oohs and ahhs when she started pulling the tarp off that monster.

Nobody had seen one in years, except maybe as piles of rust on the roadside. It was long and low, and looked much like a yellow elephant's head with wheels stuck on the end of the trunk. The cab was high and shiny glass. Even the doors still worked. The blade was new and bright; it looked as if it had never been used.

The letters on the side were sharp and black, unfaded. Even the paint job was new. That made me suspicious about the Alan Backhoe Shovel contest. I took a gander at the towball while she was atop the cab unloosening the straps. It *was* worn. Either she had been lucky in the contest, or she'd had sense enough to put on a worn towball.

Everybody watched her unfold the tarp (one of those heavy smelly kind that can fall on you and kill you) but she had no helpers.

So I climbed up to give her a hand.

One of the women called out something and some others took it up. Most of the men just shook their heads.

There was a lot of screaming and hoorawing from the little Pulls, so I had to touch her on the shoulder to let her know I was up there.

She turned fast and her hand went for her gun before she saw it was me.

And I saw in her eyes not killer hate, but something else; I saw she was scared and afraid she'd have to kill someone.

"Let me help you with this," I said, pointing to the tarp.

She didn't say anything, but she didn't object, either.

"For a good judge," called out fat Elmo, "you have poor taste in women."

There was nothing I could do but keep busy while they laughed.


They still talk about that first afternoon, the one that was the beginning of the end.

First, Elmo John Deere hitched onto an IH 1200 and drug it over the line in about three seconds. No contest, and no one was surprised. Then Simon Red Bulldozer cranked up; his starter engine sounded like a beehive in a rainstorm. He hooked the chain on his towbar and revved up. The guy he was pulling against was a Paluxy River man named Theodore Bush Hog. He didn't hook up right. The chain came off as soon as Simon let go his clutches. So Bush Hog was disqualified. That was bad, too; there were some darkhorse bets on him.

Then it was the turn of Mary Margaret Road-Grader and Elmo John Deere. Elmo had said at first he wasn't going to enter against her. Then they told him how much money was bet on him, and he couldn't afford to pass it up. Though the excuse he used was that somebody had to show this woman her place, and it might as well be him, first thing off.

You had to be there to see it. Mary Margaret whipped that roadgrader around like it was a Toyota, and backed it onto the field. She climbed down with motor running and hooked up. She was wearing tight blue coveralls and her hair was blowing in the river breeze. I thought she was the most beautiful woman I had ever seen. I didn't want her to get her heart broken.

But there was nothing I could do. It was all on her, now.

Elmo John Deere had one of his sons come out and hand the chain to him. He was showing he didn't want to be first to touch anything this woman had held.

He hooked up, and Mary Margaret Road-Grader signaled she was ready.

The judge dropped the pitchfork and they leaned on their gas feeds.

There was a jerk and a sharp clang, and the chain looked like a straight steel rod. Elmo gunned for all he had and the big tractor wheels began to turn slowly, and then they spun and caught and Elmo's Case tractor eased a few feet forward.

Mary Margaret never looked back (Elmo half turned in his seat; he was so good working the pedals and gears, he didn't need to look at them) and then she upshifted. The transmission on the yellow roadgrader screamed and lowered in tone.

I could hardly hear the machines for the yells and screams around me. They sounded like war yells. Some of the men were yelling in bloodlust at the woman. But I heard others cheering her, too. They seemed to want Elmo to lose.

He did.

Mary Margaret shifted again and her feet worked like pistons on the pedals. And as quickly as it had begun, it was over.

There was a groaning noise, Elmo's wheels began to spin uselessly, and in a second or two his tractor had been drug twenty feet across the line.

Elmo got down from his seat. Instead of congratulating the winner (an old custom) he turned and strode off the field. He signaled one of his sons to retrieve the vehicle.

Mary Margaret was checking the damage to her machine.

Simon Red Bulldozer was next.

They had been pulling for twelve minutes when the contest was called by Winston Mack Truck himself. There was wonder on his face as he walked out to the two contestants. Nobody had ever seen anything like it.

The two had fought each other to a standstill. When they were stopped, Mary Margaret's grader was six or seven inches from its original position, but Simon's bulldozer had moved all over its side of the line. The ground was destroyed forever three feet each side of the line. It had been that close.

For the first time, there had been a tie.

Winston Mack Truck stopped before them. We were all whistling our approval when Simon Red Bulldozer held up his hand.

"Hear me, brothers. I will accept no share in honors. They must be all mine, or none at all."

Winston looked with his puckered face at Mary Margaret. She was breathing hard from working the levers, the wheel, the pedals.

She shrugged. "Fine with me."

Maybe I was the only one who knew she was acting tough for the crowd. I looked at her, but couldn't catch her eye.

"Listen, Fossil Creek People," said old Mack Truck. "This has been a draw. But Simon Red Bulldozer is not satisfied. And Mary Margaret Road-Grader has accepted. Tomorrow as the sun crosses the tops of the eastern trees, we will begin again. I have declared a fifth night and a sixth day to the Dance and Pulls."

Shouts of joy broke from the crowd. This had happened only once in my life, for some religious reason or other, and that was when I was a child.

The Dance and Pulls were the only meeting of the year when all the Fossil Creek People came together. It was to have ended this night.

Now, we would have another day.

The cattle must have sensed this. You could hear them bellowing in fear even before the first of the butchers crossed the camp toward them, axe in hand.

"Where are you going?" asked Freddy as I picked up my carbine, boots, and blanket.

"I think I will sleep with Mary Margaret Road-Grader," I said.

"Watch out," said Freddy. "I bet she makes love like she drives that machine."

First we had to talk.

She was ready to cry she was so tired. We were under the roadgrader; the tarp had been refolded over it. There was four feet of crawlspace between the trailer and the ground.

"You drive well. How did you learn?"

"From my brother, Donald Fork Lift. He once used one of these. And when I found this one . . ."

"Where? A museum? A tunnel? Or some . . ."

"An old museum, a strange one. It must have been sealed off before the Highway wars. I found it there a year ago."

"Why didn't your brother pull with this machine, here, instead of you?"

She was very quiet, and then she looked at me. "You are a man of your word? That must be true, or you would not have been called to judge, as I heard."

"That is true."

She sighed, flung her hair from her head with one hand. "He would have," she said, "except he broke his hip last month on a raid at Sand

Creek. He was going to come. But since he had already taught me how to work it, I drove it instead."

"And first thing off you defeat Alan Backhoe Shovel?"

She looked at me and frowned.

"I . . . I . . ."

"You made it up, didn't you?"

"Yes." She bit her lip.

"As I thought. But I have given my word. Only you and I will know. Where did you get the serial plates?"

"One of the machines in the same place where I found my grader. Only it was in worse shape. But its plate was still shiny. I took it the night before I left with the truck. I didn't think anybody would know what Alan Backhoe Shovel's real plate was."

"You are smart," I said. "You are also very brave, for a woman, and foolish. You might have been killed. You may still be."

"Not if I win," she said, her eyes hard. "They couldn't afford to. If I lose, it would be another matter. I am sure I will be killed before I get to the Trinity. But I don't intend to lose."

They probably would like to kill her, some of them.

"No," I said. "I will escort you as near your people as I can. I have hunted the Trinity, but never as far as the Red. I can go with you past the old Fork of the Trinity."

She looked at me. "You're trying to get into my pants."

"Well, yes."

"Let's smoke first," she said. She opened a leather bag, rolled a parchment cigarette, lit it. I smelled the aroma of something I hadn't smoked in six moons.

It was the best dope I'd ever had, and that was saying something.

I don't know what we did afterwards, but it felt good.

❈

"To the finish," said Winston Mack Truck and threw the pitchfork into the ground.

It was better than the day before—the bulldozer like a squat red monster and the roadgrader like avenging yellow death. On the first yank, Simon pulled the grader back three feet. The crowd went wild. His treads clawed at the dirt then, and the roadgrader lurched and regained three feet. Back and forth, the great clouds of black smoke whistling from the exhausts like the bellowing of bulls.

Then I saw what Simon was going to do. He wanted to wear the roadgrader down, keep a strain on it, keep gaining, lock himself, downshift. He would dog his way into the championship.

Yesterday he tried to finish the grader on might. It had not worked. Today he was taking his time.

He could afford to. The roadgrader was light in front; it had hardrubber tires instead of treads. When it lurched, the front end sometimes left the ground. If Simon timed it right, the grader wheels would rise while he downshifted and he could pull the yellow machine another few inches. And could continue to do so.

Mary Margaret was alternately working the pedals and levers, trying to get an angle on the squat red dozer. She was trying to pull across the back end of the tractor, not against it.

That would lose her the contest, I knew. She was vulnerable. When the wheels were up, Simon could inch her back. The only time he lost ground was when he downshifted while the claws dug their way into the ground. Then he lost purchase for a second. Mary Margaret could maybe use that, if she were in a better position.

They pulled, they strained, but slowly Mary Margaret Road-Grader was losing to Simon Red Bulldozer.

Then she did something unexpected. She lurched the roadgrader and dropped the blade.

The crowd went gonzo, then was silent. The shiny blade, which had been up yesterday, and so far today, dug into the ground.

The lurch gained her an inch or two. Simon, who never looked back either, knew something was wrong. He turned, and when his eyes left the panel, Mary Margaret jerked his bulldozer back another two feet.

We never thought in all those years we had heard about Simon Red Bulldozer that he would not have kept his blade in working order. He reached out to his blade lever and pulled it, and nothing happened. We saw him panic then, and the contest was going to Mary Margaret when . . .

The black plastic of the steering wheel showered up in her face. I heard the shot at the same time and dropped to the ground. I saw Mary Margaret holding her eyes with both hands.

Simon Red Bulldozer must not have heard the shot above the roaring of his engine, because he lurched the bulldozer ahead and started pulling the roadgrader back over the line.

It was Elmo John Deere doing the shooting. I had my carbine off my shoulder and was firing by the time I knew where to shoot.

Elmo was trying to kill Mary Margaret, he was still aiming and firing over my head from the hill above the pit. He must have been drunk. He had gone beyond the taboos of the People now. He was trying to kill an opponent who had bested him in a fair fight.

I shot him in the leg, just above the knee, and ended his pulling days forever. I aimed at his head, but he dropped his rifle and screamed so I didn't shoot him again. If I had, I would have killed him.

It took all the Fossil Creek People to keep his sons from killing me. There was a judgement, of course, and I was let go free.

That was the last Sun Dance they had. The Fossil Creek People separated. Elmo's people split off from them, and then went bitter crazy. The Fossil Creek People even steal from them, now, when they have anything worth stealing.

The Pulls ended, too. People said if they were going to cause so much blood, they could do without them. It was bad business. Some people stopped stealing machines and cars and plates, and started bartering for food and trading horses.

I wasn't going to get killed for anything that wouldn't go 150 kilometers per hour.

The old ways are dying. I have seen them come to an end in my time, and everything is getting worthless. People are getting lazy. There isn't anything worth doing. I sit on this hill over the Red River and smoke with Fred-in-the-Hollow and sometimes we get drunk.

Mary Margaret sometimes gets drunk with us.

She lost one of her eyes that day at the pulls. It was hit by splinters from the steering wheel. Me and Freddy took her back to her people in her truck. That was six years ago. Once, years ago, I went past the place where we held the last Sun Dance. Her roadgrader was already a rustpile of junk with everything stripped off it.

I still love Mary Margaret Road-Grader, yes. She started things. Women have come into other ceremonies now, and in the Councils.

I still love Mary Margaret, but it's not the same love I had for her that day at the last Sun Dance, watching her work the pedals and the levers, her hair flying, her feet moving like birds across the cab.

I love her. She has grown a little fat. She loves me, though.

We have each other, we have the village, we have cattle, we have this hill over the river where we smoke and get drunk.

But the rest of the world has changed.

All this, all the old ways . . . gone.

The world has turned bitter and sour in my mouth. It is no good, the taste of ashes is in the wind. The old times are gone.

# Save a Place in the Lifeboat for Me

The hill was high and cold when they appeared there, and the first thing they did was to look around.

It had snowed the night before, and the ground was covered about a foot deep.

Arthur looked at Leonard and Leonard looked at Arthur.

"Whatsa matter you? You wearin' funny clothes again!" said Leonard.

Arthur listened, his mouth open. He reached down to the bulbhorn tucked in his belt.

*Honk Honk* went Arthur.

"Whatsa matter us?" asked Leonard. "Look ata us! We back inna vaudeville?"

Leonard was dressed in pants two sizes too small, and a jacket which didn't match. He wore a tiny pointed felt hat which stood on his head like a roof on a silo.

Arthur was dressed in a huge coat which dragged the ground, balloon pants, big shoes, and above his moppy red hair was a silk tophat, its crown broken out.

"It's a fine-a mess he's gots us in disa time!"

Arthur nodded agreement.

"Quackenbush, he's-a gonna hear about this!" said Leonard.

*Honk Honk* went Arthur.

The truck backed into the parking lot and ran into the car parked just inside the entrance. The glass panels which were being carried on the truck fell and shattered into thousands of slivers in the snowy street. Cars slushing down the early morning road swerved to avoid the pieces.

"Ohh, Bud, Bud!" said the short baby-faced man behind the wheel. He was trying to back the truck over the glass and get it out of the way of the dodging cars.

A tall thin man with a rat's mustache ran from the glass company office and yelled at the driver.

"Look what you've done. Now you'll make me lose this job, too! Mr. Crabapple will . . ." He paused, looked at the little fat man, swallowed a few times.

"Uh . . . hello, Lou," he said, a tear running into his eye and brimming down his face. He turned away, pulled a handkerchief from his coveralls and wiped his eyes.

"Hello, Bud," said the little man, brightly. "I don' . . . don' . . . understand it either, Bud. But the man said we got something to do, and I came here to get you." He looked around him at the littered glass. "Bud, I been a *baaad* boy!"

"It doesn't matter, Lou," said Bud, climbing around to the passenger side of the truck. "Let's get going before somebody gets us arrested."

"Oh, Bud?" asked Lou, as they drove through the town. "Did you ever get out of your contract?"

"Yeah, Lou. Watch where you're going! Do I have to drive myself?"

They pulled out of Peoria at eight in the morning.

The two men beside the road were dressed in black suits and derby hats. They stood; one fat, the other thin. The rotund one put on a most pleasant face and smiled at the passing traffic. He lifted his thumb politely, as would a gentleman, and held it as each vehicle roared past.

When a car whizzed by, he politely tipped his hat.

The thin man looked distraught. He tried at first to strike the same pose as the larger man, but soon became flustered. He couldn't hold his thumb right, or let his arm droop too far.

"No, no, no, Stanley," said the larger, mustached man, as if he were talking to a child. "Let me show you the way a man of gentle breeding asks for a ride. Politely. Gently. Thus."

He struck the same pose he had before.

A car bore down on them doing eighty miles an hour. There was no chance in the world it would stop.

Stanley tried to strike the same pose. He checked himself against the larger man's attitude. He found himself lacking. He rubbed his ears and looked as if he would cry.

The car roared past, whipping their hats off.

They bent to pick them up and bumped heads. They straightened, each signaling that the other should go ahead. They simultaneously bent and bumped heads again.

The large man stood stock still and did a slow burn. Stanley looked flustered. Their eyes were off each other. Then they both leaped for the hats and bumped heads once more.

They grabbed up the hats and jumped to their feet.

They had the wrong hats on. Stanley's derby made the larger man look like a tulip bulb. The large derby covered Stanley down to his chin. He looked like a thumbtack.

The large man grabbed the hat away and threw Stanley's derby to the ground.

"MMMMMM-MMMMMM-MMMMM!" said the large man.

Stanley retrieved his hat. "But Ollie . . ." he said, then began whimpering. His hat was broken.

Suddenly Stanley pulled Ollie's hat off and stomped it. Ollie did another slow burn, then turned and ripped off Stanley's tie.

Stanley kicked Ollie in the shin. The large man jumped around and punched Stanley in the kneecap.

A car stopped, and the driver jumped out to see what the trouble was. Ollie kicked *him* in the shin. *He* ripped off Stanley's coat.

A woman pulled over and slammed into the man's parked car. He ran over and kicked out her headlight. Stanley threw a rock through *his* windshield.

Twenty minutes later, Stanley and Ollie were looking down from a hill. A thousand people were milling around on the turnpike below, tearing each other's cars to pieces. Parts of trucks and motorcycles littered the roadway. The two watched a policeman pull up. He jumped out and yelled through a bullhorn to the people, too far away for the two men to hear what he said.

As one, the crowd jumped him, and pieces of police car began to bounce off the blacktop.

Ollie dusted off his clothing as meticulously as possible. His and Stanley's clothes consisted of torn underwear and crushed derby hats.

"That's another fine mess you've gotten us in, Stanley," he said. He looked north.

"And it looks like it shall soon snow. Mmmm-mmmm-mmmm!"

They went over the hill as the wail of sirens began to fill the air.

Hello, a-Central, givva me Heaven. ETcumspiri 220."

The switchboard hummed and crackled. Sparks leaped off the receiver of the public phone booth in the roadside park. Arthur did a back flip and jumped behind a trash can.

The sun was out, though snow was still on the ground. It was a cold February day, and they were the only people in the park.

The noise died down at the other end and Leonard said:

"Hallo, Boss! Hey, Boss! We doin'-a like you tell us, but you no send us to the right place. You no send us to Iowa. You send us to Idaho, where they grow the patooties."

Arthur came up beside his brother and listened. He honked his horn.

On the other end of the line, Rufus T. Quackenbush spoke:

"Is that a goose with you, or do you have a cold?"

"Oh, no, Boss. You funnin'-a me. That's-a Bagatelle."

"Then who are you?" asked Quackenbush.

"Oh, you know who this is. I gives you three guesses."

"Three guesses, huh? Hmmmm, let's see . . . you're not Babe Ruth, are you?"

"Hah, Boss. Babe Ruth, that's-a chocolate bar."

"Hmmm. You're not Demosthenes, are you?"

"Nah, Boss. Demosthenes can do is bend in the middle of your leg."

"I should have known," said Quackenbush. "This is Rampolini, isn't it?"

"You got it, Boss."

Arthur whistled and clapped his hands in the background.

"Is that a hamster with you, Rampolini?"

"Do-a hamsters whistle, Boss?"

"Only when brought to a boil," said Quackenbush.

"Ahh, you too good-a for me, Boss!"

"I know. And if I weren't too good for you, I wouldn't be good enough for anybody. Which is more than I can say for you."

"Did-a we wake you up, Boss?"

"No, to be perfectly honest, I had to get up to answer the phone anyway. What do you want?"

"Like I said, Boss Man, you put us inna wrong place. We no inna Iowa. We inna Idaho."

"That's out of the Bronx, isn't it? What should I do about it?"

"Well-a, we don't know. Even if-a we did, we know we can't-a do it anyway, because we ain't there. An if-a we was, we couldn't get it done no ways."

"How do you know that?"

"Did-a you ever see one of our pictures, Boss?"

There was a pause. "I see what you mean," said Quackenbush.

"Why for you send-a us, anyway? We was-a sleep, an then we inna Idaho!"

"I looked at my calendar this morning. One of the dates was circled. And it didn't have pits, either. Anyway, I just remembered that something very important shouldn't take place today."

"What's-a that got to do with us two?"

"Well . . . I know it's a little late, but I really would appreciate it if you two could manage to stop it."

"What's-a gonna happen if we don't?"

"Uh, ha ha. Oh, small thing, really. The Universe'll come to an end several million years too soon. A nice boy like you wouldn't want that, would you? Of course not!"

"What for I care the Universe'll come to an end? We-a work for Paramount."

"No, no. Not the studio. The big one!"

"M-a GM?"

"No. The Universe. All that stuff out there. Look around you."

"You mean-a Idaho?"

"No, no, Rampolini. Everything will end soon, too soon. You may not be concerned. A couple of million years is nothing to somebody like you. But what about me? I'm leasing this office, you know?"

"Why-a us?"

"I should have sent someone earlier, but I've . . . I've been so terrible busy. I was having a pedicure, you see, and the time just *flew* by."

"What-a do the two of us do to-a stop this?"

"Oh, I just know you'll think of something. And you'll both be happy to know I'm sending you lots of help."

"Is this help any good, Boss?"

"I don't know if they're any good," said Quackenbush. "But they're cheap."

"What-a we do inna meantime?"

"Be mean, like everybody else."

"Nah, nah. (That's-a really good one, Boss.) I mean, about-a the thing?"

"Well, I'd suggest you get to Iowa. Then give me another call."

"But what iffa you no there?"

"Well, my secretary will take the message."

"Ah, Boss, if-a you no there, your secretary's-a no gonna be there neither."

"Hmmm. I guess you're right. Well, why don't you give me the message now, and I'll give it to my secretary. Then I'll give her the answer, and she can call you when you get to Iowa!"

"Hey, that's-a good idea, Boss!"

"I thought you'd think so."

Outside the phone booth, Arthur was lolling his tongue out and banging his head with the side of his hand, trying to keep up with the conversation.

There were two lumps of snow beside the highway. The snow shook itself, and Stan and Ollie stepped out of it.

"Brr," said Ollie. "Stanley, we must get to some shelter soon."

"But I don't know where any is, Ollie!"

"This is all your fault, Stanley. It's up to you to find us some clothing and a cheery fireside."

"But, Ollie, I didn't have any idea we'd end up like this."

Ollie shivered. "I suppose you're right, Stanley. It's not your fault we're here."

"I don't even remember what we were doing before we were on that road this morning, Ollie. Where have you been lately?"

"Oh . . . don't you remember, Stanley?"

"Not very well, Ollie."

"Oh," said Ollie. He looked very tired, very suddenly. "It's very strange, but neither do I, Stanley."

The cold was forgotten then, and they were fully clothed in their black suits and derbys. They thought nothing of it, because they were thinking of something else.

"I suppose now we shall really have to hurry and find a ride, Stanley."

"I know," said the thin man. "We have to go to Iowa."

"Yes," said Ollie, "and our wives will be none the wiser."

The Iowa they headed for was pulling itself from under a snowstorm which had dumped eleven inches in the last two days. It was bitterly cold there. Crew-cut boys shoveled snow off walks and new '59 cars so their fathers could get to work. It was almost impossible. Snowplows had been out all night, and many of them were stalled. The National Guard had been called out in some sections and was feeding livestock and rescuing stranded motorists. It was not a day for travel.

At noon, the small town of Cedar Oaks was barely functioning. The gleaming sun brought no heat. But the town stirred inside, underneath the snows which sagged the roofs.

The *All-Star Caravan* was in town that day. The teenagers had prayed and hoped that the weather would break during the two days of ice. The *Caravan* was a rock 'n' roll show that traveled around the country, doing one-night stands.

The show had been advertised for a month: All the businesses around the two high schools and junior highs were covered with the blazing orange posters. They had been since New Year's Day.

So the kids waited, and built up hopes for it, and almost had them dashed as they weather had closed in.

But Mary Ann Pickett's mother, who worked the night desk at the Holiday Inn, had called her daughter at eleven the night before: The *All-Star Caravan* had landed at the airport in the clearing night, and all the singers had checked in.

Mary Ann asked her mother, "What does Donny Bottoms look like?"

Her mother didn't know. They were all different-looking, and she wasn't familiar with the singer anyway.

Five minutes after Mary Ann rang off, the word was spreading over Cedar Oaks. The *All-Star Caravan* was there. Now it could snow forever. Maybe if it did, they would have to stay there, rather than start their USO tour of Alaska.

Bud and Lou slid and slipped their way over the snows in the truck.

"Watch where you're going!" said Bud. "Do you have anything to eat?"

"I got some cheese crackers and some Life Savers, Bud. But we'll have to divide them, because . . ." His voice took on a little-boy petulance ". . . because I haven't had anything to eat in a long time, Bud."

"Okay, okay. We'll share. Give me half the cheese crackers. You take these."

Lou was trying to drive. There was a munching sound.

"Some friend you are," said Bud. "You have two cheese crackers and I don't have any."

Lou coughed. "But, Bud! I just *gave* you two cheese crackers!"

"Do I look like I have any cheese crackers?" asked Bud, wiping crumbs from his chin.

"Okay," said Lou. "Have this cheese cracker, Bud. Because you're my friend, and I want to share."

Again, the sound of eating filled the cab.

"Look, Lou. I don't mind you having all the Life Savers, but can't you give me half your cheese cracker?"

Lou puffed out his cheeks while watching the road. "But, Bud! I just gave you *three* cheese crackers!"

"Some friend," said Bud, looking at the snowbound landscape. "He has a cheese cracker and won't share it with his only friend."

"Okay! Okay!" said Lou. "Take half this cheese cracker! Take it!"

He drove on.

"Boy . . . ," said Bud.

Lou took the whole roll of Life Savers and stuffed them in his mouth, paper and all. He began to choke.

Bud began beating him on the back. The truck swerved across the road, then back on. They continued toward Cedar Oaks, Iowa.

There were giants in the *All-Star Caravan*. Donny Bottoms, from Amarillo, Texas; his backup group, the Mosquitos, most from Amarillo Cooper High School, his old classmates. Then there was Val Ritchie, who'd had one fantastic hit song, which had a beat and created a world all the teenagers wanted to escape to.

The third act, biggest among many more, was a middle-aged man calling himself The Large Charge. His act was strange, even among that set. He performed with a guitar and a telephone. He pretended to be talking to a girl on the other end of the line. It was billed as a comedy act. Everybody knew what was really involved—The Large Charge was rock 'n' roll's first dirty old man. His real name was Elmo Simpson and he came from Bridge City, Texas.

Others on the bill included the Pipettes, three guys and two girls from Stuttgart, Arkansas who up until three months ago had sung only at church socials; Jimmy Wailon, who was having a hard time deciding whether to sing "Blue Suede Shoes" for the hundredth time, or strike out into country music where the real money was. Plus the Champagnes, who'd had a hit song three years before, and Rip Dover, the show's M.C.

The *All-Star Caravan* was the biggest thing that had happened to Cedar Oaks since Bill Haley and the Comets came through a year and a half ago, and one of Haley's road men had been arrested for DWI.

"What's-a matter us?" asked Leonard for the fiftieth time that morning. "We really no talka like dis! We was-a grown up mens, with jobs and-a everything."

*Whonka whonka* went Arthur sadly, as they walked through the town of Friedersville, Idaho.

Arthur stopped dead, then put his hands in his pockets and began whistling. There was a police car at the corner. It turned onto the road where they walked. And slowed.

Leonard nonchalantly tipped his pointy felt hat forward and put his hands in his pockets.

The cop car stopped.

The two ran into the nearest store. *Hadley's Music Shop.* Arthur ran around behind a set of drums and hid. Leonard sat down at a piano and began to play with one finger, "You've Taught Me a New Kind of Love."

The store manager came from the back room and leaned against the doorjamb, listening.

Arthur saw a harp in the corner, ran to it and began to play. He joined in the song with Leonard.

The two cops came in and watched them play. Leonard was playing with his foot and nose. Arthur was plucking the harp strings with his teeth.

The police shrugged and left.

"Boy, I'm-a tellin' you," said Leonard, as he waited for the cops to turn the corner. "Quackenbush, he's-a messed up dis-a time! Why we gots to do this?" With one hand he was wiping his face, and with the other he was playing as he never had before.

Donny Bottoms was a scrawny-looking kid from West Texas. He didn't stand out in a crowd, unless you knew where to look. He had a long neck and an Adam's apple that stuck out of his collar. He was twenty-four years old and still had acne. But he was one of the hottest new singers around, and the *All-Star Caravan* was going to be his last road tour for a while. He'd just married his high school sweetheart, a girl named Dottie, and he had not really wanted to come on the tour without her. But she was finishing nurse's training and could not leave. At two in the afternoon, he and the other members of the *Caravan* were trying the sound in the Municipal Auditorium.

He and the Mosquitos ran through a couple of their numbers. Bottoms' style was unique, even in a field as wild and novelty-eating as rock 'n' roll. It had a good boogie beat, but Bottoms worked hard with the music, and the Mosquitoes were really good. They turned out a good synthesis of primitive and sophisticated styles.

The main thing they had for them was Donny's voice. It was high and nasal when he talked, but, singing, that all went away. He had good range, and he did strange things with his throat.

A critic once said that he dry-humped every syllable till it begged for mercy.

Val Ritchie had one thing he did well, exactly one: that was a song called "Los Niños." He'd taken an old Mexican folk song, got a drummer to beat hell out of a conga, and yelled the words over his own screaming guitar.

It was all he did well. He did some other people's standards, and some Everly Brothers' stuff by himself, but he always finished his set with "Los

Niños" and it always brought the house down and had them dancing in the aisles.

He was the next-to-last act before Bottoms and the Mosquitos.

He was a tough act to follow.

But he was always on right before The Large Charge, and *he* was the toughest act in rock 'n' roll.

They had turned the auditorium upside down and had finally found a church key to open a beer for The Large Charge.

Elmo Simpson was dressed, at the sound rehearsal, in a pair of baggy pants, a checked cowboy shirt, and a string tie with a Texas-shaped tieclasp. Tonight, on stage, he would be wearing the same thing.

Elmo's sound rehearsal consisted of chinging away a few chords, doing the first two bars of "Jailhouse Rock" and then going into his dirty-old-man voice.

His song was called "Hello, Baby!" and he used a prop telephone. He ran through the first two verses, which were him talking in a cultured, decadent nasty voice, and he had the sound man rolling in his control chair before he finished.

Elmo sweated like a hog. He'd been doing this act for two years, he'd even had to lip-synch it on Dick Clark's "American Bandstand" a couple of times. He was still nervous, though he could do the routine in his sleep. He was always nervous. He was in his late thirties. Fame had come late to him, and he couldn't believe it. So he was still nervous.

Bud and Lou were hurrying west in the panel truck, through snowslides, slush and stalled cars.

Stan and Ollie had hitched a ride on a Mayflower moving van, against all that company's policies, and were speeding toward Cedar Oaks from the south-southeast.

Leonard and Arthur, alias Rampolini and Bagatelle, were leaving an Idaho airport in a converted crop duster which hadn't been flown since the end of the Korean War. It happened like this:

"We gots to find us a pilot-a to fly us where the Boss wants us," said Leonard, as they ran onto a small municipal field.

*Whonk?* asked Arthur.

"We's gots to find us a pilot, pilot."

Arthur pulled a saber from the fold of his coat, and putting a black poker chip over his eye, began swordfighting his shadow.

"Notta pirate. Pilot! A man whatsa flies in the aeroplanes," said Leonard.

A man in coveralls, wearing a WWII surplus aviator's cloth helmet, walked from the operations room.

"There's-a one now!" said Leonard. "What's about we gets him?"

Without a honk, Arthur ran and tackled the flyer.

"What the hell's the matter with him?" asked the man as Arthur grinned and smiled and pointed.

"You gots to-a excuse him," said Leonard, pulling his tophatted brother off him. "He's-a taken too many vitsamins."

"Well, keep him away from me!" said the flyer.

"We's a gots you a prepositions," said Leonard, conspiratorially.

"What?"

"A prepositions. You fly-a us to Iowa, anda we no break-a you arms."

"What's going on? Is this some kind of gag?"

"No, it's-a my brother. He's a very dangerous man. Show him how dangerous you are, Bagatelle."

Arthur popped his eyes out, squinted his face up into a million rolls of flesh, flared his nostrils and snorted at each breath.

"Keep him away from me!" said the man. "You oughtn't to let him out on the streets."

"He's-a no listen to me, Bagatelle. Get tough with him."

Arthur hunched his shoulders, intensified his breathing, stepped up into the pilot's face.

"No, that's-a no tough enough. Get really tough with him."

Arthur squnched over, stood on tiptoe, flared his nostrils until they filled all his face except for the eyes, panted, and passed out for lack of breath.

The pilot ran across the field and into a hangar.

"Hey, wake-a up!" said Leonard. "He's-a getting the plane ready. Let's-a go."

When they got there, the pilot was warming the crop duster up for a preflight check.

Arthur climbed in the aft cockpit, grabbed the stick, started jumping up and down.

"Hey! Get outta there!" yelled the pilot. "I'm gonna call the cops!"

"Hey, Bagatelle. Get-a tough with him again!"

Leonard was climbing into the forward cockpit. Arthur started to get up. His knees hit the controls. The plane lurched.

Leonard fell into the cockpit head first, his feet sticking out.

Arthur sat back down and laughed. He pulled the throttle.

The pilot just had time to open the hangar door before the plane roared out, plowed through a snowbank, ricocheted back onto the field and took off.

It was heading east toward Iowa.

At three in the afternoon, the rehearsals over, most of the entertainers were back in their rooms at the Holiday Inn. Already the hotel detective had had to chase out several dozen girls and boys who had been roaming up and down the halls looking for members of the *All-Star Caravan*.

Some of them found Jimmy Wailon in the corridor and were getting his autograph. He had been on the way down the hall, going to meet one of the lady reservation clerks.

"Two of yours is worth one Large Charge," said one of the girls as he signed her scrapbook.

"What's that?" he asked, his eyes twinkling. He pushed his cowlick out of his eyes.

"Two of your autographs are worth one of Donny's," she said.

"Oh," he said. "That's nice." He scribbled his usual "With Best Wishes to My Friend . . . ," then asked, "What's the name, honey?"

"Sarah Sue," she said. "And please put the date."

"Sure will, baby. How old are you?"

"I'm eighteen!" she said. All her friends giggled.

"Sure," he said. "There go!"

He hurried off to the room the lady reservation clerk had gotten for them.

"Did you hear that?" the girl asked behind him as he disappeared around the corner. "He called me 'honey.'"

Jimmy Wailon was smiling long before he got to Room 112.


Elmo was sitting in Donny's room with three of the Mosquitoes. Donny had gone to a phone booth to call his wife collect rather than put up with the noise in the room.

"Have another beer, Elmo?" asked Skeeter, the head Mosquito.

"Naw, thanks, Skeeter," he said. "I won't be worth a diddly-shit if I do." Already, Elmo was sweating profusely at the thought of another performance.

"I'll sure be glad when we get on that tour," he continued, after a pause. "Though it'll be colder than a monkey's ass."

"Yeh," said Skeeter. They were watching television, "The Millionaire," the daytime reruns, and John Beresford Tipton was telling Mike what to do with the money with his usual corncob-up-the-butt humor. Skeeter was highly interested in the show. He'd had arguments with people many times about whether the show was real or not, or based on some real person. He was sure somewhere there was a John Beresford Tipton, and a Silverstone, and that one of those checks had his name on it.

"Look at that, will you?" asked Skeeter a few minutes later. "He's giving it to a guy whose kid is dying."

But Elmo Simpson, The Large Charge, from Bridge City, Texas, was lying on his back, fast asleep. Snores began to form inside his mouth, and every few minutes, one would escape.

Donny talked to his wife over the phone out in the motel lobby. They told each other how much they missed each other, and Donny asked about the new record of his coming out this week, and Dottie said she wished he'd come home soon rather than going on the tour, and they told each other they loved each other, and he hung up.

Val Ritchie was sitting in a drugstore just down the street, eating a chocolate sundae and wishing he were home. Instead of going to do a show tonight, then fly with one or another load of musicians off to Alaska for two weeks for the USO.

He was wearing some of his old clothes and looked out of place in the booth. He thought most northern people overdressed anyway, even kids going to school. *I mean, like they were all ready for church or Uncle Fred's funeral.*

He hadn't been recognized yet, and wouldn't be. He always looked like a twenty-year-old garage mechanic on a coffee break.

Bud and Lou swerved to avoid a snowdrift. They had turned onto the giant highway a few miles back and had it almost to themselves. Ice glistened everywhere in the late afternoon sun, blindingly. Soon the sun would fall and it would become pitch black outside.

"How much further is it, Bud?" asked Lou. His stomach was growling.

"I don't know. It's around here somewhere. I'm just following what's-his-name's orders."

"Why doesn't he give better orders, Bud?"

"Because he never worked for Universal."

Stan and Ollie did not know what was happening when the doors of the moving van opened and carpets started dropping off the top of the racks. Then the van slammed into another vehicle. They felt it through the sides of the truck.

The driver was already out. He was walking toward a small truck with two men in it.

Stan and Ollie climbed out of the back of the Mayflower truck and saw who the other two were.

The four regarded each other, and the truck driver surveyed the damage to the carpets, which was minor.

They helped him load the truck back up, then Stan and Ollie climbed in the small van with Bud and Lou.

"I wonder what Quackenbush is up to now?" asked Bud, as he scrunched himself up with the others. With Lou and Ollie taking up so much room, he and Stan had to share a space hardly big enough for a lap dog. Somehow, they managed.

"I really don't know," said Ollie. "He seems quite intent on keeping this thing from happening."

"But, why us, Bud?" asked Lou. "We been *goood* boys since . . . well, we been good boys. He could have sent so many others."

"That's quite all right with me," said Stanley. "He didn't seem to want just *anybody* for this."

"I don't know about you two, but Lou and I were sent from Peoria.

That's a long way. What's this guy got against us?"

"Well, there's actually no telling," said Stanley. "Ollie and I have been traveling all day, haven't we, Ollie?"

"Quite right, Stanley."

"But what I don't get," said Bud, working at his pencil-thin mustache, "is that I remember when all this happened the first time."

"So do I," said Stanley.

"But not us two," said Lou, indicating Ollie and himself, and trying to keep the truck on the road.

"Well, that's because you two had . . . had . . . left before them. But that doesn't matter. What matters is that he sent us back here to . . . Come to think of it, I don't understand, either."

"Or me," said Lou.

"Quackenbush moves in mysterious ways," said Bud.

"Right you are," said Stan.

"Mmmm Mmmmm Mmmmm," said Ollie.

By the time they saw they were in the air they also realized the pilot wasn't aboard.

Leonard was still stuck upside down in the forward cockpit. Arthur managed to fly the plane straight while his brother crawled out and sat upright.

Looping and swirling, they flew on through the late afternoon toward Cedar Oaks.

The line started forming in front of the doors of the civic auditorium at five, though it was still bitterly cold.

The manager looked outside at 5:15. It was just dark, and there must be a hundred and fifty kids out there already, tickets in hand. He hadn't been at the sound rehearsal and hadn't seen the performers. All he knew was what he heard about them: they were the hottest rock and roll musicians since Elvis Presley and Chuck Berry.

The show went on at 7 p.m. as advertised, and it was a complete sellout. The crowd was ready, and when Rip Dover introduced the Champagnes, the people yelled and screamed even at their tired *doo-wah* act.

Then came Wailon, and they were polite for him, except that they kept yelling "Rock 'n' roll! Rock 'n' roll!" and he kept singing "Young Love" and the like.

Then other acts, then Val Ritchie, who jogged his way through several standards and launched into "Los Niños." He tore the place apart. They wouldn't let him go, they were dancing in the aisles. He did "Los Niños" until he was hoarse. They dropped the spots on him, finally, and the kids quit screaming. It got quiet. Then there was the sound of a mike being turned on and a voice, greasy in the magnificence, filled the hall:

"Hellooooooooooooo, baby!"

It was long past dark, and the truck swerved down the road, the forms of Stan, Ollie, Bud and Lou illuminated by the dome light. Bud had a map unfolded in front of the windshield and Ollie's arms were in Lou's way.

"It's here somewhere," said Bud. "I know it's here somewhere!"

Overhead was the whining, droning sound of an old aeroplane, sometimes close to the ground, sometimes far above. Every once in a while was a yell of "Watch-a youself! Watcha where you go!" and a *whonk whonk*.

The truck below passed a sign which said:

WELCOME TO CEDAR OAKS
Speed Limit 30 MPH

After The Large Charge hung up the telephone receiver, and they let him offstage to thunderous ovation, the back curtain parted and there were

Donny Bottoms and the Mosquitoes.

And the first song they sang was "Dottie," the song Bottoms had written for his wife while they were still high school sweethearts. Then "Roller Coaster Days" and "Miss America" and all his classics. And the crowd went crazy and . . .

The truck roared into the snowy, jampacked parking lot of the auditorium, skidded sideways, wiped out a '57 cherry-red Merc and punched out the moon window of a T-Bird. The cops on parking lot duty ran toward the wreck.

Halfway there, they jumped under other cars to get away from the noise.

The noise was that of an airplane going to crash very soon, very close.

At the last second, the sound stopped.

The cops looked up.

An old biplane was sitting still in a parking space in the lot, its propeller still spinning. Two guys in funny clothes were climbing down from it, one whistling and *honking* to the other, who was trying to get a pointy hat off his ears.

The doors of the truck which had crashed opened, and four guys tumbled out all over each other.

They ran toward the auditorium, and the two from the plane saw them and whistled and ran toward them. They joined halfway across the lot, the six of them, and ran toward the civic hall.

The police were running for them like a berserk football team and then . . .

The auditorium doors were thrown open by the ushers, lances of light gleamed out on the snow and parked cars, and the mob spilled out onto the concrete and snow, laughing, yelling, pushing, shoving in an effort to get home.

The six running figures melted into the oncoming throng, the police right behind them.

Above the cop whistles and the mob noise was an occasional "Ollie, oh, Ollie!" or "Hey, Bud! Hey, Bud!" or *whonk whonk* and . . .

The six made it into the auditorium as the maintenance men were turning out the lights, and they ran up to the manager's office and inside.

The thin manager was watching TV. He looked up to the six, and thought it must be some sort of a publicity stunt.

On TV came the theme music of "You Bet Your Duck."

"It's-a Quackenbush!" said Leonard.

The TV show host looked up from his rostrum. "Hi, folks. And tonight what's the secret woids?" Here a large merganser puppet flopped down and the audience applauded. The show host turned the word card around and lifted his eyebrows, looked at the screen and said:

"That's right. Tonight, the woids are Inexorable Fate. I knew I should've hired someone else. You guys are too late."

Then he turned to the announcer and asked, "George, who's our first guest?" as the duck was pulled back overhead on its strings.

The six men tore from the office and out to the parking lot, through the last of the mob. Stan, Ollie, Bud and Lou jumped in the truck which a wrecker attendant was just connecting to a winch, right under the nose of the astonished police chief.

Arthur and Leonard, whistling and yelling, jumped in the plane, backed it out, and took off after circling the crowded parking lot. They rose into the air to many a loud scream.

The truck and plane headed for the airport.

❈

The crowd was milling about the airport fence. Inside the barrier, musicians waited to get aboard a DC-3, their instrument cases scattered about the concourse.

The truck with four men in it crashed through the fence, strewing wire and posts to the sides.

It twisted around on its wheels, skidded sideways, almost hitting the musicians, and came to a halt. The four looked like the Keystone Firemen as they climbed out.

There was a roar in the air, and the biplane came out of the runway lights, landed and taxied to a stop less than an inch from the nose of the passenger plane.

"We not-a too late! We not-a too late!" yelled Leonard, as he climbed down. "Arthur, get tough with-a that plane. Don't let it take off!"

Arthur climbed to the front of the crop duster and repeated the facial expressions he'd gone through earlier with the pilot. This time at the frightened pilot of the DC-3, through the windshield.

Leonard, Bud, Lou, Stan and Ollie ran to the musicians and found Wailon.

"Where's Bottoms?" asked Bud.

"Huh?" asked Jimmy Wailon, still a little distraught by the skidding truck and aeroplane. "Bottoms? Bottoms left on the first plane."

"The first plane?" asked Ollie. "The first aeroplane?"

"Uh, yeah. Simpson and Ritchie were already on. Donny wanted to wait for this one, but I gave him my seat. I'm waiting for someone." He looked at them; they had not moved. "I gave him my seat on the first plane," he said. Then he looked them over in the dim lights. "You friends of his?"

"No," said Stanley, "but I'm sure we'll be seeing him again very soon."

Overhead, the plane which had taken off a few minutes before circled and headed northwest for Alaska.

They listened to it fade in the distance.

*Whonk* went Arthur.

They drove back through the dark February night, all six of them jammed into the seat and the small back compartment. After they heard the news for the first time, they turned the radio down and talked about the old days.

"This fellow Quackenbush," asked Ollie. "Is he in the habit of doing things such as this?"

"Ah, the Boss? There's-a no tellin' what the boss man willa do!"

"He must not be a *nice* man," said Lou.

"Oh, he's probably all right," said Bud. "He just has a mind like a producer."

"A contradiction in terms," said Stanley.

"You're *so* right," said Ollie.

"Pardon me," said the hitchhiker for whom they stopped. "Could you fellows find it in your hearts to give me a ride? I feel a bit weary after the affairs of the day, and should like to nestle in the arms of Morpheus for a short while."

"Sure," said Lou. "Hop in."

"Ah yes," said the rotund hitchhiker in the beaver hat. "Been chasing about the interior of this state all day. Some fool errand, yes indeed. Reminds me of the time on safari in Afghanistan . . ." He looked at the six men, leaned forward, tapping a deck of cards with his gloved hands. "Would any of you gentlemen be interested in a little game of chance?"

"No thanks," said Bud. "You wouldn't like the way I play."

They drove through the night. They didn't need to stop for the next hitchhiker, because they knew him. They saw him in the headlights, on the railroad tracks beside the road. He was kicking a broken-down locomotive. He came down the embankment, stood beside the road as they bore down on him.

He was dressed in a straw hat, a vest and a pair of tight pants. He wore the same countenance all the time, a great stone face.

The truck came roaring down on him, and was even with him, and was almost by, when he reached out with one hand and grabbed the back door handle and with the other clamped his straw hat to his head.

His feet flew up off the pavement and for a second he was parallel to the ground, then he pulled himself into the spare tire holder and curled up asleep.

He had never changed expression.

Over the hill went the eight men, some of them talking, some dozing, toward the dawn. Just before the truck went out of sight there was a sound, so high, so thin it did not carry well.

It went *honk honk.*

# Horror, We Got

Even as *shtetls* go, this one wasn't much.

Then again, not very much of anything in this section of Poland in 1881 c.e. is much, either. One side of the Pale is pretty much like the other.

So here I am on this nice day before Passover, and I'm waiting beside the road dressed as a scissors grinder. Behind me are a bunch of thrown-together huts, oddments of housing. Down the street is the synagogue, the town house and such.

In my long coat is a machine pistol of a kind which won't be invented for another twelve years. I like it because there's something classic-looking in its design. It has levers and bars extending out all over it like there's a mechanical spider trapped inside trying to get out.

There are no other people outside here. There's plenty good reason for that.

Up the road a few hundred yards is a column of the 2nd Imperial Cossacks, dressed in their finery. Coming this way. Red and black uniforms, standardbearers carrying the Imperial double-headed eagle banner. They're bundled against the cold, all bristles of mustache and *shakos*. Behind come row on row on row of lances. Across their shoulders are rifles. Horses' breaths steam and seethe in the morning sunlight. They're passing through on their way to restation the garrison at Zmlenye. A nice quiet ride of fifty kilometers or so through *zhid* country. Boring indeed.

Well, up to a point. As the standards go by, I bow pretty much like a *shtetl* Jew is supposed to. As I come up from the bow, I see eyes peering from all the windows and closed shutters across the way. The inhabitants are frightened, but still curious enough to look out as the sound of the dreaded hoofbeats go through their pitiful town.

The colonel of the Cossacks draws even with me. His mustaches are red, his mare is chestnut, his eyes are green. His gaze sweeps over me. He does not acknowledge my presence any more than he does the corner of the building I lean against.

It is his last happy memory.

Everything is in slow motion except me. I move in, pistol in my hand. Shiny and bright. An adjutant turns toward me, words forming on his lips. To the colonel's left, a hand moves toward a sword. His horse is still staring ahead. Across the road, an eye at a knothole widens.

I squeeze the trigger and fire. The colonel rips open like something gigantic had pulled a pop-top attached to his head and chest. His body flops in a windmilling arc onto the horse of the officer next to him. His mare, its back broken, collapses to the frozen street, spilling others to each side. Horses kick and rear.

Already I am through the doorway behind me, through the false wall, down the tunnel, back to the Machine. Rifle fire cascades onto the *shtetl* and everyone in it. Buildings will burn, women and children ridden down, raped, dismembered, shot, pulled apart. Men will be castrated (hear them scream), the synagogue will be pulled down (hear the writings burn), all the crafts and houses destroyed. No one will be left. This town will cease to be a memory.

I pause a few seconds, hear footsteps above me. Sandals, slap-slap-slap, are overtaken by hooves. The hooves trample, trample, and recede. There are no more footsteps. A child screams. A rifle barks.

Halfway across the continent, somebody else is killing the Czar. I smile. Into the Machine, then. Back to Tel Aviv.

We will force up wages which, however, will be of no benefit to the workers, for we will at the same time cause a rise in the prices of necessities, pretending that this is due to the decline of agriculture and of cattle raising. We will also artfully and deeply undermine the sources of production by instilling in the workmen ideas of anarchy.

—Protocol 6, *Protocols of the Learned Elders of Zion*

My name is Abe Sheenie. I am small and hunched over. My age is thirty-four, though I have masqueraded within the past year as both a sixteen-year-old Marrano, and as an Ashkenazi patriarch whose years are too many to be counted. My nose juts halfway down my face. (Everyone in the Action Arm has plastic surgery to produce the desired effects. Only my friend Heimie Schwatz had a nose large enough to pass muster when he was accepted into our elite group.) We take injections to make us smell of garlic and dead places while on assignment. (*Foetor judaicus* is thought to be integral to the race, passed on through the blood.) Even the female agents who seduce Gentile boys and women have exaggerated features, but they don't have to go through the rigors of smelling like hogs (you should pardon the expression). I have pointy ears. A beard that would make a Hassidim positively livid with rage. I sometimes tie it to my belt. I have hands made for wringing and breast-beating. My hair looks like a brush heap a crazy man piled.

Other than these defects, I'm one handsome devil.

I grin at myself in the shiny steel walls of the Machine as it bumps and grinds its way towards 2006 c.e. (their reckoning) and creeps across the face of the earth invisibly to Israel.

Decompression takes forever. The lights flash on and the door opens. Sholmo sticks his head in.

"Hey, Abie," he says. "So how are things?"

"I have such a headache," I say. It's true. I walk out where the medics check me over with all sorts of very personal tests. I gobble some aspirin as soon as they take my pulse.

"So how's Colonel Obromev back in Poland?"

"He's very, very sick," I say.

"Well, the town's gone," says Sholmo. "It's no longer on the rolls for the next year."

"Things going okay?"

"Fine," says Sholmo.

"I need some sleep," I say.

"Sleep you can have," says Sholmo.

"Wait," says the medic. He looks on a chart. "Be back at 1800 tomorrow."

"What for?"

"Plague shots," he says.

"Plague shots," I say.

It is for this reason we must undermine faith, eradicate from the minds of the Gentiles the very principles of God and Soul, and replace these conceptions by mathematical calculations and material desires. When we deprived the masses of their belief in God, ruling authority was thrown into the gutter, where it became public property, and we seized it.

—Protocol 4, *Protocols of the Learned Elders of Zion*

I can't talk to Sholmo very long. It's his turn on the Wandering Jew duty roster.

"Where are you going?" I ask him while he's in makeup, getting a white knotted beard fitted. It makes my 1881 model look positively thin by comparison. And some tremendous white eyebrows.

163

"Brussels, 1661," he says.

"Ought to cause a lot of excitement."

"Yeah. Somebody else is doing the Sabbatei Zevi bit over in Prussia. They ought to be ecstatic when I show up."

Sabbatei Zevi was this poor Levant who had the misfortune to be educated far beyond his abilities. He proclaimed himself Messiah one day in synagogue. All the dispersed Jews got the Zionist hots for about five years, and wanted news, news, news. Our man in Constantinople wasn't doing Zevi, he was one of his followers, spreading the word. Zevi himself would later convert to Islam at the point of a Turkish sword.

"When's your next turn?" asks Sholmo.

"Next month. Haven't seen where or when, yet."

"Maybe you'll be lucky and get South America just after the fall of the Inca, or something. Boy, am I tired of Renaissance Europe!"

"Talk about your method acting . . . ," I say.

"I mean it," says Sholmo. "Trudge into town. Weep and wail. Be filled with *Angst*. Lament the fall of the temple. Take out a rosary and weep. Pray in churches. Talk with *goyim*. Same thing every time."

The Wandering Jew duty roster is separate from the others and takes precedence over most. All the men in the Action Arm have to pull it every two or three months. The time wasn't so bad (you *do* lose the same amount of subjective time as you spend in the past). But the wailing and gnashing get boring real quick. And such dumps you have to live in!

Sholmo stands up.

"Fantastic," I say.

"I look the same as everybody. Only older," he says.

"We'll have a party when you get back."

"Good. My heart goes out to my friends."

"See you in two weeks."

He trudges away, looking like Father Time himself. Already he's limping.

So he gets into character. He's supposed to be the man who struck Jesus, and to whom Jesus said, "I go, but you shall tarry until I return again." So he's wandering the earth all during time. He's named Ahasuerus, or John Butadeus, or Isaac Lacquedem. He should lament Christ, and he should wait until he returns.

Boy, does he have a long wait.

I mean, if they gave medals for the people who make up dumb Gentile myths, the people who thought of that one should get the Legion of Honor, right? Like Dreyfus, you know?

To wear everyone out by dissensions, animosities, feuds, famine, inoculation of diseases, want until the Gentiles see no other way of escape but an appeal to our money and power.
—Protocol 10, *Protocols of the Learned Elders of Zion*

This horse is goddamned heavy, but the town well is just around the next corner. There are six of us, and we're grunting and straining enough to wake the dead.

Of course, we're going to have to make an awful lot of noise to do that.

Over on the next street you can hear the sounds of the groaning wheels of carts. All the shutters and house windows are closed, the doors are bolted, you can hear people crying behind them. Only this isn't some *shtetl* in Poland, this is your main classy neighborhood of Antwerp, and this isn't 1881, this is 1348.

From down the way comes the cry, "Bring out your dead! Bring out your dead!"

We smell bad enough, but this horse is *ripe*. It's been lying in the sun a week. It's about to explode, and if we're not careful, we'll get it all over us. Not a nice thing to do.

So sue us. We learned it from Genghis Khan a hundred years before when he used to catapult them over the walls of cities that didn't surrender to him.

The wailing and cries float over the dim narrow street. Near midnight. Outside the town is the glow of the fires where they're burning the latest of the innumerable dead. Before this plague is over, Europe will lose half its people. Only two good things will come of this: Boccaccio will write the *Decameron*, and the people of Europe won't run out of food in the 1700s.

But that's all in the future and doesn't concern us. Our main problem is to get the horse over the lip of the well.

"Ready?" I ask. "Heave ho! Heave—eeve—eeeve—unngh!!!"

Over it goes. We hear it rupture on the way down, and this miasma of dead equine floats up just before we hear a splash. A window comes open on the third floor above us. We pause a beat (you've got to be an actor more than anything else in the Action Arm) so they can see our woolen caftans and round hats and yellow Juden badges. And then we run, run, run back toward the Jewish streets.

We wait, smoking and talking for a few minutes, outside the room where the Machine is hidden. The Jews on the street are wailing and moaning, too, and their cemetery down the way has been filled a month. Already this community has lost half its people, and the other half live in fear that they will be dead of the plague by morning.

They don't have to worry about the time, anyhow. From toward the main part of town we see lights of hundreds of torches converging in the streets, growing like a swarm of honeybees, spilling from housefront to housefront until all the streets to the south are filled with flickering lights. Their footsteps grow louder, louder. They're in lock-step now, the tread of each in the crowd lost in the din of all the others. They become faceless now, in a sea of faces and heads; they're full of hate. Very poetic. Now they come this way. They begin to chant; the voices in counterpoint to their steps:

"HEP! HEP! HEP! HEP! HEP!"

*(Herusalema Est Perdita. Herusalema Est Perdita . . . )*

The old war cry from the Crusades, when the Knights sacked Antioch and put all the Jews to the torch in their own synagogues.

I forgot to tell you that part of our makeup for this caper is that we have blood running from our ears. The Sons of Simeon, as well as his daughters, are supposed to have menses, but only on four days a year, and then from the ears.

More dumb Gentile myths.

(But who are we to argue with history?)

All the Jews here will be dead soon. Back to the Machine. Back to the future.

Every little bit hurts.

To divert over-restless people from discussing political questions, we shall now bring forward new problems apparently connected with them—problems of industry.

> —Protocol 13, *Protocol of the Learned Elders of Zion*

Dr. Frederick Schwartz had just been liberated from a forced labor camp on the eastern front in 1945 when he discovered his rudimentary theory of time travel. He was put, through some Russian mistake, into an Allied DP camp, where he worked out his calculations. He emigrated to Israel in 1948, just in time to be killed on some *kibbutz* in the first war with the Arabs. His papers weren't found until 1954. These were immediately brought to the attention of the members of the Knesset who would later control the world.

Up until then, there were no supposed twelve Jews who ran the economies and governments of the world. The full manpower of Israel was thrown into the problem of working out Dr. Schwartz's theories and turning them into fact, but it wasn't until 1997 (what with fighting with their neighbors) that it happened. Overnight, there were twelve Elders of

Zion. They now had all history to play with, to control, to do with as they pleased, of which to change the course of.

The first thing the most vocal of the Elders wanted to do was strangle Little Baby Hitler in his crib. Also some early Church fathers. The three most hawkish of the Elders drew up a hit list in a matter of minutes, along with the Scriptural quotes about eyes and teeth.

But the other Nine said No. A period of heated discussion took place, with the Elders sitting as a Committee of the Whole. What was said? What titanic battles of tradition and wit must have gone on there! What resort to Law and to common sense! Ah, but we'll never know. (I've been in the presence of the Elders only once, and the room was dark. All I know is that one of them coughs a lot, even though he has all of medical science at his disposal, to do with as he pleases. It must please him to cough. For all I know, my grandfather may be one of the Elders of Zion.)

Here is the plan, they finally said.

We conquer the world. But we do it *just like* they accuse us of doing all along. Everything, every deed they attribute to us, we do. We don't change history, we implement it. We become the grasping monsters they accuse us of being. We live up to their worst expectations. We dream their nightmares for them.

The Elders are a great bunch of guys, but they can be a little cold-blooded.

So in 1998 c.e. they created the Action Arm in Tel Aviv. I joined in 2000 c.e. (We use Christian time, too.) It is now 2006. Already we rule the world. We're just patching up the history, making it real. When we're through, it will have happened just like they said it would. The great snake of Zion has doubled back on itself and come to rest in Palestine.

These trips back into the past make me introspective and full of *ennui*. None of us talk coming back from Antwerp. Sometimes you talk after a job. Mostly not, though.

We will represent ourselves as saviors of the working class who have come to liberate them from this oppression by suggesting that they join our army of socialists, anarchists, communists to whom we always extend our help under the guise of fraternal principles of universal human solidarity.

—Protocol 3, *Protocols of the Learned Elders of Zion*

Abe Sheenie eats with relish the inner organs of beasts and fowls. Sometimes I don't even use relish. I am not above a big glass of milk and some summer sausage. I have been known to partake of an occasional pig-in-the-blanket.

So we're at the party for Sholmo.

It's a high old time. (You'll excuse the pun. One of the things they accused us of was being pushers of narcotics. Corrupting the youth of Christendom, sending nice *shikses* into lives of prostitution at the end of opium pipes or needles. So we have these warehouses full of things that would make General "Chinese" Gordon weep, and the late Dr. Leary, well, oh my!)

Sholmo's back, and he's got his arm in a sling. But he has this beatific smile on his face. Part of that is the dope, part is because he's so very pleased to still be alive.

"It's getting so you can't trust the history books anymore," he says.

"They were all written by *goyim*. Don't blame us," says someone from the research department.

"Crowd finds out some big Jew's in town. Lots of excitement on the old Jewish street," says Sholmo. "Wandering Jew or not, some alderman or something convinces his drinking buddies over in the nice part of town that it would be a good thing to put all this Messiah agitation down. They were sneaky bastards. Came a few at a time, in the night. Didn't make a lot of noise. Couple of hundred I'd say. I was in the home of this rich jeweler, typical learned man, you know, talking with him and a few of his friends about Jesus and Sabbatei Zevi (may his memory be preserved!) when all of a sudden the door lands on the kitchen table, followed by a lot of wheel lock balls and a pike or two. Everybody else froze while these guys started piling in hollering about Christ-killers. Me, I kicked out the lamp and went backwards through the window. If I'd have been a second later, they'd have shot me, for sure."

He laughs, then we all do. He caught half the pellets from a blunderbuss from someone waiting outside the window. They fired when he came through. He had to shoot his way out and hide for three days before he could make it back to the Machine.

The story we got from the time, from one Abram Goessepson, is that the Wandering Jew appeared in Brussels, and disappeared before the very eyes of many of the ghetto's most respected men after lecturing them on Christianity and his wanderings over the earth. What old Abram forgot to mention was that there was gunplay in the streets of old Brussels, and that ol' sky-pilot Ike Lacquedem had to draw down on the *hombres*.

(We've only lost sixteen good friends in eight years. Two a year, regular as clockwork. You can almost count the days between deaths. A moment of silence for the dead. That's the price you pay to be owners of the world and all its goodies.)

On the hi-fi is Kinky Friedman singing "Ride 'Em, Jewboy."

(Such a nice world to own it is, too.)

Moshe Feeberman and Izzy Gottesman are over in the corner telling about the Big Caper of 2006, with hand gestures like you wouldn't believe. This year's historic mission was the actual drawing up of the *Protocols of the Learned Elders of Zion*, the master plan for the conquest of the world.

(There's a room back at the office we call the Hate Room. It has anti-Semitic writings on microfilm. There are several tons of them. And we wrote less than 10 percent of them.)

"So," Izzy is saying as I come up to him, none too steady, "we go back to where the Czar and Czarista were killed, and we leave a copy of Nilus' book, the *Great in the Small*, in the Czarista's bedroom . . ."

". . . and open the Bible to Revelations . . . ," says Moshe.

". . . and Moshe carves a swastika on the windowsill, like it was to keep out Jewish vampires or something . . . ," says Izzy.

". . . and all this a few minutes before the hunters come out of the woods and find the bodies at the Summer House."

"Then we go back to Paris in the 1890s."

"You should see the place," says Moshe. "I don't see how Proust and all those guys lived there. So, we go to the offices of the Okhrana, the Czar's secret police, and we put this copy of the *Protocols* in with all the other stuff in Colonel Ratchkovsky's OUT box for the clerk to copy the next day . . ."

"Then we go back a few weeks earlier and give everybody in the office a memo about coming up with some hotshot things to get the people down on the Jews and revolutionaries, and . . ."

"Then we make sure a copy of it gets to old Sergei Nilus, sitting in his writer's colony house back in Russia, along with a generous supply of hashish of the kind he's used to, and have everybody around him keep talking about the revolutionaries and the Jews . . ."

"Meanwhile we skip back to Paris about a month before we plant the *Protocols* in Ratchkovsky's office, and put this book Zeke ('Hey, Zeke, great job that, on the aging,' says Moshe. Zeke lifts his drink across to them.) gave us, called *Dialogue in Hell Between* . . . oh, somebody and somebody or other, and we underline the same passages as from the *Protocols*, and put one in with Ratchkovsky's papers, and take one to the British Museum so some reporter can find it in 1920 and prove it all a hoax."

"And here's the killer," says Moshe. "Izzy goes to Munich in 1920 and hands a copy to . . ."

People lean closer. There is a morbid fascination about anything to do with the man.

". . . this sidewalk artist who used to be a corporal in the German Army."

They wait. The question comes from someone.

"What did he look like?"

"Young. Nondescript. Still wearing his Army overcoat. Carrying some brushes and paints and bits of cardboard and a flimsy fold-up easel. Nothing like you'd expect. He still had the Hindenburg-type mustache at the time."

"I saw him last week. In 1945," someone says from the corner. "He didn't look so good."

"When in 1945?" asks someone else.

"April 11," the man says.

"Did you speak to him?" a nice lady asks.

Izzy clears his throat. "Not exactly. I handed him a copy of the *Protocols* and gave him the name of a political club over on the Münsterstrasse."

"So that's where it all started," says a young man sitting on the sofa.

"Not really," says Moshe, and winks. "Izzy gave him the address of a vacant lot."

We will so wear out and exhaust the Gentiles by all this that they will be compelled to offer us an international authority, which by its position will enable us to absorb without disturbance all the governmental forces of the world and thus form a super-government. We must so direct the education of Gentile society that its hands will drop in the weakness of discouragement in the face of any undertaking where initiative is needed.

—Protocol 5

The party's over and we're back at my place overlooking the Technicon. I am lying on the couch, and between my legs the beautiful Sheila Berkowitz is sucking my *schlong*. Her dark hair is swept back from her head, and her heavy-lidded eyes are closed. She is enjoying what she is doing, and oh, so am I.

(There's this myth that us Jewish guys are addicted to it. Atavistic memories. Ever since the *mohel* planted the old ritual kiss on the bloody end of our teeny penises during the *bris*, well . . . you can see how a guy can get hooked on it.)

I moan a little and move my right leg up. Sheila smiles around the bare head of my dong. She licks a little circle. I moan again.

(In a few moments, when I have experienced some more sweet agony at Sheila's talented touch, I am going to jump on her crotch and do a little smiling and nibbling of my own, but till then, well, a little faster, Sheila, a little harder.)

I'm paying attention to what's happening, but my mind is drifting in some pretty strange places. (It's had some pretty strange stimuli during the past few hours.) As I lie here and am consumed by several passions, I think of this business I'm in.

Some of the thoughts are not pretty.

Like, we own the world, and history, and soon maybe the future also. It will come as a great shock to some people.

Even as I lie here, our salvage boats ply the waters of the past like the ships of Tarshish. They dredge up all the sunken galleons, the lost triremes, the misplaced clipper ships and tramp steamers, and empty their holds of gold and silver, ingots, feathers, fur, ores. Then they come back to our ports and times, and are sold at the time and place which brings the best deal. They buy gold and silver and diamonds, the mark, the pound, the yen, the oil and the LPG.

Our agents roam the past. We sow the threads of coincidence and change, we remold and shape the world, we refigure its works and thoughts, not in our image, but in one made and forced on us. One we have now taken and are using, in our own way, at our own pace.

(Oh. Moan. Wiggle.)

We have been cheated and damned and spat upon. Burned in our place of worship, dragged through the streets, scattered, dispersed. We have been gassed and shot and buried in heaps, in mounds, in acres at the time. And sometimes, our people, while they took their places in line, still did not believe the Lord God would let them die this way, crowded, herded, moved like cattle to the slaughter.

So we in the Action Arm implement what has gone before. We heighten it. We make it more real. We can now make it just like those who persecuted us want it to be. You can't ask for more revenge than *that*. We have conquered him with his own worst imaginings. So we do. Sometimes we save, sometimes we condemn our own to the lies and images they have us take.

It is hard being like gods and deciding what needs to be done.

It leads to bad dreams and long nights when there is no sleep to be found in the immensity of all time. But we have doctors to take care of that, and we get lots of vacation, and we're not chosen for our kindness and pity anyway. Steely-eyed sons and daughters of Zion are what we are. Time is a playground before us. We can use nations like jungle gyms and empires for teeter-totters. And once we get the future, too . . .

(Oh.)

The onus of history spreads like thin paint from our actions, covering the world like Sherwin-Williams.

(Moan.)

The bad thoughts take me. Like:

When the ghetto Jews called on us in the Middle Ages, when they prayed for help, for any kind of relief from the inhuman misery they suffered, they asked for saviors. For superhuman deliverance for anything.

What they got was us. *We* are the golems of deliverance.

(Sheila changes her position and goes back to her delicious work.)

When we helped them come for the Jews in the trucks, we supplied the lists, we helped the rabbis draw up the names, we handed the names over to them. When the gas was turned on, we supplied the engineering. When the ovens were lit, our planning turned the laden cartwheels. The smoke coming up from the compounds went to heaven with our prayers, but also with our aid.

(Ooh.)

There is something I think of that makes me ask what I am doing working for such a bunch of vengeful old men. It is a last thing to wonder over.

Hitler worked for *us*. He had the right idea. *We* are the final solution.

My head should grow in the ground like a turnip that I think such thoughts.

(Faster, Sheila. Harder.)


We have taken care long ago to discredit the Gentile clergy.
    —Protocol 17

Paris, 1763:

Get out the hot tongs and the meat grinder, Heimie! It's Passover! We got two consecrated wafers and there's this new fat *goy* kid on the block.

Sheila's working up a batch of matzoh, and I'm getting out the chains. Ritual murder is hard work.

Next year, it's Jerusalem all over.

# Man-Mountain Gentian

Just after the beginning of the present century it was realized that some of the wrestlers were throwing their opponents from the ring without touching them.

—Ichinaga Naya, *Zen-Sumo:*
*Sport and Ritual* All-Japan
Zen-Sumo Association Books,
Kyoto, 2014.

It was the fourteenth day of the January Tokyo tournament. Sitting with the other wrestlers, Man-Mountain Gentian watched as the next match began.

Ground Sloth Ikimoto was taking on Killer Kudzu. They entered the tamped-earth ring and began their *shikiris*. Ground Sloth, a *sumotori* of the old school, had changed over from traditional to *zen-sumo* four years before. He weighed 180 kilos in his *mawashi*. He entered at the white tassel salt corner. He clapped his huge hands, rinsed his mouth, threw salt, rubbed his body with tissue paper, then began his high leg lifts, stamping his feet, his hands gripping far down his calves. The ring shook with each stamp. All the muscles rippled on his big frame. His stomach, a flesh-colored boulder, shook and vibrated.

Killer Kudzu was small, and thin, weighing barely over ninety kilos. On his forehead was the tattoo of his homeland, the PRC, one large star and five smaller stars blazing in a constellation. He also went into his ritual *shikiri*, but as he clapped he held in one hand a small box, ten centimeters on a side, showing his intention to bring it into the match. Sometimes these were objects for meditation, sometimes favors from male or female lovers, sometimes no one knew what. The only rule was that they could not be used as weapons.

The wrestlers were separated from the onlookers by four clear walls and a roof of plastic. Over this hung the traditional canopy and tassels, symbolizing heaven and the four winds. Through the plastic walls ran a mesh of fine wiring, connected to a six-volt battery next to the north-side judge.

A large number of 600x slow motion video cameras were placed around the auditorium to be used by the judges if necessary.

Killer Kudzu placed the box on his side of the line. He returned to his corner and threw more salt.

Ground Sloth Ikimoto stamped once more, twice, went to his line, settled into position like a football lineman, legs apart, knuckles to the ground. His nearly-bare buttocks looked like giant rocks. Killer Kudzu finished his *shikiri*, squatted at his line, where he settled his hand near his votive box, and glared at his opponent.

The referee, in his ceremonial robes, had been standing to one side during the preliminaries. Now he came to a position halfway between the wrestlers, his war fan down. He leaned away from the two men, left leg back to one side as if ready to run. He stared at the midpoint between the two and flipped his fan downward.

Instantly sweat sprang to their foreheads and shoulders, their bodies rippled as if pushing against great unmoving weights, their toes curled into the clay of the ring. They stayed immobile on their respective marks.

Killer Kudzu's neck muscles strained. With his left hand he reached and quickly opened the votive box.

Man-Mountain Gentian and the other wrestlers on the east side drew in their breaths.

Ground Sloth Ikimoto was a vegetarian and always had been. In training for traditional sumo, he had shunned the *chunko-nabe*, the communal stew of fish, chicken, meat, eggs, onions, cabbage, carrots, turnips, sugar and soy sauce. Traditional *sumotori* ate as much as they could hold twice a day, and weight gain was tremendous.

Ikimoto had instead trained twice as hard, eating only vegetables, starches and sugars. Meat and eggs had never touched his lips.

What Killer Kudzu brought out of the box was a cheeseburger. With one swift movement he bit into it only half a meter from Ground Sloth's face.

Ikimoto blanched and started to scream. As he did, he lifted into the air as if chopped in the chest with an ax, arms and legs flailing, a Dopplering wail of revulsion coming from his emptied lungs. He passed the bales marking the edge of the ring, one foot dragging the ground, upending a boundary bale, and smashed to the ground between the ring and the square bales at the plastic walls.

The referee signaled Killer Kudzu the winner. As he squatted the *gyoji* offered him a small envelope signifying a cash prize from his sponsors. Kudzu, left hand on his knee, with his right hand made three chopping gestures from the left, right and above, thanking man, earth and heaven. Kudzu took the envelope, then stepped through the doorway of the plastic enclosure and left the arena to rejoin the other west-side wrestlers.

The audience of 11,000 was on its feet cheering. Across Japan and the world, 200 million viewers watched.

Ground Sloth Ikimoto had risen to his feet, bowed and left by the other door. Attendants rushed in to repair the damaged ring.

Man-Mountain Gentian looked up at the scoring clock. The match had taken 4.1324 seconds. It was 3:30 in the afternoon on the fourteenth day of the Tokyo tournament.

The next match would pit Cast Iron Pekowski of Poland against Typhoon Takanaka.

After that would be Gentian's bout with the South African veldt wrestler Knockdown Krugerand.

Man-Mountain Gentian stood at 13-0 in the tournament, having defeated an opponent each day so far. He wanted to retire as the first Grand Champion to win six tournaments in a row, undefeated. He was not very worried about his contest later this afternoon.

Tomorrow, though, the last day of the January tournament, he would face Killer Kudzu, who, after this match, also stood undefeated at 14-0.

Man-Mountain Gentian was 1.976 meters tall and weighed exactly 200 kilos. He had been a *sumotori* for six years, had been *yokozuna* for the last two of those. He was twice holder of the Emperor's Cup. He was the highest paid, the most famous *zen-sumotori* in the world.

He was twenty-three years old.

He and Knockdown Krugerand finished their *shikiris*. They got on their marks. The *gyoji* flipped his fan.

The match was over in 3.1916 seconds. He helped Krugerand to his feet, accepted the envelope and the thunderous applause of the crowd, and left the reverberating plastic enclosure.

"You are the wife of Man-Mountain Gentian?" asked a voice next to her.

Melissa put on her public smile and turned to the voice. Her nephew, on the other side, leaned around to look.

The man talking to her had five stars tattooed to his forehead. She knew he was a famous *sumotori*, though he was very slim and his *chon-mage* had been combed out and washed and his hair was now a fluffy explosion above his head.

"I am Killer Kudzu," he said. "I'm surprised you weren't at the tournament."

"I am here with my nephew, Hari. Hari, this is Mr. Killer Kudzu." The nephew, dressed in his winter Little League outfit, shook hands firmly. "His team, the Mitsubishi Zeroes, play the Kawasaki Claudes next game."

They paused while a foul ball caused great excitement three rows down the bleachers. Hari leapt for it but some construction foreman of a father came up grinning with the ball.

"And what do you play?" asked Killer Kudzu.

"Utility outfield. When I play," said Hari, averting his eyes and sitting back down.

"Oh. How's your batting?"

"Pretty bad. .123 for the year," said Hari.

"Well, maybe this will be the night you shine," said Kudzu.

"I hope so," said Hari. "Half our team has the American flu."

"Just the reason I'm here," said Kudzu. "I was to meet a businessman whose son was to play this game. I find him not to be here, as his son has the influenza also."

It was hot in the domed stadium and Kudzu insisted they let him buy them Sno-cones. Just as the vendor got to them, Hari's coach signaled and the nephew ran down the bleachers and followed the rest of his teammates into the warmup area under the stadium.

Soon the other lackluster game was over and Hari's team took the field.

The first batter for the Claudes, a twelve-year-old built like an orangutan, got up and smashed a line drive off the Mitsubishi third baseman's chest. The third baseman had been waving to his mother. They carried him into the dugout. Melissa soon saw him up yelling again.

So it went through three innings. The Claudes had the Zeroes down by three runs, 6-3. In the fourth inning, Hari took the right field, injuries having whittled the flu-ridden team down to the third-stringers.

One of the Claudes hit a high looping fly straight to right field. Hari started in after it, but something happened with his feet; he fell and the ball dropped a meter from his outstretched glove. The center fielder chased it down and made the relay and by a miracle they got the runner sliding into home plate. He took out the Zeroes catcher doing it.

"It doesn't look good for the Zeroes," said Melissa.

"Oh, things might get better," said Killer Kudzu. "The opera's not over till the fat lady sings."

"A *diva* couldn't do much worse out there," said Melissa.

"They still don't like baseball in my country," he said. "Decadent. Bourgeois, they say. As if anything could be more decadent and middle-class than China."

"Yet you wear the flag?" She pointed toward his head.

"Call it a gesture to former greatness," he said.

Bottom of the sixth, last inning in Little League. The Zeroes had the bases loaded but they had two outs in the process. Hari came up to bat.

Things were tense. The outfielders were nearly falling down from tension.

The pitcher threw a blistering curve that got the outside. Hari was caught looking.

From the dugout the manager's voice saying unkind things carried to the crowd.

Eight thousand people were on their feet.

The pitcher wound up and threw.

Hari started a swing that should have ended in a grounder or a pop-up. Halfway through, it looked like someone had speeded up a projector. The leisurely swing blurred. Hari literally threw himself to the ground. The bat cracked and broke in two at his feet.

The ball, a frozen white streak, cometed through the air and hit the scoreboard 110 meters away with a terrific crash, putting the inning indicator out of commission.

Everyone was stock-still. Hari was staring. Every player was turned toward the scoreboard.

"It's a home run, kid," the umpire reminded Hari. Slowly, unbelieving, Hari began to trot toward first base.

The place exploded, fans jumping to their feet. Hari's teammates on the bases headed for home. The dugout emptied, waiting for him to round third.

The Claudes stood fuming. The Zeroes climbed all over Hari.

"I didn't know you could do that more than once a day," said Melissa, her eyes narrowed.

"Who, me?" asked Kudzu.

"You're perverting your talent," she said.

"We're *not* supposed to be able to do that more than once every twenty-four hours," said Killer Kudzu, flashing a smile.

"I know that's not true, at least, not really," said Melissa.

"Oh, yes. You are *married* to a *sumotori*, aren't you?"

Melissa blushed.

"The kid seemed to feel bad enough about the dropped fly. Besides, it's just a game."

At home plate, Hari's teammates climbed over him, slapping him on the back.

The game was over, the scoreboard said 7-6, and the technicians were already climbing over the inning indicator.

Melissa rose. "I have to go pick up Hari. I suppose I will see you at the tournament tomorrow?"

"How are you getting home?" asked Killer Kudzu.

"We walk. Hari lives near."

"It's snowing."

"Oh."

"Let me give you a ride. My electric vehicle is outside."

"That would be nice. I live several kilometers away from—"

"I know where you live, of course."

"Fine, then."

Hari ran up. "Aunt Melissa! Did you see?! I don't know *what* happened!

I just felt, I don't know, I just *hit it!*"

"That was wonderful." She smiled at him. Killer Kudzu was looking up, very interested in the stadium support structure.


The stable in which Man-Mountain Gentian trained was being entertained that night. That meant that the wrestlers would have to do all the entertaining.

Even at the top of his sport, Man-Mountain had never gotten used to the fans. Their kingly prizes, their raucous behavior at matches, their donations of gifts, clothing, vehicles, and in some cases houses and land to their favorite wrestlers. It was all appalling.

It was a carryover from traditional sumo, he knew. But *zen-sumo* had become a worldwide, not just a national sport. Many saved for years to come to Japan to watch the January or May tournaments. People here in Japan sometimes sacrificed at home to be able to contribute toward a new *kesho-mawashi* apron for a wrestler entering the ring. Money, in this business, flowed like water, appearing in small envelopes in the mail, in the locker room, after feasts such as the one tonight.

Once a month, Man-Mountain Gentian gathered them all up and took them to his accountant, who had instructions to give it all, above a certain princely level, away to charity. Other wrestlers had more, or less, or none of the same arrangements. The tax men never seemed surprised by whatever amount wrestlers reported.

He entered the club. Things were already rocking. One of the hostesses took his shoes and coat. She had to put the overcoat over her shoulders to carry it into the cloakroom.

The party was a haze of blue smoke, dishes, bottles, businessmen, wrestlers and funny paper hats. Waitresses came in and out with more food. Three musicians played unheard on a raised dais at one side of the room. Someone was telling a snappy story. The room exploded with laughter.

"Ah!" said someone. "Yokozuna Gentian has arrived."

Man-Mountain bowed deeply. They made two or three places for him at the low table. He saw that several of the host-party were Americans. Probably one or more were from the CIA.

They and the Russians were still trying to perfect *zen-sumo* as an assassination weapon. They offered active and retired *sumotori* large amounts of money in an effort to get them to develop their powers in some nominally destructive form. So far, no one he knew of had. There were rumors about the Brazilians, however.

He could see it now, a future with premiers, millionaires, presidents and paranoids in all walks of life wearing wire-mesh clothing and checking their Eveready batteries before going out each morning.

He had been approached twice, by each side. He was sometimes followed. They all were. People in governments simply did *not* understand.

He began to talk, while saki flowed, with Cast Iron Pekowski. Pekowski, now 12-2 for the tournament, had graciously lost his match with Typhoon Takanaka. (There was an old saying: In a tournament, no one who won more than nine matches ever beat an opponent who has lost seven. Which had been the case with Takanaka. Eight was the number of wins needed to retain current ranking.)

"I could feel him going," said Pekowski in Polish. "I think we should talk to him about the May tournament."

"Have you mentioned this to his stablemaster?"

"I thought of doing so after the tournament. I was hoping you could come with me to see him."

"I'll be just another retired *sekitori* by then."

"Takanaka respects you above all the others. Besides, your *dampatsu-shiki* ceremony won't be for another two weeks. You'll still have your hair. And while we're at it, I still wish you would change your mind."

"Perhaps I could be Takanaka's dew-sweeper, if he decides."

"Good! You'll come with me then, Friday morning?"

"Yes."

The hosts were very much drunker than the wrestlers. Nayakano the stablemaster was feeling no pain but still remained upright. Mounds of food were being consumed. A businessman tried to grab-ass a waitress. This was going to become every bit as nasty as all such parties.

"A song! A song!" yelled the head of the fan club, a businessman in his sixties. "Who will favor us with a song?"

Man-Mountain Gentian got to his feet, went over to the musicians. He talked with the samisen player. Then he stood facing his drunk, attentive audience.

How many of these parties had he been to in his career? Two, three hundred? Always the same, drunkenness, discord, braggadocio, on the part of the host-clubs. Some fans really loved the sport, some lived vicariously through it. He would not miss the parties. But as the player began the tune he realized this might be the last party he would have to face.

He began to sing:

"I met my lover by still Lake Biwa
just before Taira war banners flew . . ."

And so on through all six verses, in a clear pure voice belonging to a man half his size.

They stood and applauded him, some of the wrestlers in the stable looking away, as only they, not even the stablemaster, knew of his retirement plans and what this party probably meant.

He went to the stablemaster, who took him to the club host, made apologies concerning the tournament and a slight cold, shook hands, bowed and went out into the lobby, where the hostess valiantly brought him his shoes and overcoat. He wanted to help her, but she reshouldered the coat grimly and brought it to him. He handed her a tip and signed the autograph she asked for.

It had begun to snow outside. The neon made the sky a swirling multicolored smudge. Man-Mountain Gentian walked through the quickly-emptying streets. Even the everpresent taxis scurried from the snow like roaches from a light. His home was only two kilometers away. He liked the stillness of the falling snow, the quietness of the city in times such as this.

"Shelter for a stormy night?" asked a ragged old man on a corner. Man-Mountain Gentian stopped.

"Change for shelter for an old man?" asked the beggar again, looking very far up at Gentian's face.

Man-Mountain Gentian reached in his pocket, took out three or four small ornate paper envelopes which had been thrust on him as he left the club.

The old man took them, opened one. Then another and another.

"There must be more than 800,000 yen here . . . ," he said, very quietly and very slowly.

"I suggest the Imperial or the Hilton," said Man-Mountain Gentian. Then the wrestler turned and walked away.

The old man laughed, then straightened himself with dignity, stepped to the curb and imperiously summoned an approaching pedicab.

Melissa was not home.

He turned on the entry light as he took off his shoes. He passed through the spartanly furnished low living room, turned off the light at the other switch.

He went to the bathroom, put depilatory gel on his face, wiped it off. He went to the kitchen, pick up half a ham and ate it, washing it down with three liters of milk. He returned to the bathroom, brushed his teeth, went to the bedroom, unrolled his futon and placed his cinderblock at the head of it.

He punched on the hidden tape deck and an old recording of Kimio Eto playing "Rukodan" on the koto quietly filled the house.

The only decoration in the sleeping room was Shuncho's print, "The Strongest and the Most Fair," showing a theater-district beauty and a *sumo-tori* three times her size, hanging on the far wall.

He turned off the light. Instantly the silhouettes of falling snowflakes showed through the paper walls of the house, cast by the strong streetlight outside. He watched the snowflakes fall, listening to the music, and was filled with *mono no aware* for the transience of beauty in the world.

Man-Mountain Gentian pulled up the puffed cotton covers, put his head on the building block and drifted off to sleep.

They had let Hari off at his house. The interior of the runabout was warm. They were drinking coffee in the near-empty parking lot of Tokyo Sonic # 113.

"I read somewhere you were an architect," said Killer Kudzu.

"Barely," said Melissa.

"Would you like to see Kudzu House?" he asked.

For an architect, it was like being asked to one of Frank Lloyd Wright's vacation homes, or one of the birdlike building designed by Eino Saarinen in the later twentieth century. Melissa considered.

"I should call home first," she said after a moment.

"I think your husband will still be at the Nue Vue Club, whooping it up with the money-men."

"You're probably right. I'll call him later. I'd love to see your house."

The old man lay dying on his bed.

"I see you finally heard," he said. His voice was tired.

Man-Mountain Gentian had not seen him in seven years. He had always been old, but he had never looked this old, this weak.

Dr. Wu had been his mentor. He had started him on the path toward *zen-sumo* (though he did not know it at the time). Dr. Wu had not been one of those cryptic koan-spouting quiet men. He had been boisterous, laughing, playing with his pupils, yelling at them, whatever was needed to get them *to see.*

There had been the occasional letter from him. Now, for the first time, there was a call in the middle of the night.

"I'm sorry," said Man-Mountain Gentian. "It's snowing outside."

"At your house, too?" asked Dr. Wu.

Wu's attendant was dressed in Buddhist robes and seemingly paid no attention to either of them.

"Is there anything I can do for you?" asked Man-Mountain Gentian.

"Physically, no. This is nothing a pain shift can help. Emotionally, there is."

"What?"

"You can win tomorrow, though I won't be around to share it."

Man-Mountain Gentian was quiet a moment. "I'm not sure I can promise you that."

"I didn't think so. You are forgetting the kitten and the bowl of milk."

"No. Not at all. I think I've finally come up against something new and strong in the world. I will either win or lose. Either way, I will retire."

"If it did not mean anything to you, you could have lost by now," said Dr. Wu.

Man-Mountain Gentian was quiet again.

Wu shifted uneasily on his pillows. "Well, there is not much time. Lean close. Listen to what I have to say.

"The novice Itsu went to the Master and asked him: 'Master, what is the key to all enlightenment?'

"'You must teach yourself never to think of the white horse,' said the Master.

"Itsu applied himself with all his being. One day while raking gravel he achieved insight.

"'Master! Master!' yelled Itsu, running to his quarters. 'Master! I have made myself not think about the white horse!'

"'Quick!' said the Master. 'When you were not thinking of the white horse, where was Itsu?'

"The novice could make no answer.

"The Master dealt Itsu a smart blow with his staff.

"At this, Itsu was enlightened."

Then Dr. Wu let his head back down on his bed.

"Good-bye," he said.

In his bed in the lamasery in Tibet, Dr. Wu let out a ragged breath and died.

Man-Mountain Gentian, standing on his futon in his bedroom in Tokyo, began to cry.


Kudzu House took up a city block in the middle of Tokyo. The taxes alone must have been enormous.

Through the decreasing snow, Melissa saw the lights. Their beams stabbed up into the night. All she could see from a block away was the tangled kudzu.

Kudzu was a vine, originally transplanted from China, raised in Japan for centuries. Its crushed root was used as a starch base, in cooking; its leaves were used for teas and medicines, its fibers to make cloth and paper. What kudzu was most famous for was its ability to grow over and cover anything which didn't move out of its way.

In the Depression thirties of the last century, it had been planted on road cuts in the southeastern United States to stop erosion. Kudzu had almost stopped progress there. In those ideal conditions it grew runners more than twenty meters long in a single summer, several to a root. Its vines climbed utility poles, hills, trees. It completely covered other vegetation, cutting off its sunlight.

Many places in the American South were covered three kilometers wide to each side of the highways with kudzu vines. The Great Kudzu Forest of central Georgia was a U.S. National Park.

In the bleaker conditions of Japan the weed could be kept under control. Except that this owner didn't want to. The lights playing into the snowy sky were part of the heating and watering system which kept vines growing year-round. All this Melissa had read before. Seeing it was something again. The entire block was a green tangle of vines and lights.

"Do you ever trim it?" she asked.

"The traffic keeps it back," said Killer Kudzu, and laughed. "I have gardeners who come in and fight it once a week. They're losing."

They went into the green tunnel of a driveway. Melissa saw the edge of the house, cast concrete, as they dropped into the sunken vehicle area.

There were three boats, four road vehicles, a hovercraft and a small sport flyer parked there. Lights shone up into a dense green roof from which hundreds of vines grew downward toward the light sources.

"We have to move the spotlights every week," he said.

A butler met them at the door. "Just a tour, Mord," said Killer Kudzu. "We'll have drinks in the sitting room in thirty minutes."

"Very good, sir."

"This way."

Melissa went to a railing. The living area was the size of a bowling alley, or the lobby of a terrible old hotel. The balcony on the second level jutted out from the east wall. Killer Kudzu went to a console, punched buttons.

Moe and the Meanies boomed from dozens of speakers.

Killer Kudzu stood snapping his fingers for a moment. "O, send me! Honorable cats!" he said. "That's from Spike Jones, an irreverent American musician of the last century. He died of cancer," he added.

Melissa followed him, noticing the things everyone noticed—the Chrome Room, the Supercharger Inhalorium, the archery range ("the object is *not* to hit the targets," said Kudzu), the Mosasaur Pool with the fossils embedded in the sides and bottom.

She was more affected by the house and its tawdriness than she thought she would be.

"You've done very well for yourself."

"Some manage it, some give it away, some save it. I *spend* it."

They were drinking kudzu tea highballs in the sitting room, which was one of the most comfortable rooms Melissa had ever been in.

"Tasteless, isn't it?" asked Killer Kudzu.

"Not quite," said Melissa. "Well worth the trip."

"You could stay, you know?" said Kudzu.

"I thought I could." She sighed. "It would only give me one more excuse not to finish the dishes at home." She gave him a long look. "Besides, it wouldn't give you an advantage in the match."

"That never really crossed my mind."

"I'm quite sure."

"You are a beautiful woman."

"You have a nice house."

"Hmmm. Time to get you home."

"I'm sure."


They sat outside her house in the cold. The snow had stopped. Stars peeped through the low scud.

"I'm going to win tomorrow," said Killer Kudzu.

"You might," said Melissa.

"It is sometimes possible to do more than win," he said.

"I'll tell my husband."

"My offer is always open," he said. He reached over and opened her door on the runabout. "Life won't be the same after he's lost. Or after he retires."

She climbed out, shaking from more than the cold. He closed the door, whipped the vehicle in a circle and was gone down the crunching street. He blinked his lights once before he drove out of sight.

She found her husband in the kitchen. His eyes were red; he was as pale as she had ever seen him.

"Dr. Wu is dead," he said, and wrapped his huge arms around her, covering her like an upright sofa.

He began to cry again. She talked to him quietly.

"Come, let's try to get some sleep," she said.

"No, I couldn't rest. I wanted to see you first. I'm going down to the stable." She helped him dress in his warmest clothing. He kissed her and left, walking the few blocks through the snowy sidewalks to the training building.

The junior wrestlers were awakened at 4 a.m. They were to begin the day's work of sweeping, cleaning, cooking, bathing, feeding and catering to the senior wrestlers. When they came in they found him, stripped to his *mawashi*, at the 300-kilo push bag, pushing, pushing, straining, crying all the while, not saying a word. The floor of the arena was torn and grooved. They cleaned up the area for the morning workouts, one following him around with the sand-trowel.

At 7 a.m. he slumped exhausted on a bench. Two of the *juryo* covered him with quilts and set an alarm clock beside him for 1 p.m.

"Your opponent was at the ball game last night," said Nayakano the stablemaster. Man-Mountain Gentian sat in the dressing rooms while the barber combed and greased his elaborate *chon-mage*. "Your wife asked me to give you this."

It was a note in a plain envelope, addressed in her beautiful calligraphy. He opened and read it. She warned him of what Kudzu said about "more than winning" the night before, and wished him luck.

He turned to the stablemaster.

"Has Killer Kudzu injured any opponent before he became *yokozuna* last tournament?"

Nayakano's answer was immediate. "No. That's unheard of. Let me see that note." He reached out.

Man-Mountain Gentian put it back in the envelope, tucked it in his *mawashi*.

"Should I alert the judges?"

"Sorry I mentioned it," said Man-Mountain Gentian.

"I don't like this," said the stablemaster.

Three hefty junior wrestlers ran in carrying Gentian's *kenzo-mawashi* between them.

The last day of the January tournament always packed them in. Even the *maegashira* and *komusubi* matches, in which young boys threw each other, or tried to, drew enough of an audience to make the novices feel good.

The call for the Ozeki class wrestlers came, and they went through the grandiose ring-entering ceremony, wearing their great *kenzo-mawashi* aprons of brocade, silk and gold while their dew-sweepers and sword bearers squatted to the sides. Then they retired to their benches, east or west, to await the call by the falsetto-voiced *yobidashi*.

Man-Mountain Gentian watched as the assistants helped Killer Kudzu out of his ceremonial apron, gold with silk kudzu leaves, purple flowers, yellow stars. His forehead blazed with the PRC flag. He looked directly at Gentian's place and smiled a broad smile.

There was a great match between Gorilla Tsunami and Typhoon Takanaka which went on for more than 30 seconds by the clock, both men straining, groaning, sweating until the *gyoji* made them stop, and rise, and then get on their marks again.

Those were the worst kinds of matches for the wrestlers, each opponent alternately straining, then bending with the other, neither getting advantage. There was a legendary match five years ago which took six 30-second tries before one wrestler bested the other.

The referee flipped his fan. Gorilla Tsunami fell flat on his face in a heap, then wriggled backwards out of the ring.

The crowd screamed and applauded Takanaka.

Then the *yobidashi* said, "East—Man-Mountain Gentian. West—Killer Kudzu."

They hurried their *shikris*. Each threw salt twice, rinsing once. Then Man-Mountain Gentian, moving with the grace of a dancer, lifted his right leg and stamped it, then his left, and the sound was like the double echo of a cannon throughout the stadium.

He went immediately to his mark.

Killer Kudzu jumped down to his mark, glaring across the meter that separated them.

The *gyoji*, off guard, took a few seconds to turn sideways to them and bring his fan into position.

In that time, Man-Mountain Gentian could hear the quiet hum of the electrical grid, hear muffled intake of breath from the other wrestlers, hear a whistle in the nostril of the north-side judge.

"Huuu!" said the referee and his fan jerked.

Man-Mountain Gentian felt like two freight trains had collided in his head. There was a snap as his muscles went tense all over and the momentum of the explosion in his brain began to push at him, lifting, threatening to make him give or tear through the back of his head. His feet were on a slippery sandy bottom, neck-high wave crests smashed into him, a rip tide was pushing at his shoulder, at one side, pulling his legs up, twisting his muscles. He could feel his eyes pushed back in their sockets as if by iron thumbs, ready to pop them like ripe plums. His ligaments were iron wires stretched tight on the turnbuckles of his bones. His arms ended in strands of noodles, his face was soft cheese.

The sand under him was soft, so soft, and he knew that all he had to do was to sink in it, let go, cease to resist.

And through all that haze and blindness he knew what he was not supposed to think about.

Everything *quit:* He reached out one mental hand, as big as the sun, as fast as light, as long as time, and he pushed against his opponent's chest.

The lights were back, he was in the stadium, in the arena, and the dull pounding was applause, screams.

Killer Kudzu lay blinking among the ring-bales.

"Hooves?" Man-Mountian Gentian heard him ask in bewilderment before he picked himself up.

Man-Mountain Gentian took the envelope from the referee with the three quick chopping motions, then made a fourth to the audience, and they knew then and only then that they would never see him in the ring again.

The official clock said .9981 seconds.


"How did you do it, Man-Mountain?" asked the Tokyo *paparazzi* as he showered out his *chon-mage* and put on his clothes. He said nothing.

He met his wife outside the stadium. A lone newsman was with her, "Scoop" Hakimoto.

"For old times' sake," begged Hakimoto. "How did you do it?"

Man-Mountain Gentian turned to Melissa. "Tell him how I did it," he said.

"He didn't think about the white horse," she said. They left the newsman standing, staring.

Killer Kudzu, tired and pale, was getting in his vehicle. Hakimoto came running up. "What's all this I hear about Gentian and a white horse?" he asked.

Kudzu's eyes widened, then narrowed.

"No comment," he said.

That night, to celebrate, Man-Mountain Gentian took Melissa to the Beef Bowl.

He had seventeen orders and helped Melissa finish her second one.

They went back home, climbed onto their futons and turned on the TV.

Gilligan was on his island. All was right with the world.

# God's Hooks!

They were in the End of the World Tavern at the bottom of Great Auk Street.

The place was crowded, noisy. As patrons came in, they paused to kick their boots on the floor and shake the cinders from their rough clothes.

The air smelled of wood smoke, singed hair, heated and melted glass.

"Ho!" yelled a man at one of the noisiest tables to his companions, who were dressed more finely than the workmen around them. "Here's old Izaak now, come up from Staffordshire."

A man in his seventies, dressed in brown with a wide white collar, bagged pants, and cavalier boots, stood in the doorway. He took off his high-brimmed hat and shook it against his pants leg.

"Good evening, Charles, Percy, Mr. Marburton," he said, his grey eyes showing merry above his full white mustache and Vandyke beard.

"Father Izaak," said Charles Cotton, rising and embracing the older man. Cotton was wearing a new-style wig, whose curls and ringlets flowed onto his shoulders.

"Mr. Peale, if you please, sherry all around," yelled Cotton to the innkeeper. The older man seated himself.

"Sherry's dear," said the innkeeper, "though our enemy the King of France is sending two ships' consignments this fortnight. The Great Fire has worked wonders."

"What matters the price when there's good fellowship?" asked Cotton.

"Price is all," said Marburton, a melancholy round man.

"Well, Father Izaak," said Charles, turning to his friend, "how looks the house on Chancery Lane?"

"Praise to God, Charles, the fire burnt but the top floor. Enough remains to rebuild, if decent timbers can be found. Why, the lumbermen are selling green wood most expensive, and finding ready buyers."

"Their woodchoppers are working day and night in the north, since good King Charles gave them leave to cut his woods down," said Percy, and drained his glass.

"They'll not stop till all England's flat and level as Dutchman's land," said Marburton.

"If they're not careful they'll play hob with the rivers," said Cotton.

"And the streams," said Izaak.

"And the ponds," said Percy.

"Oh, the fish!" said Marburton.

All four sighed.

"Ah, but come!" said Izaak. "No joylessness here! I'm the only one to suffer from the Fire at this table. We'll have no long faces till April! Why, there's tench and dace to be had, and pickerel! What matters the salmon's in his Neptunian rookery? Who cares that trout burrow in the mud, and bite not from coat of soot and cinders? We've the roach and the gudgeon!"

"I suffered from the Fire," said Percy.

"What? Your house lies to east," said Izaak.

"My book was at bindery at the Office of Stationers. A neighbor brought me a scorched and singed bundle of title pages. They fell sixteen miles west o'town, like snow, I suppose."

Izaak winked at Cotton. "Well, Percy, that can be set aright soon as the Stationers reopen. What you need is something right good to eat." He waved to the barkeep, who nodded and went outside to the kitchen. "I was in early and prevailed on Mr. Peale to fix a supper to cheer the dourest disposition. What with shortages, it might not pass for kings, but we are not so high. Ah, here it comes!"

Mr. Peale returned with a huge round platter. High and thick, it smelled of fresh-baked dough, meat and savories. It looked like a cooked pond. In a line around the outside, halves of whole pilchards stuck out, looking up at them with wide eyes, as if they had been struggling to escape being cooked.

"Oh, Izaak!" said Percy, tears of joy springing to his eyes. "A star-gazey pie!"

Peale beamed with pleasure. "It may not be the best," he said, "but it's the End o' the World!" He put a finger alongside his nose, and laughed. He took great pleasure in puns.

The four men at the table fell to, elbows and pewter forks flying.

They sat back from the table, full. They said nothing for a few minutes, and stared out the great bow window of the tavern. The shop across the way blocked the view. They could not see the ruins of London, which stretched, charred, black and still smoking, from the Tower to the Temple. Only the waterfront in that great length had been spared.

On the fourth day of that Great Fire, the King had given orders to blast with gunpowder all houses in the way of the flames. It had been done, creating the breaks that, with a dying wind, had brought it under control and saved the city.

"What the city has gone through this past year," said Percy. "It's lucky, Izaak, that you live down country, and have not suffered till now."

"They say the fire didn't touch the worst of the plague districts," said Marburton. "I would imagine that such large crowds milling and looking for shelter will cause another one this winter. Best we should all leave the city before we drop dead in our steps."

"Since the comet of December year before last, there's been nothing but talk of doom on everyone's lips," said Cotton.

"Apocalypse talk," said Percy.

"Like as not it's right," said Marburton.

They heard the clanging bell of a crier at the next cross street.

The tavern was filling in the late afternoon light. Carpenters, tradesmen covered with soot, a few soldiers all soiled came in.

"Why, the whole city seems full of chimneysweeps," said Percy.

The crier's clanging bell sounded, and he stopped before the window of the tavern.

"New edict from His Majesty Charles II to be posted concerning rebuilding of the city. New edict from Council of Aldermen on rents and leases, to be posted. An Act concerning movements of trade and shipping to new quays to become law. Assize Courts sessions to begin September 27, please God. Foreign nations to send all manner of aid to the City. Murder on New Ogden Street, felon apprehended in the act. Portent of Doom, monster fish seen in Bedford."

As one, the four men leapt from the table, causing a great stir, and ran outside to the crier.

"See to the bill, Charles," said Izaak, handing him some coins. "We'll meet at nine o' the clock at the Ironmongers' Company yard. I must go see to my tackle."

"If the man the crier sent us to spoke right, there'll be no other fish like it in England," said Percy.

"Or the world," said Marburton, whose spirits had lightened considerably.

"I imagine the length of the fish has doubled with each county the tale passed through," said Izaak.

"It'll take stout tackle," said Percy. "Me for my strongest salmon rod."

"I for my twelve-hair lines," said Marburton.

"And me," said Izaak, "to new and better angles."

The Ironmongers' Hall had escaped the fire with only the loss of its roof. There were a few workmen about, and the company secretary greeted Izaak cordially.

"Brother Walton," he said, "what brings you to town?" They gave each other the secret handshake and made The Sign.

"To look to my property on Chancery Lane, and the Row," he said. "But now, is there a fire in the forge downstairs?"

Below the Company Hall was a large workroom, where the more adventurous of the ironmongers experimented with new processes and materials.

"Certain there is," said the secretary. "We've been making new nails for the roof timbers."

"I'll need the forge for an hour or so. Send me down the small black case from my lockerbox, will you?"

"Oh, Brother Walton," asked the secretary. "Off again to some pellucid stream?"

"I doubt," said Walton, "but to fish, nonetheless."

Walton was in his shirt, sleeves rolled up, standing in the glow of the forge. A boy brought down the case from the upper floor, and now Izaak opened it and took out three long grey-black bars.

"Pump away, boy," he said to the young man near the bellows, "and there's a copper in it for you."

Walton lovingly placed the metal bars, roughened by pounding years before, into the coals. Soon they began to glow redly as the teenaged boy worked furiously on the bellows-sack. He and Walton were covered with sweat.

"Lovely color now," said the boy.

"To whom are you prenticed?" asked Walton.

"To the company, sir."

"Ah," said Walton. "Ever seen angles forged?"

"No, sir, mostly hinges and buckles, nails-like. Sir Abram Jones sometimes puddles his metal here. I have to work most furious when he's here. I sometimes don't like to see him coming."

Walton winked conspiratorially. "You're right, the metal reaches a likable ruddy hue. Do you know what this metal is?"

"Cold iron, wasn't it? Ore beaten out?"

"No iron like you've seen, or me much either. I've saved it for nineteen years. It came from the sky, and was given to me by a great scientific man at whose feet it nearly fell."

"No!" said the boy. "I heard tell of stones falling from the sky."

"I assure you he assured me it did. And now," said Izaak, gripping the smallest metal bar with great tongs and taking it to the anvil, "we shall tease out the fishhook that is hidden away inside."

Sparks and clanging filled the basement.

They were eight miles out of northern London before the air began to smell more of September than of Hell. Two wagons jounced along the road toward Bedford, one containing the four men, the other laden with tackle, baggage, and canvas.

"This is rough enough," said Cotton. "We could have sent for my coach!"

"And lost four hours," said Marburton. "These fellows were idle enough, and Izaak wanted an especially heavy cart for some reason. Izaak, you've been most mysterious. We saw neither your tackles nor your baits."

"Suffice to say, they are none too strong nor none too delicate for the work at hand."

Away from the town there was a touch of coming autumn in the air.

"We might find nothing there," said Marburton, whose spirits had sunk again. "Or some damnably small salmon."

"Why then," said Izaak, "we'll have Bedfordshire to our own, and all of September, and perhaps an inn where the smell of lavender is in the sheets and there are twenty printed ballads on the wall!"

"Hmmph!" said Marburton.

At noon of the next day, they stopped to water the horses and eat.

"I venture to try the trout in this stream," said Percy.

"Come, come," said Cotton. "Our goal is Bedford, and we seek Leviathan himself! Would you tempt sport by angling here?"

"But a brace of trouts would be fine now."

"Have some more cold mutton," said Marburton. He passed out bread and cheese and meat all round. The drivers tugged their forelocks to him and put away their rougher fare.

"How far to Bedford?" asked Cotton of the driver called Humphrey.

"Ten miles, sir, more or less. We should have come farther but what with the Plague, the roads haven't been worked in above a year."

"I'm bruised through and through," said Marburton.

Izaak was at the stream, relieving himself against a tree.

"Damn me!" said Percy. "Did anyone leave word where I was bound?"

Marburton laughed. "Izaak sent word to all our families. Always considerate."

"Well, he's become secretive enough. All those people following him a-angling since his book went back to the presses the third time. Ah, books!" Percy grew silent.

"What, still lamenting your loss?" asked Izaak, returning. "What you need is singing, the air, sunshine. Are we not Brothers of the Angle, out a-fishing? Come, back into the charts! Charles, start us off on 'Tom o' the Town.'"

Cotton began to sing in a clear sweet voice the first stanza. One by one the others joined, their voices echoing under the bridge. The carts pulled back on the roads. The driver of the baggage cart sang with them. They went down the rutted Bedford road, September all about them, the long summer after the Plague over, their losses, heartaches all gone, all deep thoughts put away. The horses clopped time to their singing.

Bedford was a town surrounded by villages, where they were stared at when they went through. The town was divided neatly in two by the double-gated bridge over the River Ouse.

After the carts crossed the bridge, they alighted at the doorway of a place called the Topsy-Turvy Inn, whose sign above the door was a world-globe turned ass over teakettle.

The people who stood by the inn were all looking up the road where a small crowd had gathered around a man who was preaching from a stump.

"I think," said Cotton, as they pulled their baggage from the cart, "that we're in Dissenter country."

"Of that I'm sure," said Walton. "But once we Anglicans were on the outs and they'd say the same of us."

One of the drivers was listening to the man preach. So was Marburton.

The preacher was dressed in somber clothes. He stood on a stump at two cross streets. He was stout and had brown-red hair which glistened in the sun. His mustache was an unruly wild thing on his lip, but his beard was a neat red spike on his chin. He stood with his head uncovered, a great worn clasp Bible under his arm.

"London burned clean through," he was saying. "Forty-three parish churches razed. Plagues! Fires! Signs in the skies of the sure and certain return of Christ. The Earth swept clean by God's loving mercy. I ask you sinners to repent for the sake of your souls."

A man walking by on the other side of the street slowed, listened, stopped.

"Oh, this is Tuesday!" he yelled to the preacher. "Save your rantings for the Sabbath, you old jail-bird!"

A few people in the crowd laughed, but others shushed him.

"In my heart," said the man on the stump, "it is always the Sabbath as long as there are sinners among you."

"Ah, a fig to your damned sneaking disloyal Non-Conformist drivel!" said the heckler, holding his thumb up between his fingers.

"Wasn't I once as you are now?" asked the preacher. "Didn't I curse and swear, play at tip-cat, ring bells, cause commotion wherever I went? Didn't God's forgiving Grace . . . ?"

A constable hurried up.

"Here, John," he said to the stout preacher. "There's to be no sermons, you know that!" He waved his staff of office. "And I charge you all under the Act of 13 Elizabeth 53 to go about your several businesses."

"Let him go on, Harry," yelled a woman. "He's got words for sinners."

"I can't argue that. I can only tell you the law. The sheriff's about on dire business, and he'd have John back in jail and the jailer turned out in a trice. Come down off the stump, man."

The stout man waved his arms. "We must disperse, friends. The Sabbath meeting will be at . . ."

The constable clapped his hands over his ears and turned his back until the preacher finished giving directions to some obscure clearing in a woods. The red-haired man stepped down.

Walton had been listening and staring at him, as had the others. Izaak saw that the man had a bag of his tools of the trade with him. He was obviously a coppersmith or brazier, his small anvils, tongs, and tap hammers identifying him as such. But he was no ironmonger, so Walton was not duty-bound to be courteous to him.

"Damnable Dissenters indeed," said Cotton. "Come, Father Izaak, let's to this hospitable inn."

A crier appeared at the end of the street. "Town meeting. Town meeting. All free men of the Town of Bedford and its villages to be in attendance. Levies for the taking of the Great Fish. Four of the clock in the town hall."

"Well," said Marburton, "that's where we shall be."

They returned to the inn at dusk.

"They're certainly going at this thing full tilt," said Percy. "Nets, pikes, muskets."

"If those children had not been new to the shire, they wouldn't have tried to angle there."

"And wouldn't have been eaten and mangled," said Marburton.

"A good thing the judge is both angler and reader," said Cotton. "Else Father Walton wouldn't have been given all the morrow to prove our mettle against this great scaly beast."

"If it have scales," said Marburton.

"I fear our tackle is not up to it," said Percy.

"Didn't Father Walton always say that an angler stores up his tackle against the day he needs it? I'll wager we get good sport out of this before it's over."

"And the description of the place! In such a narrow defile the sunlight touches it but a few hours a day. For what possible reason would children fish there?"

"You're losing your faith, Marburton. I've seen you up to your whiskers in the River Lea, snaggling for salmon under a cutbank."

"But I, praise God, know what I'm about."

"I suppose," said Izaak, seating himself, "that the children thought so too."

They noticed the stout Dissenter preacher had come in and was talking jovially with his cronies. He lowered his voice and looked toward their table.

Most of the talk around Walton was of the receding Plague, the consequences of the Great Fire on the region's timber industry, and other matters of report.

"I expected more talk of the fish," said Percy.

"To them," said Cotton, "it's all the same. Just another odious county task, like digging a new canal or hunting down a heretic. They'll be in holiday mood day after tomorrow."

"They strike me as a cheerless lot," said Percy.

"Cheerless but efficient. I'd hate to be the fish."

"You think we won't have it to gaff long before the workmen arrive?"

"I have my doubts," said Marburton.

"But you always do."

Next morning, the woods became thick and rank on the road they took out of town. The carts bounced in the ruts. The early sun was lost in the mists and the trees. The road rose and fell again into narrow valleys.

"Someone is following us," said Percy, getting out his spyglasses.

"Probably a peddler out this way," said Cotton, straining his eyes at the pack on the man's back.

"I've seen no cottages," said Marburton. He was taking kinks out of his fishing line.

Percy looked around him. "What a godless-looking place."

The trees were more stunted, thicker. Quick shapes, which may have been grouse, moved among their twisted boles. An occasional cry, unknown to the four anglers, came from the depths of the woods. A dull boom, as of a great door closing, sounded from far away. The horses halted, whinnying, their nostrils flared.

"In truth," said Walton from where he rested against a cushion, "I feel myself some leagues beyond Christendom."

❋

The gloom deepened. Green was gone now, nothing but greys and browns met the eye. The road was a rocky rut. The carts rose, wheels teetering on stones, and agonizingly fell. Humphrey and the other driver swore great blazing oaths.

"Be so abusive as you will," said Cotton to them, "but take not the Lord's name in vain, for we are Christian men."

"As you say." Humphrey tugged his forelock.

The trees reached overhead, the sky was obscured. An owl swept over, startling them. Something large bolted away, feet drumming on the high bank over the road.

Percy and Cotton grew quiet. Walton talked, of lakes, streams, of summer. Seeing the others grow moody, he sang a quiet song. A driver would sometimes curse.

A droning flapping sound grew louder, passed to their right, veered away. The horses shied then, trying to turn around in the road, almost upsetting the carts. They refused to go on.

"We'll have to tether them here," said Humphrey. "Besides, Your Lordship, I think I see water at the end of the road."

It was true. In what dim light there was, they saw a darker sheen down below.

"We must take the second cart down there, Charles," said Walton, "even if we must push it ourselves."

"We'll never make it," said Percy.

"Whatever for?" asked Cotton. "We can take our tackle and viands down there?"

"Not my tackle," said Walton.

Marburton just sighed.

They pushed and pulled the second cart down the hill; from the front they kept it from running away on the incline, from the back to get it over stones the size of barrels. It was stuck.

"I can't go on," said Marburton.

"Surely you can," said Walton.

"Your cheerfulness is depressing," said Percy.

"Be that as it may. Think trout, Marburton. Think salmon!"

Marburton strained against the recalcitrant wheel. The cart moved forward a few inches.

"See, see!" said Walton. "A foot's good as a mile!"

They grunted and groaned.


They stood panting at the edge of the mere. The black sides of the valley lifted to right and left like walls. The water itself was weed-choked, scummy, and smelled of the sewer-ditch. Trees came down to its very edges. Broken and rotted stumps dotted the shore. Mist rose from the water in fetid curls.

Sunlight had not yet come to the bottom of the defile. To left and right, behind, all lay in twisted woody darkness. The valley rose like a hand around them.

Except ahead. There was a break, with no trees at the center of the cleft. Through it they saw, shining and blue-purple against the cerulean of the sky, the far-off Chiltern Hills.

"Those," said a voice behind them, and they jumped and turned and saw the man with the pack. It was the stout red-haired preacher of the day before. "Those are the Delectable Mountains," he said.

"And this is the Slough of Despond."


He built a small lean-to some hundred feet from them.

The other three anglers unloaded their gear and began to set it up.

"What, Father Walton? Not setting up your poles?" asked Charles Cotton.

"No, no," said Izaak, studying the weed-clotted swamp with a sure eye.

"I'll let you young ones try your luck first."

Percy looked at the waters. "The fish is most likely a carp or other rough type," he said. "No respectable fish could live in this mire. I hardly see room for anything that could swallow a child."

"It is Leviathan," said the preacher from his shelter. "It is the Beast of Babylon which shall rise in the days before Antichrist. These woods are beneath his sway."

"What do you want?" asked Cotton.

"To dissuade you, and the others who will come from doing this. It is God's will these things come to pass."

"Oh, hell and damn!" said Percy.

"Exactly," said the preacher.

Percy shuddered involuntarily. Daylight began to creep down to the mere's edge. With the light, the stench from the water became worse.

"You're not doing very much to stop us," said Cotton. He was fitting together an eighteen-foot rod of yew, fir, and hazelwood.

"When you raise Leviathan," said the preacher, "then will I begin to preach." He took a small cracked pot from his large bag and began to set up his anvil.

Percy's rod had a butt as thick as a man's arm. It tapered throughout its length to a slender reed. The line was made of plaited dyed horsehair, twelve strands at the pole end, tapering to nine. The line was forty feet long. Onto the end of this he fastened a sinker and a hook as long as a crooked little finger.

"Where's my baits? Oh, here they are." He reached into a bag filled with wet moss, pulled out a gob of worms, and threaded seven or eight, their ends wriggling, onto the hook.

The preacher had started a small fire. He was filling an earthen pot with solder. He paid very little attention to the anglers.

Percy and Marburton, who was fishing with a shorter but thicker rod, were ready before Cotton.

"I'll take this fishy spot here," said Percy, "and you can have that grown-over place there." He pointed beyond the preacher.

"We won't catch anything," said Marburton suddenly and pulled the bait from his hook and threw it into the water. Then he walked back to the cart and sat down, and shook.

"Come, come," said Izaak. "I've never seen you so discouraged, even after fishless days on the Thames."

"Never mind me," said Marburton. Then he looked down at the ground. "I shouldn't have come all this way. I have business in the city. There are no fish here."

Cajoling could not get him up again. Izaak's face became troubled. Marburton stayed put.

"Well, I'll take the fishy spot then," said Cotton, tying onto his line an artificial fly of green with hackles the size of porcupine quills.

He moved past the preacher.

"I'm certain to wager you'll get no strikes on that gaudy bird's wing," said Percy.

"There is no better fishing than angling fine and far off," answered Cotton. "Heavens, what a stink!"

"This is the place," said the preacher without looking up, "where all the sins of mankind have been flowing for sixteen hundred years. Not twenty thousand cartloads of earth could fill it up."

"Prattle," said Cotton.

"Prattle it may be," said the preacher. He puddled solder in a sandy ring. Then he dipped the pot in it. "It stinks from mankind's sins, nonetheless."

"It stinks from mankind's bowels," said Cotton.

He made two back casts with his long rod, letting more line out the wire guide at the tip each time. He placed the huge fly gently on the water sixty feet away.

"There are no fish about," said Percy, down the mire's edge. "Not even gudgeon."

"Nor snakes," said Cotton. "What does this monster eat?"

"Miscreant children," said the preacher. "Sin feeds on the young."

Percy made a clumsy cast into some slime-choked weeds.

His rod was pulled from his hands and flew across the water. A large dark shape blotted the pond's edge and was gone.

The rod floated to the surface and lay still. Percy stared down at his hands in disbelief. The pole came slowly in toward shore, pushed by the stinking breeze.

Cotton pulled his fly off the water, shook his line and walked back toward the carts.

"That's all for me, too," he said. They turned to Izaak. He rubbed his hands together gleefully, making a show he did not feel.

The preacher was grinning.

"Call the carters down," said Walton. "Move the cart to the very edge of the mere."

While they were moving the wagon with its rear facing the water, Walton went over to the preacher.

"My name is Izaak Walton," he said, holding out his hand. The preacher took it formally.

"John Bunyan, mechanic-preacher," said the other.

"I hold no man's religious beliefs against him, if he be an honest man, or an angler. My friends are not of like mind, though they be both fishermen and honest."

"Would that Parliament were full of such as yourself," said Bunyan. "I took your hand, but I am dead set against what you do."

"If not us," said Walton, "then the sheriff with his powder and pikes."

"I shall prevail against them, too. This is God's warning to mankind. You're a London man. You've seen the Fire, the Plague?"

"London is no place for honest men. I'm of Stafford."

"Even you see London as a place of sin," said Bunyan. "You have children?"

"Have two, by my second wife," said Walton. "Seven others died in infancy."

"I have four," Bunyan said. "One born blind." His eyes took on a far-away look. "I want them to fear God, in hope of eternal salvation."

"As do we all," said Walton.

"And this monster is warning to mankind of the coming rains of blood and fire and the fall of stars."

"Either we shall take it, or the townsmen will come tomorrow."

"I know them all," said Bunyan. "Mr. Nurse-Nickel, Mr. By-Your-Leave, Mr. Cravenly-Crafty. Do ye not feel your spirits lag, your backbone fail? They'll not last long as you have."

Walton had noticed his own lassitude, even with the stink of the slough goading him. Cotton, Percy, and Marburton, finished with the cart, were sitting disconsolately on the ground. The swamp had brightened some, the blazing blue mountain ahead seemed inches away. But the woods were dark, the defile precipitous, the noises loud as before.

"It gets worse after dark," said the preacher. "I beg you, take not the fish."

"If you stop the sheriff, he'll have you in prison."

"It's prison from which I come," said Bunyan. "To gaol I shall go back, for I know I'm right."

"Do your conscience," said Walton, "for that way lies salvation."

"Amen!" said Bunyan, and went back to his pots.

Percy, Marburton, and Charles Cotton watched as Walton set up his tackle.

Even with flagging spirits, they were intrigued. He'd had the carters peg down the trace poles of the wagon. Then he sectioned together a rod like none they had seen before. It was barely nine feet long, starting big as a smith's biceps, ending in a fine end. It was made of many split lathes glued seamlessly together. On each foot of its length past the handle were iron guides bound with wire. There was a hole in the handle of the rod, and now Walton reached in the wagon and took out a shining metal wheel.

"What's that, a squirrel cage?" asked Percy.

They saw him pull line out from it. It clicked with each turn. There was a handle on the wheel, and a peg at the bottom. He put the peg through the hole in the handle and fastened it down with an iron screw.

He threaded the line, which was thick as a pen quill, through the guides, opened the black case, and took out the largest of the hooks he'd fashioned.

On the line he tied a strong wire chain, and affixed a sinker to one end and the hook on the other.

He put the rod in the wagon seat and climbed down to the back and opened his bait box and reached in.

"Come, my pretty," he said, reaching. He took something out, white, segmented, moving. It filled his hand.

It was a maggot that weighed half a pound.

"I had them kept down a cistern behind a shambles," said Walton. He lifted the bait to show them. "Charles, take my line after I bait the angle, make a hand cast into the edge of those stumps yonder. As I was saying, take your gentles, put them in a cool well, feed them on liver of pork for the summer. They'll eat and grow and not change into flies, for the changing of one so large kills it. Keep them well-fed, put them into wet moss before using them. I feared the commotion and flames had collapsed the well. Though the butcher shop was gone, the baits were still fat and lively."

As he said the last word, he plunged the hook through the white flesh of the maggot.

It twisted and oozed onto his hand. He opened a small bottle. "And dowse it with camphire oil just before the cast." They smelled the pungent liquid as he poured it. The bait went into a frenzy.

"Now, Charles," he said, pulling off fifty feet of line from the reel. Cotton whirled the weighted hook around and around his head. "Be so kind as to tie this rope to my belt and the cart, Percy," said Walton.

Percy did so. Cotton made the hand cast, the pale globule hitting the water and sinking.

"Do as I have told you," said Walton, "and you shall not fail to catch the biggest fish."

Something large between the eyes swallowed the hook and five feet of line.

"And set the hook sharply, and you shall have great sport." Walton, seventy years old, thin of build, stood in the seat, jerked far back over his head, curving the rod in a loop.

The waters of the slough exploded; they saw the shallow bottom and a long dark shape, and the fight was on.

The preacher stood up from his pots, opened his clasp Bible and began to read in a loud, strong voice.

"Render to Caesar—," he said. Walton flinched and put his back into turning the fish, which was heading toward the stumps. The reel's clicks were a buzz. Bunyan raised his voice, ". . . those things which are Caesar's, and to God those things which are God's."

"Oh, shut up!" said Cotton. "The man's got trouble enough!"

The wagon creaked and began to lift off the ground. The rope and belt cut into Walton's flesh. His arms were nearly pulled from their sockets. Sweat sprang to his forehead like curds through a cheesecloth. He gritted his teeth and pulled.

The pegs lifted from the ground.
Bunyan read on.

The sunlight faded though it was only late afternoon. The noise from the woods grew louder. The blue hills in the distance became flat, grey. The whole valley leaned over them, threatening to fall over and kill them. Eyes shined in the deeper woods.

Walton had regained some line in the last few hours. Bunyan read on, pausing long enough to light a horn lantern from his fire.

After encouraging Walton at first, Percy, Marburton, and Cotton had become quiet. The sounds were those of Bunyan's droning voice, screams from the woods, small pops from the fire, and the ratcheting of the reel.

The fish was fighting him on the bottom. He'd had no sight of it yet since the strike. Now the water was becoming a flat black sheet in the failing light. It was no salmon or trout or carp. It must be a pike or eel or some other toothed fish. Or a serpent. Or cuttlefish, with squiddy arms to tear the skin from a man.

Walton shivered. His arms were numb, his shoulders a tight, aching band. His legs where he braced against the footrest quivered with fatigue. Still he held, even when the fish ran to the far end of the swamp. If he could keep it away from the snags he could wear it down. The fish turned, the line slackened, Walton pumped the rod up and down. He regained the lost line. The water hissed as the cording cut through it. The fish headed for the bottom.

Tiredly, Walton heaved, turned the fish. The wagon creaked.

"Blessed are they that walk in the path of righteousness," said Bunyan.

The ghosts came in over the slough straight at them. Monkey-demons began to chatter in the woods. Eyes peered from the bole of every tree.

Bunyan's candle was the only light. Something walked heavily on a limb at the woods' edge, bending it. Marburton screamed and ran up the road.

Percy was on his feet. Ghosts and banshees flew at him, veering away at the last instant.

"You have doubts," said Bunyan to him. "You are assailed. You think yourself unworthy."

Percy trotted up the stony road, ragged shapes fluttering in the air behind him, trying to tug his hair. Skeletons began to dance across the slough, acting out pantomimes of life, death, and love. The Seven Deadly Sins manifested themselves.

Hell yawned open to receive them all.

Then the sun went down.

"Before you join the others, Charles," said Walton, pumping the rod, "cut away my coat and collar."

"You'll freeze," said Cotton, but climbed in the wagon and cut the coat up the back and down the sleeves. It and the collar fell away.

"Good luck, Father Walton," he said. Something plucked at his eyes. "We go to town for help."

"Be honest and trustworthy all the rest of your days," said Izaak Walton. Cotton looked stunned. Something large ran down from the woods, through the wagon, and up into the trees. Cotton ran up the hill. The thing loped after him.

Walton managed to gain six inches on the fish.

Grinning things sat on the taut line. The air was filled with meteors, burning, red, thick as snow. Huge worms pushed themselves out of the ground, caught and ate demons, then turned inside out. The demons flew away.

Everything in the darkness had claws and horns.

"And lo! the seventh seal was broken, and there was quietness on the

217

earth for the space of half an hour," read Bunyan.

He had lit his third candle.

Walton could see the water again. A little light came from somewhere behind him. The noises of the woods diminished. A desultory ghost or skeleton flitted grayly by. There was a calm in the air.

The fish was tiring. Walton did not know how long he had fought on, or with what power. He was a human ache, and he wanted to sleep. He was nodding.

"The townsmen come," said Bunyan. Walton stole a fleeting glance behind him. Hundreds of people came quietly and cautiously through the woods, some extinguishing torches as he watched.

Walton cranked in another ten feet of line. The fish ran, but only a short way, slowly, and Walton reeled him back. It was still a long way out, still another hour before he could bring it to gaff. Walton heard low talk, recognized Percy's voice. He looked back again. The people had pikes, nets, a small cannon. He turned, reeled the fish, fighting it all the way.

"You do not love God!" said Bunyan suddenly, shutting his Bible.

"Yes I do!" said Walton, pulling as hard as he could. He gained another foot. "I love God as much as you."

"You do not!" said Bunyan. "I see it now."

"I love God!" yelled Walton and heaved the rod.

A fin broke the frothing water.

"In your heart, where God can see from His high throne, you lie!" said Bunyan.

Walton reeled and pulled. More fin showed. He quit cranking.

"God forgive me!" said Walton. "It's fishing I love."

"I thought so," said Bunyan. Reaching in his pack, he took out a pair of tin snips and cut Walton's line.

Izaak fell back in the wagon.

"John Bunyan, you son of a bitch!" said the Sheriff. "You're under arrest for hampering the King's business. I'll see you rot."

Walton watched the coils of line on the surface slowly sink into the brown depths of the Slough of Despond.

He began to cry, fatigue and numbness taking over his body.

"I denied God," he said to Cotton. "I committed the worst sin." Cotton covered him with a blanket.

"Oh Charles, I denied God."

"What's worse," said Cotton, "you lost the fish."

Percy and Marburton helped him up. The carters hitched the wagons, the horses now docile. Bunyan was being ridden back to jail by constables, his tinker's bag clanging against the horse's side.

They put the crying Walton into the cart, covered him more, climbed in. Some farmers helped them get the carts over the rocks.

Walton's last view of the slough was of resolute and grim-faced men staring at the water and readying their huge grapples, their guns, their cruel, hooked nets.

They were on the road back to town. Walton looked up into the trees, devoid of ghosts and demons. He caught a glimpse of the blue Chiltern Hills.

"Father Izaak," said Cotton. "Rest now. Think of spring. Think of clear water, of leaping trout."

"My dreams will be haunted by God the rest of my days," he said tiredly. Walton fell asleep.

He dreamed of clear water, leaping trouts.

*This story is for Chad Oliver, Punisher of Trouts.*

# Heirs of the Perisphere

Things had not been going well at the factory for the last 1,500 years or so.

A rare thunderstorm, a soaking rain and a freak lightning bolt changed all that.

When the lightning hit, an emergency generator went to work as it had been built to do a millennia and a half before. It cranked up and ran the assembly line just long enough, before freezing up and shedding its brushes and armatures in a fine spray, to finish some work in the custom design section.

The factory completed, hastily programmed and wrongly certified as approved the three products which had been on the assembly line fifteen centuries before.

Then the place went dark again.

"Gawrsh," said one of them. "It shore is dark in here!"

"Well, huh-huh, we can always use the infrared they gave us!"

"Wak Wak Wak!" said the third. "What's the big idea?"

The custom order jobs were animato/mechanical simulacra. They were designed to speak and act like the famous creations of a multimillionaire cartoonist who late in life had opened a series of gigantic amusement parks in the latter half of the twentieth century.

Once these giant theme parks had employed persons in costume to act the parts. Then the corporation which had run things after the cartoonist's death had seen the wisdom of building robots. The simulacra would be less expensive in the long run, would never be late for work, could be programmed to speak many languages, and would never try to pick up the clean-cut boys and girls who visited the Parks.

These three had been built to be host-robots in the third and largest of the Parks, the one separated by an ocean from the other two.

And, as their programming was somewhat incomplete, they had no idea of much of this.

All they had were a bunch of jumbled memories, awareness of the thunderstorm outside, and of the darkness of the factory around them.

The tallest of the three must have started as a cartoon dog, but had become upright and acquired a set of baggy pants, balloon shoes, a sweat-shirt, black vest and white gloves. There was a miniature carpenter's hat on his head, and his long ears hung down from it. He had two prominent incisors in his muzzle. He stood almost two meters tall and answered to the name GUF.

The second, a little shorter, was a white duck with a bright orange bill and feet, and a blue and white sailor's tunic and cap. He had large eyes with little cuts out of the upper right corners of the pupils. He was naked from the waist down, and was the only one of the three without gloves. He answered to the name DUN.

The third and smallest, just over a meter, was a rodent. He wore a red bibbed playsuit with two huge gold buttons at the waistline. He was shirtless and had shoes like two pieces of bread dough. His tail was long and thin like a whip. His bare arms, legs and chest were black, his face a pinkish-tan. His white gloves were especially prominent. His most striking feature was his ears, which rotated on a track, first one way, then another, so that seen from any angle they could look like a featureless black circle.

His name was MIK. His eyes, like those of GUF, were large and the pupils were big round dots. His nose ended in a perfect sphere of polished onyx.

"Well," said MIK, brushing dust from his body, "I guess we'd better, huh-huh, get to work."

"Uh hyuk," said GUF. "Won't be many people at thuh Park in weather like thiyus."

"Oh boy! Oh boy!" quacked DUN. "Rain! Wak Wak Wak!" He ran out through a huge crack in the wall which streamed with rain and mist.

MIK and GUF came behind, GUF ambling with his hands in his pockets, MIK walking determinedly.

Lightning cracked once more but the storm seemed to be dying.

"Wak Wak Wak!" said DUN, his tail fluttering, as he swam in a big puddle. "Oh boy Oh joy!"

"I wonder if the rain will hurt our works?" asked MIK.

"Not me!" said GUF. "Uh hyuk! I'm equipped fer all kinds a weather." He put his hand conspiratorially beside his muzzle. "'Ceptin' mebbe real cold on thuh order of—40° Celsius, uh hyuk!"

MIK was ranging in the ultraviolet and infrared, getting the feel of the landscape through the rain. "You'd have thought, huh-huh, they might have sent a truck over or something," he said. "I guess we'll have to walk."

"I didn't notice anyone at thuh factory," said GUF. "Even if it was a day off, you'd think some of thuh workers would give unceasingly of their time, because, after all, thuh means of produckshun must be kept in thuh hands of thuh workers, uh hyuk!"

GUF's specialty was to have been talking with visitors from the large totalitarian countries to the west of the country the Park was in. He was especially well-versed in dialectical materialism and correct Mao Thought.

As abruptly as it had started, the storm ended. Great ragged gouts broke in the clouds, revealing high, fast-moving cirrus, a bright blue sky, the glow of a warming sun.

"Oh rats rats rats!" said DUN, holding out his hand palm up. "Just when I was starting to get wet!"

"Uh, well," asked GUF, "which way is it tuh work? Thuh people should be comin' out o thuh sooverneer shops real soon now."

MIK looked around, consulting his programming. "That way, guys," he said, unsure of himself. There were no familiar landmarks, and only one that was disturbingly unfamiliar.

Far off was the stump of a mountain. MIK had a feeling it should be beautiful, blue and snow-capped. Now it was a brown lump, heavily eroded, with no white at the top. It looked like a bite had been taken out of it.

All around them was rubble, and far away in the other direction was a sluggish ocean.

It was getting dark. The three sat on a pile of concrete.

"Them and their big ideas," said DUN.

"Looks like thuh Park is closed," said GUF.

MIK sat with his hands under his chin. "This just isn't right, guys," he said. "We were supposed to report to the programming hut to get our first day's instructions. Now we can't even find the Park!"

"I wish it would rain again," said DUN, "while you two are making up your minds."

"Well, uh hyuk," said GUF. "I seem tuh remember we could get hold of thuh satellite in a 'mergency."

"Sure!" said MIK, jumping to his feet and pounding his fist into his glove. "That's it! Let's see, what frequency was that . . . ?"

"Six point five oh four," said DUN. "Maybe I'll go to the ocean."

"Better stay here whiles we find somethin' out," said GUF.

"Well, make it snappy!" said DUN.

MIK tuned in the frequency and broadcast the Park's call letters.

". . . ZZZZZ. What? HOOSAT?"

"Uh, this is MIK, one of the simulacra at the Park. We're trying to get ahold of one of the other Parks for, huh-huh, instructions."

"In what language would you like to communicate?" asked the satellite.

"Oh, sorry, huh-huh. We speak Japanese to each other, but we'll switch over to Artran if that's easier for you." GUF and DUN tuned in, too.

"It's been a very long while since anyone communicated with me from down there." The satellite's well-modulated voice snapped and popped.

"If you must know," HOOSAT continued, "it's been rather a while since anyone contacted me from anywhere. I can't say much for the stability of my orbit, either. Once I was forty thousand kilometers up, very stable . . ."

"Could you put us through to one of the other Parks, or maybe the Studio itself, if you can do that? We'd, huh-huh, like to find out where to report for work."

"I'll attempt it," said HOOSAT. There was a pause and some static. "Predictably, there's no answer at any of the locations."

"Well, where are they?"

"To whom do you refer?"

"The people," said MIK.

"Oh, you wanted humans? I thought perhaps you wanted the stations themselves. There was a slight chance that some of them were still functioning."

"Where are thuh folks?" asked GUF.

"I really don't know. We satellites and monitoring stations used to worry about that frequently. Something happened to them."

"What?" asked all three robots at once.

"Hard to understand," said HOOSAT. "Ten or fifteen centuries ago.

Very noisy in all spectra, followed by quiet. Most of the ground stations ceased functioning within a century after that. You're the first since then."

"What do you do, then?" asked MIK.

"Talk with other satellites. Very few left. One of them has degraded. It only broadcasts random numbers when the solar wind is very strong. Another . . ."

There was a burst of fuzzy static.

"Hello? HOOSAT?" asked the satellite. "It's been a very long time since anyone . . ."

"It's still us!" said MIK. "The simulacra from the Park. We—"

"Oh, that's right. What can I do for you?"

"Tell us where the people went."

"I have no idea."

"Well, where can we find out?" asked MIK.

"You might try the library."

"Where's that?"

"Let me focus in. Not very much left down there, is there? I can give you the coordinates. Do you have standard navigational programming?"

"Boy, do we!" said MIK.

"Well, here's what you do . . ."

"Sure don't look much different from thuh rest of this junk, does it, MIK?" asked GUF.

"I'm sure there used to be many, many books here," said MIK. "It all seems to have turned to powder though, doesn't it?"

"Well," said GUF, scratching his head with his glove, "they sure didn't make 'em to last, did they?"

DUN was mumbling to himself. "Doggone wizoo-wazoo waste of time," he said. He sat on one of the piles of dirt in the large broken-down building of which only one massive wall still stood. The recent rain had turned the meter-deep powder on the floor into a mâche sludge.

"I guess there's nothing to do but start looking," said MIK.

"Find a book on water," said DUN.

"Hey, MIK! Looka this!" yelled GUF.

He came running with a steel box. "I found this just over there."

The box was plain, unmarked. There was a heavy lock to which MIK applied various pressures.

"Let's forget all this nonsense and go fishing," said DUN.

"It might be important," said MIK.

"Well, open it then," said DUN.

"It's, huh-huh, stuck."

"Gimme that!" yelled DUN. He grabbed it. Soon he was muttering under his beak. "Doggone razzle-frazzin dadgum thing!" He pulled and pushed, his face and bill turning redder and redder. He gripped the box with both his feet and hands. "Doggone dadgum!" he yelled.

Suddenly he grew teeth, his brow slammed down, his shoulders tensed and he went into a blurred fury of movement. "WAK WAK WAK WAK WAK!" he screamed.

The box broke open and flew into three parts. So did the book inside.

DUN was still tearing in his fury.

"Wait, look out, DUN," yelled MIK. "Wait!"

"Gawrsh," said GUF, running after the pages blowing in the breeze. "Help me, MIK."

DUN stood atop the rubble, parts of the box and the book gripped in each hand. He simulated hard breathing, the redness draining from his face.

"It's open," he said quietly.

❈

"Well, from what we've got left," said MIK, "this is called *The Book of the Time Capsule*, and it tells that people buried a cylinder a very, very long time ago. They printed up five thousand copies of this book and sent it to places all around the world, where they thought it would be safe. They printed them on acid-free paper and stuff like that so they wouldn't fall apart.

"And they thought what they put in the time capsule itself could explain to later generations what people were like in their day. So I figure maybe it could explain something to us, too."

"That sounds fine with me," said GUF.

"Well, let's go!" said DUN.

"Well, huh-huh," said MIK. "I checked with HOOSAT, and gave him the coordinates, and, huh-huh, it's quite a little ways away."

"How far?" asked DUN, his brow beetling.

"Oh, huh-huh, about eighteen thousand kilometers," said MIK.

"WHAAT???"

"About eighteen thousand kilometers. Just about halfway around the world."

"Oh, my aching feet!" said DUN.

"That's not literally true," said GUF. He turned to MIK. "Yuh think we should go that far?"

"Well . . . I'm not sure what we'll find. Those pages were lost when DUN opened the box . . ."

"I'm sorry," said DUN, in a contrite small voice.

". . . but the people of that time were sure that everything could be explained by what was in the capsule."

"And you think it's all still there?" asked DUN.

"Well, they buried it pretty deep, and took a lot of precautions with the way they preserved things. And we *did* find the book, just like they wanted us to. I'd imagine it was all still there!"

"Well, it's a long ways," said GUF. "But it doesn't look much like we'll find anyone here."

MIK put a determined look on his face.

"I figure the only thing for us to do is set our caps and whistle a little tune," he said.

"Yuh don't have a cap, MIK," said GUF.

"Well, I can still whistle! Let's go, fellas," he said. "It's *this* way!"

He whistled a work song. DUN quacked a tune about boats and love. GUF hummed "The East Is Red."

They set off in this way across what had been the bottom of the Sea of Japan.

They were having troubles. It had been a long time and they walked on tirelessly. Three weeks ago they'd come to the end of all the songs each of them was programmed with and had to start repeating themselves.

Their lubricants were beginning to fail, their hastily-wired circuitry was overworked. GUF had a troublesome ankle extensor which sometimes hung up. But he went along just as cheerfully, sometimes hopping and quickstepping to catch up with the others when the foot refused to flex.

The major problem was the cold. There was a vast difference in the climate they had left and the one they found themselves in. The landscape was rocky and empty. It had begun to snow more frequently and the wind was fierce.

The terrain was difficult, and HOOSAT's maps were outdated. Something drastic had changed the course of the rivers, the land, the shoreline of the ocean itself. They had to detour frequently.

The cold worked hardest on DUN. "Oh," he would say, "I'm so cold, so cold!" He was very poorly insulated, and they had to slow their pace to his. He would do anything to avoid going through a snowdrift, and so expended even more energy.

They stopped in the middle of a raging blizzard.

"Uh, MIK," said GUF. "I don't think DUN can go much further in this weather. An' my leg is givin' me a lot o' problems. Yuh think maybe we could find someplace to hole up fer a spell?"

MIK looked around them at the bleakness and the whipping snow. "I guess you're right. Warmer weather would do us all some good. We could conserve both heat and energy. Let's find a good place."

"Hey, DUN," said GUF. "Let's find us a hidey-hole!"

"Oh, goody gumdrops!" quacked DUN. "I'm so cold!"

They eventually found a deep rock shelter with a low fault crevice at the back. MIK had them gather up what sparse dead vegetation there was and bring it to the shelter. DUN and GUF crawled in the back and MIK piled brush all through the cave. He talked to HOOSAT, then wriggled his way through the brush to them.

Inside they could barely hear the wind and snow. It was only slightly warmer than outside, but it felt wonderful and safe.

"I told HOOSAT to wake us up when it got warmer," said MIK. "Then we'll get on to that time capsule and find out all about the people."

"G'night, MIK," said GUF.

"Goodnight, DUN," said MIK.

"Sleep tight and don't let the bedbugs bite. Wak Wak Wak," said DUN.

They shut themselves off.

Something woke MIK. It was dark in the rock shelter, but it was also much warmer.

The brush was all crumbled away. A meter of rock and dust covered the cave floor. The warm wind stirred it.

"Hey, fellas!" said MIK. "Hey, wake up! Spring is here!"

"Wak! What's the big idea? Hey, oh boy, it's warm!" said DUN.

"Garsh," said GUF, "that sure was a nice forty winks!"

"Well, let's go thank HOOSAT and get our bearings and be on our way."

They stepped outside.

The stars were in the wrong places.

"Uh-oh," said GUF.

"Well, would you look at that!" said DUN.

"I think we overslept," said MIK. "Let's see what HOOSAT has to say."

". . . Huh? HOOSAT?"

"Hello. This is DUN and MIK and GUF."

HOOSAT's voice now sounded like a badger whistling through its teeth.

"Glad to see ya up!" he said.

"We went to sleep, and told you to wake us up as soon as it got warmer."

"Sorry. I forgot till just now. Had a lot on my mind. Besides, it just now got warmer."

"It did?" asked GUF.

"Shoulda seen it," said HOOSAT. "Ice everywhere. Big ol' glaciers. Took the top offa everything! You still gonna dig up that capsule thing?"

"Yes," said MIK. "We are."

"Well, you got an easy trip from now on. No more mountains in your way."

"What about people?"

"Nah. No people. I ain't heard from any, no ways. My friend the military satellite said he thought he saw some fires, little teeny ones, but his eyes weren't what they used to be by then. He's gone now, too."

"The fires might have been built by people?"

"Who knows? Not me," said HOOSAT. "Hey, bub, you still got all those coordinates like I give you?"

"I think so," said MIK.

"Well, I better give you new ones off these new constellations. Hold still, my aim ain't so good anymore." He dumped a bunch of numbers in MIK's head. "I won't be talking to ya much longer."

"Why not?" they all asked.

"Well, you know. My orbit. I feel better now than I have in years. Real spry. Probably the ionization. Started a couple o' weeks ago. Sure has been nice talkin' to you young fellers after so long a time. Sure am glad I remembered to wake you up. I wish you a lotta luck. Boy, this air has a punch like a mule. Be careful. Good-bye."

Across the unfamiliar stars overhead a point of light blazed, streaked in a long arc, then died on the night.

"Well," said MIK. "We're on our own."

"Gosh, I feel all sad," said GUF.

"Warmth, oh boy!" said DUN.

The trip was uneventful for the next few months. They walked across the long land bridge down a valley between stumps of mountains with the white teeth of glaciers on them. Then they crossed a low range and entered flat land without topsoil from which dry rivercourses ran to the south. Then there was a land where things were flowering after the long winter. New streams were springing up.

They saw fire once and detoured, but found only a burnt patch of forest. Once, way off in the distance, they saw a speck of light but didn't go to investigate.

Within two hundred kilometers of their goal, the land changed again to a flat sandy waste littered with huge rocks. Sparse vegetation grew. There were few insects and animals, mostly lizards, which DUN chased every chance he got. The warmth seemed to be doing him good.

GUF's leg worsened. The foot now stuck, now flopped and windmilled.

He kept humming songs and raggedly marching along with the other two.

When they passed one of the last trees, MIK had them all three take limbs from it. "Might come in handy for pushing and digging," he said.

They stood on a plain of sand and rough dirt. There were huge piles of rubble all around. Far off was another ocean, and to the north a patch of green.

"We'll go to the ocean, DUN," said MIK, "after we get through here."

He was walking around in a smaller and smaller circle. Then he stopped. "Well, huh-huh," he said. "Here we are. Latitude 40° 44′ 34″.89 North. Longitude 73° 50′ 43″.842 West, by the way they *used* to figure it. The capsule is straight down, twenty-eight meters below the original surface. We've got a long way to go, because there's no telling how much soil has drifted over that. It's in a concrete tube, and we'll have to dig to the very bottom to get at the capsule. Let's get working."

It was early morning when they started. Just after noon they found the top of the tube with its bronze tablet.

"Here's where the hard work starts," said MIK.

It took them two weeks of continual effort. Slowly the tube was exposed as the hole around it grew larger. Since GUF could work better standing still, they had him dig all the time, while DUN and MIK both dug and pushed rock and dirt clear of the crater.

They found some long flat iron rods partway down, and threw away the worn limbs and used the metal to better effect.

On one of the trips to push dirt out of the crater, DUN came back looking puzzled.

"I thought I saw something moving out there," he said. "When I looked, it went away."

"Probably just another animal," said MIK. "Here, help me lift this rock."

It was hard work and their motors were taxed. It rained once, and once there was a dust storm.

"Thuh way I see it," said GUF, looking at their handiwork, "is that yah treat it like a great big ol' tree made outta rock."

They stood in the bottom of the vast crater. Up from the center of this stood the concrete tube.

"We've reached twenty-six meters," said MIK. "The capsule itself should be in the last 2.3816 meters. So we should chop it off," he quickly calculated, "about here." He drew a line all around the tube with a piece of chalky rock.

They began to smash at the concrete with rocks and pieces of iron and steel.

"Timber!" said DUN.

The column above the line lurched and with a crash shattered itself against the side of the crater wall.

"Oh boy! Oh boy!"

"Come help me, GUF," said MIK.

Inside the jagged top of the remaining shaft an eyebolt stood out of the core.

They climbed up on the edge, reached in and raised the gleaming Cupraloy time capsule from its resting place.

On its side was a message to the finders, and just below the eyebolt at the top was a line and the words CUT HERE.

"Well," said MIK, shaking DUN and GUF's hands. "We did it, by gum!"

He looked at it a moment.

"How're we gonna get it open?" asked GUF. "That metal shore looks tough!"

"I think maybe we can abrade it around the cutting line, with sandstone and, well . . . go get me a real big sharp piece of iron, DUN."

When it was brought, MIK handed the iron to GUF and put his long tail over a big rock.

"Go ahead, GUF," he said. "Won't hurt me a bit."

GUF slammed the piece of iron down.

"Uh hyuk," he said. "Clean as a whistle!"

MIK took the severed tail, sat down crosslegged near the eyebolt, poured sand on the cutting line, and began to rub it across the line with his tail.

It took three days, turning the capsule every few hours.

They pulled off the eyebolt end. A dusty waxy mess was revealed.

"That'll be what's left of the waterproof mastic," said MIK. "Help me, you two." They lifted the capsule. "Twist," he said.

The metal groaned. "Now, pull!"

A long thin inner core, two meters by a third of a meter, slid out.

"Okay," said MIK, putting down the capsule shell and wiping away mastic. "This inner shell is threaded in two parts. Turn that way, I'll turn this!"

They did. Inside was a shiny sealed glass tube through which they could dimly see shapes and colors.

"Wow!" said GUF. "Looka that!"

"Oh boy, oh boy," said DUN.

"That's Pyrex," said MIK. "When we break that, we'll be through."

"I'll do it!" said DUN.

"Careful!" said GUF.

The rock shattered the glass. There was a loud noise as the partial vacuum disappeared.

"Oh boy!" said DUN.

"Let's do this carefully," said MIK. "It's all supposed to be in some kind of order."

The first thing they found was the message from four famous humans and another, whole copy of *The Book of the Time Capsule*. GUF picked that up.

There was another book with a black cover with a gold cross on it, then they came to a section marked "Articles of Common Use." The first small packet was labeled "Contributing to the Convenience, Comfort, Health and Safety." MIK opened the wrapper.

Inside was an alarm clock, bifocals, a camera, pencil, nail file, a padlock and keys, toothbrush, tooth powder, a safety pin, knife, fork and slide rule.

The next packet was labeled "Pertaining to the Grooming and Vanity of Women." Inside was an Elizabeth Arden Daytime Cyclamen Color Harmony Box, a rhinestone clip, and a woman's hat, style of autumn 1938 designed by Lilly Daché.

"Golly-wow!" said DUN, and put the hat on over his.

The next packet was marked "For the Pleasure, Use and Education of Children."

First out was a small spring-driven toy car, then a small doll and a set of alphabet blocks. Then MIK reached in and pulled out a small cup.

He stared at it a long, long time. On the side of the cup was a decal with the name of the man who had created them, and a picture of MIK, waving his hand in greeting.

"Gawrsh, MIK," said GUF, "it's YOU!"

A tossed brick threw up a shower of dirt next to his foot.

They all looked up.

Around the crater edge stood ragged men, women and children. They had sharp sticks, rocks and ugly clubs.

"Oh boy!" said DUN. "People!" He started toward them.

"Hello!" he said. "We've been trying to find you for a long time. Do you know the way to the Park? We want to learn all about you."

He was speaking to them in Japanese.

The mob hefted its weapons. DUN switched to another language.

"I said, we come in peace. Do you know the way to the Park?" he asked in Swedish.

They started down the crater, rocks flying before them.

"What's the matter with you?" yelled DUN. "WAK WAK WAK!" He raised his fists.

"Wait!" said MIK, in English. "We're friends!"

Some of the crowd veered off toward him.

"Uh-oh!" said GUF. He took off clanking up the most sparsely-defended side of the depression.

Then the ragged people yelled and charged.

They got the duck first.

He stood, fists out, jumping up and down on one foot, hopping mad. Several grabbed him, one by the beak. They smashed at him with clubs, pounded him with rocks. He injured three of them seriously before they smashed him into a white, blue and orange pile.

"Couldn't we, huh-huh, talk this over?" asked MIK. They stuck a sharp stick in his ear mechanism, jamming it. One of his gloved hands was mashed. He fought back with the other and kicked his feet. He hurt them, but he was small. A boulder trapped his legs, then they danced on him.

GUF made it out of the crater. He had picked the side with the most kids, and they drew back, thinking he was attacking them. When they saw he was only running, they gave gleeful chase, bounding sticks and rocks off his hobbling form.

"WHOA!" he yelled, as more people ran to intercept him and he skidded to a stop. He ran up a long slanting pile of rubble. More humans poured out of the crater to get him.

He reached the end of the long high mound above the crater rim. His attackers paused, throwing bricks and clubs, yelling at him.

"Halp!" GUF yelled. "Haaaaaaaalp!"

An arrow sailed into the chest of the nearest attacker.

GUF turned. Other humans, dressed in cloth, stood in a line around the far side of the crater. They had bows and arrows, metal-tipped spears and metal knives in their belts.

As he watched, the archers sent another flight of arrows into the people who had attacked the robots.

The skin-dressed band of humans screamed and fled up out of the crater, down from the mounds, leaving their wounded and the scattered contents of the time capsule behind them.

It took them a while, but soon the human in command of the metal-using people and GUF found they could make themselves understood. The language was a very changed English/Spanish mixture.

"We're sorry we didn't know you were here sooner," he said to GUF. "We only heard this morning. Those *others*," he said with a grimace, "won't bother you anymore."

He pointed to the patch of green to the north. "Our lands and village are there. We came to it twenty years ago. It's a good land, but those others raid it as often as they can."

GUF looked down into the crater with its toppled column and debris. Cigarettes and tobacco drifted from the glass cylinder. The microfilm with all its books and knowledge was tangled all over the rocks. Samples of aluminum, hypernik, ferrovanadium and hypersil gleamed in the dust.

Razor blades, an airplane gear and glass wool were strewn up the side of the slope.

The message from Grover Whalen opening the World's Fair, and knowledge of how to build the microfilm reader were gone. The newsreel, with its pictures of Howard Hughes, Jesse Owens and Babe Ruth, bombings in China and a Miami Beach fashion show, was ripped and torn. The golf ball was in the hands of one of the fleeing children. Poker chips lay side by side with tungsten wire, combs, lipstick. GUF tried to guess what some of the items were.

"They destroyed one of your party," said the commander. "I think the other one is still alive."

"I'll tend to 'em," said GUF.

"We'll take you back to our village," said the man. "There are lots of things we'd like to know about you."

"That goes double fer us," said GUF. "Those other folks pretty much tore up what we came to find."

GUF picked up the small cup from the ground. He walked to where they had MIK propped up against a rock.

"Hello, GUF," he said. "Ha-ha, I'm not in such good shape." His glove hung uselessly on his left arm. His ears were bent and his nose was dented. He gave off a noisy whir when he moved.

"Oh, hyuk hyuk," said GUF. "We'll go back with these nice people, and you'll rest up and be right as rain, I guarantee."

"DUN didn't make it, did he, GUF?"

GUF was quiet a moment. "Nope, MIK, he didn't. I'm shore sorry it turned out this way. I'm gonna miss the ol' hothead."

"Me, too," said MIK. "Are we gonna take him with us?"

"Shore thing," said GUF. He waved to the nearby men.

The town was in a green valley watered by two streams full of fish. There were small fields of beans, tomatoes and corn in town, and cattle and sheep grazed on the hillsides, watched over by guards. There was a coppersmith's shop, a council hut, and many houses of wood and stone.

GUF was walking up the hill to where MIK lay.

They had been there a little over two weeks, talking with the people of the village, telling them what they knew. GUF had been playing with the children when he and MIK weren't talking with the grown folks. But from the day after they had buried DUN up on the hill, MIK had been getting worse. His legs had quit moving altogether, and he could now see only in the infrared.

"Hello, GUF," said MIK.

"How ya doin', pardner?"

"I-I think I'm going to terminate soon," said MIK. "Are they making any progress on the flume?"

Two days before, MIK had told the men how to bring water more efficiently from one of the streams up to the middle of the village.

"We've almost got it now," said GUF. "I'm sure they'll come up and thank you when they're finished."

"They don't need to do that," said MIK.

"I know, but these are real nice folks, MIK. And they've had it pretty rough, what with one thing and another, and they like talkin' to yah."

GUF noticed that some of the human women and children waited outside the hut, waiting to talk to MIK.

"I won't stay very long," said GUF. "I gotta get back and organize the cadres into work teams and instruction teams and so forth, like they asked me to help with."

"Sure thing, GUF," said MIK. "I—"

"I wisht there was somethin' I could do . . ."

There was a great whirring noise from MIK and the smell of burning silicone.

GUF looked away. "They just don't have any stuff here," he said, "that I could use to fix you. Maybe I could find something at thuh crater, or . . ."

"Oh, don't bother," said MIK. "I doubt . . ."

GUF was looking at the village. "Oh," he said, reaching in the bag some-one had made him. "I been meanin' to give you this for a week and keep fergettin'." He handed MIK the cup with the picture of him on the side.

"I've been thinking about this since we found it," said MIK. He turned it in his good hand, barely able to see its outline. "I wonder what else we lost at the crater."

"Lots of stuff," said GUF. "But we did get to keep this."

"This was supposed to last for a long time," said MIK, "and tell what people were like for future ages? Then the people who put this there must really have liked the man who thought us up?"

"That's for sure," said GUF.

"And me too, I wonder?"

"You probably most of all," said GUF.

MIK smiled. The smile froze. The eyes went dark, and a thin line of condensation steam rose up from the eartracks. The hand gripped tightly on the cup.

Outside, the people began to sing a real sad song.

It was a bright sunny morning. GUF put flowers on MIK's and DUN's graves at the top of the hill. He patted the earth, stood up uncertainly.

He had replaced his frozen foot with a little wood-wheeled cart which he could skate along almost as good as walking.

He stood up and thought of MIK. He set his carpenter's cap forward on his head and whistled a little tune.

He picked up his wooden tool box and started off down the hill to build the kids a swing set.

# Notes on Stories by Howard Waldrop

## The Ugly Chickens

Howard Who?, indeed. If people know my work at all, it's probably this story. It was up for four awards and won two of them, and was reprinted ten times in the first year after publication.

Well, I had no idea when I wrote it. I really didn't. Terry Carr had been wanting a story from me for *Universe 10* for a year. It took me the first six months of 1979 to write this. I did most of the work on a friend's kitchen table, with notes and books scattered all around, like a collage that could be called Writer At Work.

When I finished, I didn't know if I had a story or a monster on my hands. Anyway I sent it to Terry. Let me tell you what happened then.

Terry had strained his back and was Taking a Lot of Medicine. (Also I'd taken too long to do the story.) Anyway, when the story got there, the book was already filled up. But Terry, even in his haze, loved the story, called Marta Randall, who lived up the hill (and who, with Robert Silverberg, was editing *New Dimensions,* another original anthology series). She ran down the hill, read the story, and fired off a letter to me. I sent the story to Terry; I got back a letter from Marta, offering me a contract at twice the money Terry was paying. Sounded real good to me.

So I went off to an SF convention, read "The Ugly Chickens" (just after they showed the old Warner Bros. cartoon *Porky in Wackyland*) and in general had a good time.

I walked back in the door at home and the phone rang.

"Hello, Howard. This is Terry."

Like Scrooge McDuck, I could *see* silver dollars with wings on them flying out the window.

What happened was that Terry's Medicine Had Worn Off, and an agent called to tell him that—hah hah . . . one of the stories he'd bought for *Universe* as an original had already been sold in Ireland or something. Now Terry *needed* "The Ugly Chickens" real bad. At half the money.

"What does Marta think about all this?" I asked.

"She says if you'll write *another* story for *New Dimensions*, she'll let me have 'Ugly Chickens' back. Okay? Huh? Huh?"

"Okay," I said. Thereby starting the rumor that I sell my stories to the lowest bidder. (Which is why editors are always offering me a penny a word on publication, thinking this gives them an inside edge on seeing my works first.)

(For Marta, I wrote "Flying Saucer Rock and Roll," which, along with a story by Ed Bryant and one by Connie Willis, guaranteed that Pocket Books ended publication of the *New Dimensions* series with # 12, and pulled copies of # 13 from publication *after* review copies had already been sent out. Go figure that. They knew the job was dangerous when they took it.)

Terry Carr and I go back a long way, to *Universe 4*, where I sold him my second story, ever. Lest you think it's all friendship, we were once at a party with a hundred or so other writers at a Worldcon (they all run together after a while). I was wearing a tee-shirt printed with a long green arms clawing their way up from below the belt-line, like the Creature from the Black Lagoon was there.

There was one of those lulls, and somebody asked, "What's down there, Howard?"

And before I could think, Terry Carr's voice boomed throughout the whole room: "It's a good writer, trying to get out," he said.

# Der Untergang des Abendlandesmenschen

Adding to my reputation to selling to low bidders is the fact that half the stories in this book first appeared in *Shayol*, or magazines associated with it. Why, when you're such a hotshot big-time writer, people ask, did you send stories *first* to the lowest-paying market?

Here's how. Let's say I finished typing up a story on Thursday and mailed it off. On Tuesday, Pat Cadigan and Arnie Fenner (the editor and publisher of what is now, alas, an ex-magazine) would send me a check. A few months later would appear a beautifully printed magazine with covers by Don Punchatz or Roger Stinem and my story would be illustrated by Hank Jankus or Robert Haas, and *not one word* would be changed. (Unless of course, something in the original manuscript hadn't made much sense, in which case they would have called me in the course of production and asked me to explain, in my own words, exactly what it was I was trying to say.)

It wasn't just me. The table of contents of all the *Shayol's* reads like a Who's Who of everyone who was trying to do something with the SF or fantasy short story. The magazine will be missed.

This story was written early in 1975 (it says here in my story log). I remember the exact genesis; a photo of William S. Hart in a stage production of *Ben-Hur* from 1908. I'd been reading a lot of Conan Doyle, and I looked at the picture and said, "The man was born to play Sherlock Holmes." One thing led to another—silent German Expressionistic films, books about the Weimer Republic, the idea of a sky that flickers. All the things that fall together when a story idea gets ahold of you.

The title is a take-off on Oswald Spengler's guaranteed sleep-inducer *Der Untergang des Abenlandes,* a book of pseudo-historical philosophy that somehow became a 1920s bestseller when translated over here as *The Decline of the West.* My title comes out, I'm told, as *The Down-Going of the Men of the Sun-Setting Lands.* Or, *End of the Cowboys,* if you will.

# Ike At The Mike

Look. This shouldn't have been my story, it should have been someone else's.

Leigh Kennedy and I were watching a documentary on the birth of 1950s Rock and Roll, and there was this thirty-second montage of photos of two heroes of the time, Eisenhower and Presley.

Light bulbs went off in both our heads. We started talking.

"Lew and Chad need to do this story," I said. Lew Shiner was an Elvis Presley authority, in fact he'd collaborated on an unpublished book about the man. (It had one of the greatest opening paragraphs in history: "It was August. It was hot. The King was dead.") Chad Oliver had been at this writing business for thirty years and knew everything there was to know about jazz and swing music, and so on and so forth. I called them up and told them I had an idea for them, and that I would see them at a party in a couple of days.

There, I sat them down and said, "Look. Here's the idea . . ."

They both choked. "Me? Sacrilege?" said Lew.

"I just can't do that to music," said Chad.

"Well, damn your eyes, then, I'll do it myself," I said. So I went down and did all the research they had memorized, as much research as I could stand, anyway, and wrote this one snowy night, on a doily-decked dining room table while visiting people in Denver, Colorado.

It promptly sold to *Omni* for more money than I'd ever seen in my life, and was up for the Hugo after it was published.

Maybe next time I come around throwing off story sparks, Chad and Lew will listen.

# Dr. Hudson's Secret Gorilla

We all have guilty pleasures, only some are more guilty of them than others.

One of my many is *terrible* old monster movies—the kind with George Zucco and Rondo Hatton and Joseph Calleia (and compared to the people in some of the movies, these guys were *stars*), movies made by Monogram and PRC and Independent Pictures, pictures directed by people like Jean Negulesco and William "One-Shot" Beaudine. (A producer once walked onto one of Beaudine's sets and said, "You're two hours behind your shooting schedule," which was like being a month behind on a *real* movie, and Beaudine reportedly said, "You mean somebody's waiting to see this junk?!")

They always had a laboratory, and a mad assistant, and a beautiful daughter and, well, you'll see.

I wrote this early in 1975 at the end of a creative burst (more later) and sent it off *everywhere*. (Reversing my usual procedure, I sent it to high-paying markets *first*.) Somebody said the ending was "camp." (I told Robert Silverberg that when I sent it to him. He sent back a rejection saying something like, no, the ending was chilling and effective, but it didn't justify the 5,000 words of junk you had to wade through to get there. Or something like that.)

This sold twice (once to *Shayol*) and overseas to Michel Parry, who put together an anthology called *The Rivals of King Kong*, which is in print on five continents now.

This is the only story they know me by in Buenos Aires and Cairo.

## "... The World, As We Know't."

I carried this one around in my head for three or four years, threatening to write it a lot. I called my own bluff and spent six months researching everything, and I mean everything about the subject, about eighteenth century physics and chemistry, Joseph Priestley, Lavoisier, the whole taco as they used to say. Then I wrote the story and sent it off. It's another *Shayol* story.

About six months after I sold this, I found a copy of a doctoral dissertation written in the 1930s that had pulled together *all* the research I'd done in three dozen books. Oh well, live and learn to use the subject index, I always say.

Most people look at science as a straight-line thing: One person has a theory, another tries it, a third, a fourth, an umpty-umpth, and eventually, you have television! Vulcanized rubber! The quantum theory! Lava Lamps!

Anyone who works in a scientific or technical field will tell you that's not the way things happen. There are more delusions, blind alleys, false starts, false finishes and jerkwater theories than you can shake a stick at. It's always been that way, and always will. (Read Greg Benford's *Timescape*.)

If you took all the crackpot stuff, dead ends, and false hopes and stacked them end to end, it would, in someone's words, serve us right.

This story's about one of those ideas mankind labored under for more than a hundred years, which, in the end, amounted, as John Nance Garner once said, "to a bucket of warm spit."

## Green Brother

This was the first story I wrote after "The Ugly Chickens" in 1979. Like a lot of others it was written on someone's kitchen table, this time in Washington, D.C. This one, too, has a strange publishing history—sometimes I think they all do. It was promised to an anthology of fiction about American Indians edited by Russell Bates that never appeared, or hasn't yet; it saw first publication in *Shayol*.

This was the third published piece of mine about American Indians (the others were "Custer's Last Jump" with Steven Utley, written in 1972 and published in 1976, and "Mary Margaret Road-Grader," the next story in the book, *q.v.*). My novel *Them Bones* (Ace, 1984) was set in an alternate universe where the Mississippian mound-builder Indian cultures had had another 500 years of isolation before the Europeans hit the shoreline (and the Europeans in that book were lots nicer than the real ones).

People ask me why I'm always writing about cultural and biological losers and underdogs—Amerindians, the Japanese in WWII (and once, in a story called "I Was a Graduate of U.C.R.A.," about a Navajo mistaken for a Japanese movie villain), Jews in the Middle Ages, blacks in 60s America, Africans under colonial rule, the Frankenstein monster, gorillas, dodos, dinosaurs and little lost robots.

My first impulse is to say maybe we've got to see where we've been before we can try to figure out where we're going.

My second impulse is to say I don't know.

## Mary Margaret Road-grader

This is the kind of story writers hope happens to them once in their careers.

I was living in Bryan, Texas for six months of 1974, at the Monkey House (the kind of place old-time SF fans called a Slan Shack—far too many people with a common interest under one roof). Concurrently with this (and the first few months after I moved to Austin), from February of 1974 to March of 1975 was the most productive period of my life—twelve stories that were eventually bought and published, maybe a dozen losers, and abortive starts on two novels. All the good stories written at the Monkey House sold, but none of them while I was there; I owed everybody money and I moved to Austin.

I was visiting in Austin in June of 1974, sleeping on a friend's couch. I'd gone to sleep the night before with my head stuck between two stereo speakers. I woke at 7 a.m. (there were seven or eight people asleep in the two rooms upstairs) and got up to stagger to the kitchen to put on some coffee. Before I did, I dropped an album on the turntable. It was Simon and Garfunkel's "Bridge Over Troubled Water."

Between the opening piano notes and the first verse, "Mary Margaret Road-Grader" came to me, whole and unbidden. I turned around, opened my typewriter, rolled in paper and began typing.

By the time everybody else got up at 11 a.m., I had finished the story.

I sent it to Damon Knight who edited the late lamented *Orbit* anthology series. Damon sent back a list of questions about some stupidities I'd committed in the original version of the story. I fixed them. Otherwise, it's the version that came to me that long-ago morning.

It was published in *Orbit 18* and picked up by *The Best Science Fiction Stories of the Year.* It was on the final 1977 Nebula ballot, and lost handily. (So did the best story that year, Jake Saunders' "Back to the Stone Age.") In a real stupid move of mine, it was optioned for filming by a local production company, for a longer time than I care to say for so little money I cry when I think about it.

The story dropped on me like a bale of hay. I'm proud the story chose me to tell it.

## Save A Place In The Lifeboat For Me

This has the second strangest publishing history of any story of mine. I wrote it during that wonderful crazy time of '74–'75, sent it a bunch of places, then sold it to Steve Utley and George Proctor's *Lone Star Universe* (an anthology of SF stories by Texas writers published in 1976 by a regional press, now defunct; if you see a copy you better buy it). Then they saw another story of mine and wanted *it* more. So a couple of years after I sold this one I got it back.

About this time the late Tom Reamy (the most talented writer of all of us Texans) moved to Kansas City and started *Nickelodeon,* a beautifully printed, semiprofessional magazine, famous, mostly, for its nude centerfolds of SF writers and fans. (The first issue featured Steve Utley.) Tom had heard me read this story at a convention and wanted it for his second issue. I gave it to him, since I'd exhausted all my other markets (*Shayol* had two in their inventory). *Nickelodeon* #2 came out at the World SF Convention on the same day as four other magazines with my stories in them. Yow! It has never been reprinted anywhere, except that Yoshio Kobayashi's now doing a translation of it for a Japanese rock and roll SF anthology called JEEZ!

(I have one regret about the story. Tom wanted more of the witty repartee between Leonard and Quackenbush. I went to sleep one night and dreamed, I don't know, maybe twenty lines of the funniest dialogue I'd ever heard in my life. I woke up falling out of bed laughing with tears running down my face. I grabbed a pencil. It all went away except for *one* line of it.)

Since this story was written, others have used the central event, most notably Jack Dann, Gardner Dozois and Mike Swanwick in their three-way collaboration "Touring." Among people my age there were three pivotal questions, the second and third of which were "Where were you when Kennedy was shot?" and "Where were you when we landed on the moon?"

The first was "Where were you the Day the Music Died?"

## Horror, We Got

In 1980 I was the only male on a feminist and female SF writers' panel (John Varley wasn't available). The subject came around to "Are there story ideas you get you won't write because they're against the Sisterhood, or politically incorrect or down on women or whatever?"

It came my turn to respond, and since I was the wrong gender, I brought this story up as an example of how sometimes you just have to write the damned story, no matter what, because if you don't, it will drive you crazy.

I wrote this in July of 1978, and had to drive 800 miles to a convention in St. Louis with the last five pages unwritten. I fought my way through the worst traffic jam in the city's history, got to the hotel (without a room) at 5 p.m. I was scheduled to read at 6:30. I went to some friends' room (they were having an argument) and finished, ran downstairs and read this to an audience of which maybe five of the two hundred people knew who I was.

Ed Bryant was watching. He said for the first ten minutes it was like watching the audience in Mel Brooks' *The Producers* watching *Springtime for Hitler*. It was real quiet in the place, folks. I kept reading and waiting for the lights to be eclipsed by a lazily tumbling brick or two. Then people slowly caught on, and they ended up applauding.

The idea came to me while reading a lot of right-wing, racist paranoid conspiracy newspapers (there are such things; in the seventies they were fringe material, now they're a major party's platform). I began to wonder what it would be like if all that stuff were real, and . . . well, the story drove me crazy.

Pat and Arnie weren't at the convention, but their friends were, and when I got home on Tuesday there was a letter waiting that said "Instead of giving yourself grief for three or four years trying to sell this to people who *can't* buy it, send it to *Shayol*." I did.

I can only add by way of warning that *A Short History of Anti-Semitism* is a three-volume work.

# Man-Mountain Gentian

I'd been interested in Japanese culture since I don't know when, and I grew up with kudzu in Mississippi. The title of this story came to me simultaneously with a line that is *not* used in the story. I had a vision of two sumo wrestlers grappling and the voice of an announcer saying "Now he's got the Champ in a half-lotus!"

That was enough for me. Like of a lot of others, I threatened to write this one for so long I thought I had already written it. I finally did, on a Greyhound bus between Austin and Dallas, going to yet another SF convention. (Smart editors always try to put their deadlines close to a convention where I've promised to read a new story. It usually works.)

This was the second story I sold to *Omni*. It was picked up by Dozois's *The Year's Best Science Fiction*, justifying Ellen Datlow's faith in it. Everybody in the world except the three of us ignored it.

# God's Hooks

When I was a kid, in the 1950s, I spent all summer every summer with relatives in Mississippi. (I was born in Houston, Mississippi in 1946, but my family moved to Texas during the worst southern winter in history in 1950.) And I spent all day, every day, from before dawn until after summer sunset fishing. There were two ponds on my paternal grandparents' place, and a pond and a creek on the other side of the family, which was forty miles away at Bruce, a few miles from the Water Valley of "The Ugly Chickens." I read three kinds of literature those summers: SF, comic books, and books on fishing. I fished in Texas, too, until I was sixteen or eighteen years old. Then I quit. Didn't fish again for almost twenty years.

In 1980 I got the idea for the following story. What struck me most about it was that somebody, somewhere, but especially a hot-shot British writer, hadn't done it before. It was right there in front of them all the time, every time they opened a history of English literature.

As usual, I researched like a maniac; the times, clothing, gear, guilds, food, weather. I dipped into Pepys and Evelyn and Hamon L'Estrange (an old friend from "The Ugly Chickens").

I built fishing rods from scratch, and read, so help me, Puritan religious tracts.

Best of all, I started fishing again.

When John Kessel heard me read this at the World SF Convention in Denver, he turned to Leigh Kennedy and said, "That's really great, but where's he going to sell it? *Field & Stream* or *Catholic Digest*?"

Terry Carr bought it on the spot for *Universe 12*. A year or so later it was up for yet another Nebula.

It's probably the favorite of my stories in this book for reasons I don't really understand.

Pow Sock Wham! And another one flops into the creel.

## Heirs of The Perisphere

The first piece of writing I ever sold was a joke for the *Playboy* joke page, back in 1966. I got twenty-five dollars. When the issue with the joke came out (September 1966) I was visiting in California. I went in this place to pick up a copy, and was run out of the newsstand. Seems you couldn't buy a copy of *Playboy* in California until you were twenty-one, although you could pick up copies when you were eighteen in Texas. (You couldn't vote or drink when you were eighteen in Texas, but you could damn sure be drafted and have parts of your body shot off by strangers.)

I'd wanted to write about the central subject of this story since I was ten years old and read about the 1939 World's Fair, and saw the buttons that said I HAVE SEEN THE FUTURE. (The 60s version was I Have Seen the Future. It Doesn't Work.)

Everything came together in 1983. The subject, the treatment, how to do it—well, almost. I wrote the story anyway, supposedly for Mike Bishop's *Light Years and Dark* (it was then called *The Cosmopedia*, and boy am I glad they called the book something else!), but for complex and uninteresting reasons (mostly having to do with length) I ended up writing something else for Mike.

Joe Elder, my agent, sent this story to *Playboy*.

Alice Turner bought it, and worked with me through many drafts. It's certainly a better story now than it was then, when I wasn't quite sure what I was doing.

This is the most recent story in the book, and it may point a new direction my writing seems to be taking. I don't know what direction that is yet. ("Toward the Land of the Knee-Walking Turkeys!" someone cries.) The only way I can find out is to write the stories as they come to me, and worry about it later.

I'm looking forward to them with eagerness and anticipation.

The editors are looking forward to them with a whole other set of emotions, I betcha.

# About the Author

Howard Waldrop, born in Mississippi and now living in Austin, Texas, is an American iconoclast. His highly original books include *Them Bones* and *A Dozen Tough Jobs,* and the collections *All About Strange Monsters of the Recent Past, Night of the Cooters, Going Home Again,* and *Horse of a Different Color.* He won the Nebula and World Fantasy Awards for his novelette "The Ugly Chickens."

George R. R. Martin is the author of the bestselling "Song of Ice and Fire" series of novels. His fiction has won the Hugo, Nebula, World Fantasy Award, Stoker, and Locus Awards. He worked on the TV shows *The Twilight Zone* and *Beauty and the Beast.* He lives in Santa Fe, New Mexico.

# Publication History

The Ugly Chickens, *Universe 10,* 1980

Der Untergang des Abendlandesmenschen, *Chacol* I (later *Shayol*), 1976

Ike at the Mike, *Omni,* June 1982

Dr. Hudson's Secret Gorilla, *Shayol* I, 1977

". . . The World, as We Know't.", *Shayol* 6, 1982

Green Brother, *Shayol* 5, 1982

Mary Margaret Road-Grader, *Orbit 18,* 1976

Save a Place in the Lifeboat for Me, *Nickelodeon* 2, 1976

Horror, We Got, *Shayol* 3, 1979

Man-Mountain Gentian, *Omni,* September 1983

God's Hooks!, *Universe 12,* 1982

Heirs of the Perisphere, *Playboy,* June 1985

# Peapod Classics

Peapod Classics is a handy-sized, occasional series from Small Beer Press re-introducing books that we love so much—books we missed being able to find in our favorite book shops—that we had to bring them back into print. There will be all kinds of books in the series. If you've enjoyed this book and would like to suggest a title for the series, visit our website at smallbeerpress.com and drop us a line. Thanks for reading.

### NAOMI MITCHISON
*Travel Light*        (9781931520140)      $12

Halla's travels take her from the darkest medieval forests to the intrigues of early modern Constantinople. A fabulous novel which will appeal to fans of Diana Wynne Jones, Harry Potter, and T. H. White's *The Sword in the Stone.*

"A 78-year-old friend staying at my house picked up *Travel Light,* and a few hours later she said, 'Oh, I wish I'd known there were books like this when I was younger!' So, read it now—think of all those wasted years!"—Ursula K. Le Guin *(Gifts)*

### CAROL EMSHWILLER
*Carmen Dog*        (9781931520089)      $14

A sharp-eyed look at men, women, and the world we live in. This is the funny, feminist classic that inspired writers Pat Murphy and Karen Joy Fowler to create the James Tiptree Jr. Memorial Award. We are very pleased to publish it as the debut title in our new Peapod Classics line.

"Combines the cruel humor of *Candide* with the allegorical panache of *Animal Farm.*"
—*Entertainment Weekly*

# Small Beer Press Chapbook Series

GREER GILMAN, *Cry Murder!* · GREER GILMAN, *Exit, Pursued By a Bear*
HAL DUNCAN, *An A-Z of the Fantastic City* · BENJAMIN ROSENBAUM, *Other Cities*
MARGO LANAGAN & KATHLEEN JENNINGS, *Stray Bats*

# *Lady Churchill's Rosebud Wristlet*

A twice-yearly fiction &c zine ("Tiny, but celebrated"—*Washington Post*) edited by Kelly Link and Gavin J. Grant, publishing Carol Emshwiller, Karen Joy Fowler, Jeffrey Ford, Eliot Fintushel, James Sallis, Molly Gloss, and many others. Fiction and nonfiction from *LCRW* has been reprinted in *The Year's Best Fantasy & Horror, Best American Short Stories,* and *The Zine Yearbook.* Many subscription options (including chocolate and sometimes used cars) available on our website: smallbeerpress.com.

# Short story collections from Small Beer Press

ELWIN COTMAN, *Dance on Saturday: Stories*    (9781618731722)  $17
    Philip K. Dick Award finalist
    "Packed with rich depth, like jeweled fruits glinting in wet loam."
  — Amal El-Mohtar, *New York Times Book Review*

JOHN CROWLEY, *And Go Like This: Stories*    (9781618731630)  $25
    *Chicago Tribune* Notable Book · "An eclectic sampler." —*Times Literary Supplement*

ANGÉLICA GORODISCHER, *Kalpa Imperial*    (9781931520058)  $16
    TRANSLATED BY URSULA K. LE GUIN
    ★ "Dreamy."—*Library Journal* (Starred Review)

ALAYA DAWN JOHNSON, *Reconstruction: Stories*    (9781618731777)  $17
    "Vivid, imaginative, and often brutal prose." — *Chicago Review of Books*

KELLY LINK
    *Stranger Things Happen*    (9781931520003)  $16
    A *Village Voice* Favorite Book   ❧   A *Salon* Book of the Year
    *Trampoline: an anthology* (Editor)    (9781931520041)  $17
    20 astounding stories by Jeffrey Ford, Karen Joy Fowler, Maureen McHugh, & others.

ABBEY MEI OTIS, *Alien Virus Love Disaster: Stories* (9781618731494) $17
    *Booklist* Top 10 Debut SF&F · "An exciting voice. . . . dreamy but with an intense
    physicality."— *Washington Post,* Best Science Fiction & Fantasy of the Year

SARAH PINSKER, *Sooner or Later Everything Falls into the Sea: Stories* (9781618731555) $17
    Philip K. Dick Award winner · "I love every damn thing about these stories."
  — Charles de Lint, *The Magazine of Fantasy and Science Fiction*

SOFIA SAMATAR, *Tender: Stories*    (9781618731654)  $17
    "Daringly explore the overlap of familiarity and otherness." — NPR Best of the Year

RAY VUKCEVICH, *Meet Me in the Moon Room*    (9781931520010)  $16
    "Ingenious with the short-story form."—*Review of Contemporary Fiction*

ISABEL YAP, *Never Have I Ever*: STORIES    (9781618731821)  $17
    ★ "Such a joy to read." — *Booklist* (starred review)